MW00592805

THE Sibling Connection

THE *Sibling* *Connection*

SEEDS OF LIFE AND DEATH

ROY FANTI

Library of Congress

ISBN 0-9648883-3-5 (limited edition)

Printed in the United States of America
October 1995

THE Sibling Connection

CHAPTER 1

Grown men aren't suppose to cry. Women can cry. Sissies always cry. But, grown men just don't! They've learned, from early childhood, to suppress their deepest sorrows behind a stoic facade of insensitivity. They know how to bury, internally, their agonizing emotions of pain and hurt with a coffin-like silence that inhibits any external release of heart-felt grief. Cruelly, grown men are expected to manifest only the strong, herculean, Rock of Gibraltar image of man, in their life-long quest to become a man's man.

And with all his determination, Bill Price struggled to hold back the dam of tears welling inside his tortured body. Tried with all his might. But failed miserably . . . as he now began to sob uncontrollably. This failure was then compounded by the involuntary expulsion of ear piercing, wailing moans from a pathetically distraught, and grievously suffering human being.

Alas, once the tears started to flow, there was no way to halt their progression towards a climatic crescendo that resembled that following the birth of an avalanche. Initially, Bill's distressful outbursts built momentum slowly but, the sudden shock of the reality of the tragedy that now confronted him rapidly accelerated his woeful exclamations. His tears drained incessantly down his sallow cheeks, through the porous channels of an unshaven, seven day old, stubbled beard and onto an 8x10 inch photograph that he clutched tightly with his palsy-like shaking hands . . . as his weeping brown eyes looked longingly and adoringly at it.

Soon the picture's image became blurred by the never ending cascade of teardrops that inundated its glossy surface. And, as the cherished image it portrayed faded from view, Bill's mind drifted back in time. Back to only two and a half years ago. Back to the sanctuary of his faded shadows of yesterday that safe-harbored the happiest days of his young life.

Days that began on a particular morning, in February of '37, as he drove along narrow East Hudson Street on his way to a 9 o'clock sales appointment with a group of doctors at the Hartford Hospital. His new, black, Lincoln Zephyr-2 seater was purring like a contented kitten, as it plodded through powdery light snow which had been falling since dawn . . . and which covered the normally grimy, city streets and sidewalks with a cleansing, fluffy white blanket . . . one that kept healing itself under the gouging wounds of the sporadic vehicle traffic now stirring on the main arteries . . . one which Bill and his Lincoln seemed to relish . . . with the same enthusiasm that youngsters always display while sledding during winter snowstorms.

Although only twenty six years of age and, in spite of the Great Depression that the world was experiencing, Bill was essentially free of all financial worries, portraying a man enjoying life, his work, and his prospects for a happy future. One who had almost everything going for him . . . his money . . . his looks . . . especially his looks. For he was a strikingly handsome man with dark brown, wavy hair, complimenting warm brown, magnetic eyes. A man whose presence always commanded attention whenever he entered any room. And, why not? He possessed the sinewy 6'-2" frame of a well trained prize fighter . . . honed into shape with a rigid exercise regimen that included country club golf and competitive tennis on weekends.

But . . . Bill certainly deserved all his good fortune. Not born rich, he molded a self-made man who arduously worked his way

4

through Yale University by doing menial odd jobs to pay for his room, board, and tuition. Then, after graduating magna cum laude, he continued to apply his tireless energy and talents as a superb salesman, rapidly climbing the executive ladder to become the New England Regional Vice President for the Better Casualty and Life Insurance Company in only four years. Although a very eligible and a popular bachelor . . . Bill remained single . . . wondering if he would ever find a woman who could turn his head or his heart.

The City of Hartford was just coming to life with the start of a new winter day as Bill approached the Hospital grounds . . . early as usual, as always . . . for his scheduled meeting. Promptness was another of his virtues. To him, it simply was a matter of good business sense . . . as well as good common sense and good upbringing. After all, time was a valuable commodity to his breed of clients and respecting theirs oftentimes was the extra competitive edge that won him the sale of a policy over his rivals.

Exactly 8:15 Bill casually observed, as he flipped his left wrist to see the face of his gold watch. Still 45 minutes to kill. "Plenty of time to have a hot cup of coffee," he concluded silently, as he parked his car in the unplowed lot and walked slowly through the ankle high snow drifts to the hospital foyer.

Bill paused inside the marbled lobby just long enough to shake the clinging snow from his pant legs and to brush a few lingering specks of melting flakes from his hair and off the shoulders of his gray tweed overcoat . . . before moving over to the elevator on his journey to the basement cafeteria.

Within seconds of pushing the down button, the door opened. As he stepped in, Bill was instantly recognized by one of its passengers, Dr. Jordon Brown, Chief Obstetrician, . . . a long standing, satisfied client, and personal friend.

"Bill! What a pleasant surprise!"

But Dr. Brown's warm salutation was lost on Bill . . . whose attention immediately diverted and was focused onto a stunning blond nurse standing next to the doctor.

5

"She's absolutely beautiful," Bill thought, as his pleased eyes scanned what he perceived to be a perfectly contoured 5'-6" body veiled under a form fitting, traditional white uniform . . . his unblushing imagination allowing him to perceive her seductive elegance in its natural state.

Initially, Dr. Brown seemed puzzled by Bill's lack of response to his greeting but, after astutely following the direction of Bill's enraptured stare, he instinctively understood the reason for his distracted frame of mind. Appreciating the obvious, Dr. Brown felt that introductions would certainly be in order. So, he graciously tried to comply.

"Bill. I'd like you to meet Karen Yohansen. She has just assisted me with one of those unexpected . . . expected emergency deliveries, and is now off duty. We're both going down for breakfast. Care to join us?"

Bill's delayed . . . but slow . . . affirmative nod pleased Dr. Brown, who still erroneously believed that Bill's reciprocal welcoming conversation would soon follow. So he waited . . . and waited . . . but no response was forthcoming because Bill's and Karen's eyes now seemed welded in a hypnotic trance . . . his brown intently focused on her Calypso sea of crystal blue.

The elevator was going down . . . but Bill's emotions were obviously skyrocketing.

Jordan treated. An event that Bill never would have permitted under more normal composure. But today his actions reflected those of a sixteen year old on his first date . . . as did Karen's . . . as she consciously exhibited flirtatious eyes and a Mona Lisa teasing smile that further accentuated her deep cheek dimples. It's not surprising that their casual coffee conversation continued long after Dr. Brown excused himself when he was paged to report to surgery.

Bill may have thought he was a confirmed bachelor, but when Karen, in a relaxed moment, took off her cap and let her long, taffy blonde hair drape softly down her back to her waist, he was permanently hooked. How could anyone resist the innocent, almost

6

naive, aura that she projected and which now held him spellbound? A confirmed bachelor? Certainly not anymore. For even his scheduled 9 o'clock meeting eluded him. And, for the first time, he was not only late . . . but he was also flirting with love.

Their courtship was intense. And, in May, after only three months of dating, Bill proposed under a full moon. They eloped the next day to bind in marriage the kind of devotion and love all dream about . . . but so few actually share. One consummated the night before . . . for life.

Karen gave up her promising nursing career to cater exclusively to the needs of Bill and their sumptuous eight room Colonial home, nestled on ten acres of rolling hills in Cromwell, Connecticut. Naturally, Bill spoiled her at every opportunity. And on her 24th birthday, on Christmas day, gave her the keys to a new, green, Studebaker President, 4-door sedan. While visual symbols of his growing financial wealth became ever apparent . . . Karen now was his real source of pride and happiness . . . not his money. And when on Valentine's Day in '38, she told him she might be pregnant . . . confirmed that week by Dr. Brown . . . he was absolutely ecstatic. Both looked forward to the upcoming event with excited enthusiasm and anticipation, with only one exception on Karen's part. Every month Bill had to travel for approximately two consecutive weeks throughout New England to visit with Branch managers, to generate new business, and to expand existing accounts. Ever since they were married, Karen would always accompany Bill on these trips, as neither wanted to be separated from each other for such long periods. Besides, for Karen it seemed as if she was on one continuous honeymoon as Bill always adjusted his itinerary to allow them at least three or four days of each trip for sightseeing and vacationing.

Not only did they eat at the fanciest restaurants, and sleep in the finest hotels, but their several trips to date provided them with breathtaking panoramic views of picturesque Cape Cod, from the lower shore of Falmouth to the undulating dunes at the tip of

Provincetown, and of the awe inspiring rocky Maine coast, stretching from Old Portsmouth to Bar Harbor. Most memorable, however, for Karen was their late September trip . . . "following the rainbow" as she delighted in saying over and over again . . . as the autumn leaves of New Hampshire and Vermont exploded into a spectacular, spectral array of fall foliage.

Neither would ever forget how Mother Nature's trees, dancing to the soothing tickle of a soft breeze majestically fluttered in a masterful blend of yellow, red, orange, and purple hues. Both Bill and Karen were so overwhelmed by its colorful beauty, they vowed to make a return Mecca to see this memorable garden of Eden next year.

These trips provided such treasures of togetherness, both of them eagerly looked forward to those yet to come. Karen, who never traveled outside of Connecticut before Bill came into her life, cherished them so much she hoped they would never stop. But stop they did. And abruptly in May . . . during her fourth month of pregnancy. Actually it was Bill, not her doctor, who insisted she stay at home because of her pregnancy. Very reluctantly, and privately in tears, Karen acquiesced . . . for the sake of their unborn child.

Karen tried to adjust to Bill's absence during June . . . but couldn't, as time weighed heavily on her mind. She tried to relieve some of her boredom by volunteering her services at the Hartford Hospital. And while renewing old acquaintances and keeping active in the maternity ward did help pass the days, the long evenings without Bill still depressed her . . . even though she tried to consume the hours, til exhaustion, by knitting and decorating the nursery. Worse yet, by the time August rolled around her swelling had become so pronounced even this volunteer work had to be completely curtailed . . . under Dr. Brown's mandate this time. As a consequence, the ensuing monotony became ever more unbearable . . . and only the constant thought of the expected birth in mid-October made her loneliness for Bill tolerable.

In mid-September, Bill was once again preparing to leave on

a trip. This time, however, it was his movements that were slow and uncoordinated as he began to pack his bag. Something was obviously troubling him. Deep wrinkles that periodically creased his brow gave away the fact that he was a person in conflict within himself. One moment he'd be decided and unhesitatingly place a shirt or tie in his luggage . . . but the next moment would find him pausing, as if uncertain, and unpacking. His deep apprehension couldn't be camouflaged . . . especially from the very person that he was so distressed about . . . Karen!

Bill knew Karen was starting her ninth month and an uneasy feeling tortured his mind . . . a premonition that this prearranged business commitment was calling it too close for comfort and should be canceled. Karen sensed Bill's bothered mind and made every effort, while assisting him in selecting his clothes, to be light and gay in her conversation to dispel his fears. To no avail. For as he closed his bag and started to buckle its straps, he stopped abruptly. Turning to face her, he said in a very worrisome tone,

"I'm not going . . . Not this time. I just don't feel right about leaving you so close to your delivery date."

Then, Bill in further justification of his apprehensive mood, added,

"What if the baby comes prematurely? What then?"

Karen glowed with appreciation of Bill's concern for her . . . and while she so desperately wanted him to stay, she knew she had to allay his anxiety by conveying the opposite impression.

"Stop being such an old mother's hen," she chuckled convincingly. "According to Dr. Brown, there's still a full month to go. Besides . . . have you forgotten? I was a damn good nurse before you married me."

Then, to reinforce her self praise, she quickly added,

"Still am and you know it. I can take care of myself in any emergency."

For a clincher, she nonchalantly pointed out,

"Anyway, the hospital is only 15 miles away. I could get

9

there in less than a half hour if necessary, even if I had to drive myself. With my medical training and experience, I'd certainly know enough to get there in plenty of time."

Karen's rebuttal remarks were persuasive. And as Bill mulled over the logic of her comments, his tensions noticeably eased . . . enough at least for him to smile meekly with a sheepish grin, realizing he probably was being unnecessarily alarmed.

"I guess you're right darling. I feel a bit foolish. But, I don't want anything to happen to you . . . or, our baby."

"Oh, Bill . . . that's why I love you so much!", Karen exclaimed joyfully. "But stop fretting this instant. Nothing is going to happen. Believe me when I say that."

Somewhat reassured now, Bill finished strapping the buckles of his bags and, then, Karen and he left the master bedroom, arm in arm, descended the long spiral, mahogany staircase, and walked slowly through the large country kitchen and out the back door to the Lincoln parked on the gravel driveway. After carefully placing his luggage in the car, Bill turned back towards Karen and sighed,

"I wish you were coming with me . . . Like old times."

Remembering their promise of last September, Karen's blue eyes reddened from the gush of tears she could no longer restrain. All efforts on her part to gallantly suppress the flow by repeatedly blinking her long curly blonde lashes also failed.

Since she was unsuccessful in impeding the resultant stream, which now was running down her cheeks, she offered no resistance to Bill as he lifted her chin towards him, and gently brushed them dry with his linen handkerchief. Then, when he bent over to kiss her, she impulsively threw outstretched arms around his neck and clung on tenaciously. They embraced for a long moment . . . neither wanting to part lips and begin the separation.

Finally, Bill moved his right hand to Karen's waist and ever so lightly started to pat her extended belly. With a boyish gleam in his moistened eyes, he humorously observed,

"The way Jonathon keeps on growing . . . pretty soon I won't be able to reach your honey lips to kiss you."

Jonathon! There never was any doubt that the baby was to be called Jonathon. Bill instantly took a liking to the name as soon, as Karen suggested it.

"Jonathon Price", he exclaimed exuberantly with expanded chest. "Sounds distinguished. A name he can wear proudly. I like it Karen . . . Let's call him Jonathon."

So from that moment on two things were taken for granted. Their child would be a boy, and he was a Jonathon.

Glancing upwards as he reached for the Lincoln's car door handle, Bill noticed a thin band of wispy, white clouds off in the distant western horizon. While opening the door and lowering his tall frame to get in, he casually remarked,

"Looks as if we'll finally have a little rain to break the dry spell before the week's over."

In retrospect, that prophecy turned out to be the understatement of the decade.

After rolling down his side window and starting his car, Bill reluctantly began to move away. His right hand held tightly onto the steering wheel, while his left hand repeatedly oscillated . . . first, far out of the opened window and, then, onto his puckered lips, as he commenced waving love-kisses to Karen.

"Remember. I'll phone you every afternoon around supper-time," he shouted above the engine clatter.

Now both continued waving farewell and throwing kisses to each other as his Lincoln crawled down the long, narrow, winding, gravel-stone driveway, stopped momentarily, and then turned East onto the macadam roadway. Chugging towards Boston, it and Bill quickly vanished from sight.

Forlornly, Karen slowly ambled along the cobblestone brick path towards her house . . . every so often pausing to look back over her shoulder, hoping against hope, that somehow she would see Bill

11

returning to her. But only disappointment greeted each backward glance. Although never complaining to Bill, Karen just couldn't get use to this work cycle that lately took her husband away from her two weeks out of four. And the stark realization that he was gone again, rekindled the strong depression that always surfaced on his first day of departure. If anything, today's feeling of remorse was even worse than all the others. For as she reentered the kitchen and carefully latched the door, she lamented weepfully,

"It's like having a marriage only half the time."

Of course Karen knew she was basking in selfpity. But being alone had always been one of her phobias. And the fact that her nearest neighbors lived over a half a mile away only amplified her feeling of isolation . . . particularly today. That was one reason why she so enjoyed her volunteer work at the hospital. Just watching the newborns always lifted her down spirits, and revived such pleasant memories of her nursing career assisting doctors with these deliveries. Actually, Karen was so fascinated with the birth process, she always considered that assigned duty as sheer pleasure, rather than work.

Suddenly, out of blue, she felt a mild kick . . . followed by yet another. These 'remember me' kicks of Jonathon did wonders to temporarily alter Karen's despondent mood to one of high expectation.

"Just one month to go," she whispered, lowering her head as if conversing with her unborn child. Then placing both hands on her round, distended stomach she sighed impatiently,

"I can't wait!"

CHAPTER 2

Violent tornado like winds swept across Joe Walker's ramshackled farmhouse . . . provoking it to creak and moan as it swayed menacingly under nature's latest onslaught. Surely, the next strong gust would blow it apart.

The loud, wrenching noise of weathered pine-boards, straining arduously to rip and peel themselves totally free from loosened rusty nails, suddenly woke Joe with a startle. Groggily he listened to the heavy pitter-patter tones cascading off the roof of his seventy year old shack, then impulsively, he released a curt smile which quickly spread across his thirty year old stubbled face. A smile stimulated by a mistaken belief that, at last, a long overdue rain must be inundating his farmland.

He almost cried out with sheer ecstasy over this welcomed event. However, Joe's brief moment of joy rapidly degenerated into another of acute disappointment when he recognized the all too familiar echoes of thousands of sand pellets ricocheting off his already pitted roof and pock-marked wooden structure .

"Shit!" He now uttered quietly, under his breath . . . displaying an uncontrollable annoyance over the reality that yet another dust storm was ravishing the countryside.

Ever so slowly, Joe, still only half-awake, maneuvered his naked, lanky, 5' 11", muscular frame from under a musty top sheet soaked through with his body perspiration. The stench of his smelly human sweat, caused by a hot September night's unbearable heat, filled his nostrils with disgust.

Just getting up, sitting on the edge of his badly warped straw mattress, and putting calloused feet on the bare wooden floor was a chore for him this morning. His whole body seemed leaded as he raised himself upright, lumbered trance-like over to the shoulder-high kitchen window, and peered out motionlessly for several minutes.

Before too long, his prematurely balding head began to oscillate from side to side with a rhythmic motion that appeared synchronized to the pinging chimes of specks of sand which bounced randomly across the floor, after being driven by the unrelenting force of the wind through numerous cracks in the ceiling and walls.

Joe stared transfixed for several minutes at the caked earth that stretched like an endless sea of parched wasteland to the horizon and far beyond. His almost mesmerized eyes captured nothing but the sickening sight of denuded farmland. Soil-raped into infertility by the wanton appetite of a never ending dry spell that was now devouring the great agricultural plains of the Midwest at an alarming rate.

Unable to contain his pent-up furor any longer, Joe abruptly exclaimed with a quivering tremor in his normally deep, steady alto voice,

"Great God Almighty! . . . Another day of this God damn drought.

In obvious disgust, he jerked down the torn green window shade . . . trying ever so defiantly but, futilely . . . to shut out the whole truth of a world decaying all around him. Joe knew, even though he now turned his back on reality, that he faced another day without any hope for the onset of rain so critically needed to save his withering crops. Another day, enduring swirling winds relentlessly bent on carrying aloft the last remnants of topsoil that only four years ago adorned his fifteen acres of prime, fertile, productive farmland.

But, in turning away, Joe now faced his twenty-three-year-old

14

wife, Sue, who up before dawn was busy scrapping together their meager breakfast. Quickly, he shut his saddened lids, trying to conceal his blurring brown eyes from her.

Without mumbling any word of greeting . . . Joe drifted listlessly back towards the disheveled bed to get dressed. While putting on his tattle-tale, gray undershirt and thread-bare, denim blue coveralls, he unwillingly began reflecting on their last few miserable years together. Years of trying to eke out just a survival existence . . . seeding and reseeding soil. Soil equally as barren as Sue, who only last week had aborted again.

Lately, it pained Joe to even look at Sue. Frail and weakened in body and spirit by her third miscarriage in two years, she projected a pathetic, down-trodden image with tousled, long black hair, sallow skin and deep sunken hazel eyes . . . just a dark shadow of her former self . . . no longer portraying the natural beauty and youthful vibrance that first attracted him to her. Now, her ghost-like, skeletal features haunted Joe and punishingly served as an all too frequent reminder of his own inadequacy as a man to provide for her in the manner promised when she became his teen age bride in March of '33.

Born to be a mother, Sue's maternal instincts had always flamed an insatiable desire to have a child. However, the last vestige of hope for motherhood was prematurely sucked from her heart with the latest hemorrhaging expulsion from her womb of a three month old fetus. The Doctor's grim prognosis that she probably never would be able to bear children cut more deeply than a sharp butcher's knife. And, forever deeply scarred her psychologically . . . devastating her feeling of self-worth.

Nature was cruel . . . no rain . . . no crops . . . no children. No wonder Sue's hope was dying . . . along with the soil . . . along with Joe's will to keep trying.

When Joe finished dressing, he again dragged himself into the open kitchen area and quietly sat down at the small round table, seating himself directly across from Sue. This morning, both mirrored each other's mood of dejection. Each was responding mechanically, as usual, to a daily routine that for some time had cycled within an ever deepening rut. Only the fragrance of hot-brewed coffee being poured into his oversized ceramic mug revived Joe's dull senses.

As he now unconsciously stroked the brown bristles of a week old unkempt beard with the nervously kneading fingers of his left hand, Joe noted with a guilty discomfort that he had not as yet spoken a word to Sue . . . nor she to him. But all their days seemed like that lately. Each was so beset with inner griefs and turmoils, neither bothered to take any initiative to exchange even trivial dialogue.

Apparently, their vocal cords also were afflicted with the same lethargic inertness that enveloped both of them.Thus, their conversations were scarce . . . like the rains . . . like the breakfast meals. In fact, days had past since either had enjoyed the simple luxury of a sizzling slice of bacon, or a couple of fried eggs. Instead, hard corn biscuits and coffee were their only source of nourishment between dawn and dusk.

Truly, nothing seemed to be changing for them . . . not the meals . . . not the weather. And certainly not their dim chances for a better tomorrow.

Still hungry after gulping down his small dry biscuit, Joe unconsciously reached for another . . . but suddenly paused, with his grasping left hand suspended in mid-air. Timely, he had caught himself about to take Sue's, which as yet had not been touched, and probably wouldn't have been eaten by her anyway. Nevertheless, Joe couldn't bring himself to having it.

"God! She certainly needs nourishment more than I do," Joe thought as he lowered his arm empty handed. Then, expelling a white lie . . . without fooling Sue . . . he meekly uttered his first audible words,

"I'm just not that hungry, today."

Next, placing both of his large, grubby hands on the rim of

the gouged oak table, he slowly pushed his big chair backward, while continuing his terse remarks.

"Thank God, the winds are subsiding. Time for me to get out there and rework the fields."

With that he promptly rose and took a few long strides toward the door . . . before stopping abruptly. Frozen in space, he pondered for a brief moment, then turned, and strode briskly back toward Sue. Having also stood up, Sue now watched Joe's sudden unexpected action with bewilderment as he wrapped his powerful arms around her thin waist and easily lifted her tiny 5'-2" body upward until their pensive eyes look longing into each others at level contact. Uncharacteristically, he now proceeded to lean forward and tenderly kiss her melancholy lips . . . before trying to console her sadness by softly whispering,

"Now, don't you fret anymore, honey. We'll have lots of children, someday . . . even if we have to adopt them."

Without meaning to, Joe had pierced the bowels of her deep anguish with these words. No longer able to hold back the reservoir of tears that had dammed inside her for so long, Sue spontaneously burst out crying . . . and in so doing witnessed for the first time in her married life tears brimming, then, flowing unrestrained down Joe's whiskered cheeks. Both sobbed pitifully for an eternal moment while clinging like climbing ivy to each other. Both were un-ashamedly feeling to the core each others hurts and disappointments. Both clung tenaciously to the only thing they had that they were still sure of . . . each other.

Finally, Sue softly cupped Joe's moistened face with her shaking hands and held their trembling lips together . . . until each had regained some control of their upset emotions. Now, in a heroic gesture, she unlocked lips . . . forced a reluctant smile . . . and gently commanded,

"Put me down Joe—I'm O.K. now."

The fact that this Summer of '38 was so dry and that a severe drought was plaguing most of the Nation was of small consolation to Joe, who was trapped inside the periphery of the Nation's ever expanding dust bowl. His years of struggling and working his farm in central Kansas, twelve hours a day . . . seven days a week . . . now were only yielding crops of heartache and poverty. Unfortunately, today offered no more hope than any of their yesterdays . . . with perhaps one small exception. Joe felt somewhat relieved that this morning, in their tears, he and Sue had partially bridged their chasms of internal despair. He could only pray that both might now begin to better comfort each other's personal distress.

For this reason, in spite of the fact he was laboriously pushing his hand plow through caked earth in the blistering heat of midday, and sweat was oozing from every micro inch of his drenched body . . . his mental attitude was surprisingly improved.

Reaching the crest of a small knoll, Joe, who was panting like a dog in heat, stopped to catch a deep breath. And while mopping his soggy brow with an already soaked kerchief, his gaunt cheeks broadened with a snide smirk.

"Here I am drowning in my own sweat!" he pathetically observed, "But, there's not a single drop of water for my dying crops."

Then, as he casually glanced towards the west over his left shoulder, Joe winced as if struck by a doubled bolt of lightning . . . refusing, at first, to believe his horrified eyes which were sharply focused on a cyclonic cloud now forming and darkening the sky in the near horizon. The tears that quickly swelled inside nearly choked him . . . long before the dust swirls had arrived. Totally disillusioned now by the inevitable, Joe disgustedly heaved his plow aside, and in one continuous motion swiftly bent over at the waist, reached down, grabbed a fistful of loose, sandy soil and, in a fit of defiant anger, flung it with all his might towards the heavens. Then in a rage, as if suddenly gone berserk, he tossed himself face downward onto the ground and now began mercilessly pounding the soil with clenched fists . . . over . . . and over . . . and over again for several minutes, while all the time, simultaneously, wailing like a baby. When he looked again and noticed the dust cloud whipping closer and descending in his direction, he cried out loudly to the heavens,

"God! . . . I can't take it anymore. You've punished me long enough. What have I ever done to deserve your fuck'en wrath?"

It was ages before Joe ceased his crazed behavior and even made a feeble attempt to get up. When he finally did, his motions were awkward and unstable . . . so reminiscent of a man wobbling recklessly in a drunken stupor. Sobbing still, with his head hung low, he now began an aimless trek back toward his shack . . . periodically kicking the sandy turf in a useless, rebellious gesture of retaliation against his unlucky fate.

Nature's elements had finally defeated him . . . Joe was a broken man . . . a stark reminder of how fragile the human body is under unrelenting stress.

Meanwhile Sue, who was closely watching Joe's tirade through the open front cabin door, suddenly felt physically sick . . . became nauseous, and began dry-heaving. Although in obvious pain, she bravely clasped her arms across her aching stomach muscles and started to run out to Joe's aid. But, as she staggered onto their decrepit wooden porch, her emotionally paralyzed legs crumbled . . . along with her will . . . and she collapsed in a state of agonizing grief.

At the crack of dawn the next morning, September 15, 1938, Joe and Sue hastily packed the best of their worthless belongings onto their dilapidated '27 old, blue, Ford pick-up truck, abandoned the farm and everything else on it, and headed east to New England to begin over again.

"At least that part of the country still has crops to pick," Joe said unconvincingly.

CHAPTER 3

Bill had been so right about the rain. Only he was so wrong about when it would start and how much would fall.

For after the cirrus clouds moved in late Monday, the blazing sun dimmed, before being blotted out entirely by the bone-chilling drizzle which soon followed and which fell continuously all day Tuesday and into Wednesday morning. Tedium quickly set in for Karen, who was victimized by the bad weather and forced to remain indoors instead of enjoying the small pleasures of puttering in her garden and taking short walks as planned. As a consequence, her spirit became as dull as the damp days and only brightened, momentarily, when the noon radio forecasters promised clearing by later in the day. What the basis was for such optimism, however, remained forever a mystery to Karen because by then the rain was coming down even harder. But this obvious fact didn't seem to phase the weathermen, who falsely predicted sunshine again on Thursday before succumbing to visual observation techniques and, correctly foreboded heavy rains continuing through Friday.

As the hours churned ever more slowly, the gloomy days abraded Karen's taut nerves and fermented an unhealthy pent-up frustration due to her confinement and inactivity which greatly amplified the desolation which surrounded her. This forced isolation, coupled together with the accompanying locked-in boredom, took its toll and shortly brought on the usual stir crazy symptoms exhibited by those cooped up in a claustrophobic environment for an extended time period.

"It's smothering me," she moaned.

So when Bill called . . . as he did faithfully each day . . . who could blame her for being such a chatter box and rambling on and on endlessly with the man she idolized as if he was in the same room with her. On these brief daily occasions, time accelerated so rapidly that many minutes of conversation seemed compressed into only fleeting seconds but, once Bill hung up, time again became viscous and dragged on as before. With each passing day . . . as she became lonelier and lonelier and missed him more and more . . . she found it harder and harder to resist the urge of telling Bill to terminate his trip and to come home.

By Wednesday the 21st of September, Bill had been gone nine days . . . during the latter five of which the heavy rain continued to fall unabated. Despite meteorological evidence to the contrary, Karen naively had hoped that when she awoke on that particular morning she'd finally be greeted with a long overdue sunrise. But, when she rubbed open her sleepy blue eyes, she had to contend, instead, with an unpleasant surprise . . . a sudden sharp twinge in her stomach muscles.

"Just gas," she groaned matter of factly . . . denying herself the reality of a more plausible explanation. Then, dismissing the incident from her mind as if it never happened, she began the drudgery of another rainy day . . . Breakfast was purposely light . . . So was the housework . . . And, so was the next twinge around 9 A.M. . . . Karen seem somewhat perplexed, and while not overly concerned, as yet, did decide nevertheless to relax . . . just to be on the safe side . . . by sitting down on her expansive living room sofa and putting the finishing touches on a blue bunting she had knitted for Jonathon. Then tiring, she gingerly raised her legs up and with some effort placed them flat on the soft, brown, velvet cushions. Just worming herself into a comfortable position was a real chore for her these days, Her maneuvering lately was so difficult and required so much energy, she couldn't help but feel that her awkward actions mimicked those of the tremendously fat lady in a circus.

"Jonathon's going to be one huge baby!" she speculated.

Finally, as she settled into a cozy position, Karen found herself being lulled to sleep by the musical chimes coming from the antique grandfather clock in the hallway . . . ten distinct gongs . . . followed by one distinct, moderate pain. Deeply creasing her forehead, Karen uttered aloud apprehensively,

"It can't be!"

Now, trying to convince herself as to the veracity of her impetuous remark she calculated and recalculated the pregnancy cycle . . . over and over again in her mind.

"At least two weeks," she concluded. "Maybe more."

However, Karen's false prophesy didn't negate the random, but shorter intervals between spasms that she now experienced. No longer able to ignore them, she began to mentally note their frequency of occurrence. And at 2:30, when the spasms were only about 45 minutes apart, she almost came to truth with reality.

She was fine again, until about 3:15, when the phone rang. With some effort, she picked up the phone's receiver on the end table and answered. As expected it was Bill . . . and, as always, his voice was cheerful. Hers, she quickly decided, must convey the same impression.

After the usual brief moments of "hello's" and small talk about the miserable weather, Bill asked thoughtfully,

"How are you feeling, honey?"

Karen didn't mean to pause so long before responding, but unfortunately she did, probably an unintentional reaction to the falsehood she didn't want to utter, but now was . . . and quite convincingly too . . . at least so she thought.

"I'm feeling just fine, Bill."

How she kept from screaming out those few words was no small miracle because, simultaneously, she had to fight off the pain of a harder contraction this time. Karen realized she had to break off the conversation with Bill as soon as possible before an unmuffled pain spilled the truth to him. She knew that if he had any inkling of her distress, he would drop everything and come rushing home to her pellmell . . . in spite of the bad weather and the fact that he was over two hundred miles away in Augusta, Maine. She wanted so to avoid that since she feared he could get hurt or killed in an accident on the rain slick highways. Therefore, she knew she had to suffocate her conscience once more and reiterate her previous lie,

"I'm really feeling great Bill," And jovially added, "In fact if this rain ever let's up, I just might go out and wash my car."

Bill's spontaneous laughter made Karen happy because it gave her the opportunity she was looking for to bring their conversation to a pleasant end. Now it was Bill's turn to complain about having to hang up but, under Karen's strong urging, the usual . . . "miss you . . . love you" farewells were tenderly expressed.

Audibly, Karen sighed with relief over her success in terminating the call without Bill discovering that she was experiencing signs of early labor pains. Now contemplating her next move, she repeatedly drummed her fingers anxiously on the telephone, as if debating with herself whether or not she should call the doctor. Finally, she lifted her hand off the receiver . . . her hesitancy, this time, being the normal reaction of individuals not to prematurely cry wolf. However, the extreme harshness of the next contraction removed the last lingering doubt from her distressed mind and convinced her at last that this was no false alarm.

"Less than forty minutes apart," she blurted anxiously. "God!. There isn't much time."

She began scolding herself for delaying so long when all of her nurse's training should have motivated her to much quicker action.

"But, it's so different when it's happening to you," she weakly argued in her own defense.

Hastily, she dialed her doctor's office. And when, after two rings, his nurse answered, she let out a long audible breath before asking nervously,

"Betty . . . This is Karen Price . Is Dr. Brown there?"

"No, Karen. He isn't," came back the quick response. "He's still at the hospital. Is anything wrong?"she questioned, sensing from Karen's jittery voice that something was the matter.

"Yes!" Karen said emphatically. "I'm in labor. I shouldn't be. But, I am! My contractions are coming about 40 minutes apart."

Jolted by this disturbing news, Betty immediately interrupted to take charge of a situation that she had confronted eons of times before.

"Karen . . . just hold on for a few seconds while I contact Dr. Brown on the other phone for instructions. He undoubtedly will want you to meet him at the hospital immediately. Now, don't hang up while I try to find out exactly what he wants to do."

A weak smile swept across Karen's weary face as she replied, "Don't worry . . . I won't."

She could hear Betty's dialing over her receiver . . . until suddenly . . . her line went dead. Believing she had been inadvertently disconnected, Karen immediately redialed Dr. Brown's office. This time, however, she didn't hear any rings . . . or even a busy signal . . . just deathly silence . . . followed then by only the shrieking, reverberating echo of her own trembling voice as she kept pleading into the mouthpiece,

"Hello . . . hello . . . HELLO!"

Again and again she redialed . . . each time with the same negative result . . . each time dead silence . . . each time more fright as Karen's heart pounded in accelerated beat, stimulated by the awareness that now she was totally isolated from the outside world, and by the realization that her phobia had gotten a toe hold and now was playing havoc with her panicked mind.

She might have continued her dialing mania forever . . . if it wasn't for the fact she was forced to throw the receiver down in order to grab her stomach, trying desperately to fight off once more the pain of an intense contraction. She whimpered unashamedly, before bursting out with a cry of anguish.

"Oh . . . my God!"

There wasn't any doubt at all in Karen's mind that Jonathon would be born very soon, maybe in an hour . . . certainly not more than two or three at most.

She had to do something . . . anything to save his life. Having the baby at home was her first thought, but she knew that Bill was adamantly opposed to that course of action. Whenever she suggested it to him during her pregnancy, he would snap back and say,

"No! Put that thought right out of your mind. Jonathon's going to be born in a hospital . . . just in case there are any complications for either of you."

Experience had taught her the wisdom of Bill's remark, and besides . . . if anything happened to Jonathon because she did . . . she never would forgive herself. As much as she knew Bill loved her, she couldn't help but wonder if he ever would forgive her if she deliberately ignored his warning. Her indecision was tormenting her.

"God!" she screamed. "Help me to do the right thing."

Gathering her wits, and some small control of her frazzled emotions, she walked over to the large baywindow of the living room, opened the drapes and attempted to peer out through the rain smeared panes. A cold shiver raced across her goose-pimpled body. The weather outside was ominous. Once again she seemed frozen into inactivity by an indecisive mind debating her only two alternatives.

Suddenly, Karen realized that she had only one choice that she could live with . . . she had to get to the hospital . . . and without delay.

"Before its too late," she cried.

Hurriedly, she unconsciously grabbed the baby's blue bunting on her way out of the living room, moved to the vestibule closet in the front hallway and took out her pink cashmere sweater, tan raincoat, and black rubber boots.

Just as quickly, she slipped these on . . . all except the boots which she disgustedly threw back into the closet after clumsily struggling for several precious moments to pull them over her shoes . . . realizing finally that in her maternal state it was impossible to reach below her knees without sitting and laboriously lifting and contorting her feet.

Then she removed an umbrella from its wrought iron stand and, on the run, snatched her alligator pocketbook off of the kitchen table . . . as she continued her unbroken motion towards the back door. Unlatching it, she paused a moment . . . as if to brace herself for the upcoming battle with the elements. Mustering her courage, she swung open the door . . . only to be driven back a few steps by the unexpected force of the fierce wind.

Arching her frame, as if she was climbing up a steep hill, she pushed forward again while simultaneously trying to open the umbrella, but it remained closed, in spite of her strained effort to make it unfurl. Refusing to give up, she twisted her body around a hundred and eighty degrees, and tried once again . . . only to witness, to her dismay, the strong gale currents immediately ballooning the umbrella wide open . . . like a parachute . . . before its radial frame of ribs cascaded forward and blew out. Totally dejected, she tossed the useless, mangled instrument onto the kitchen floor. After struggling unsuccessfully to close the backdoor, she turned and braced herself to leave. Buffeted mercilessly by the wind and rain that showed no respect for her pending motherhood, Karen literally had to inch her way to the Studebaker . . . all the time her hair and outer wear absorbing water like a sponge. At last, she reached the car, yanked open the door, awkwardly got in, and then somehow was able to pull it shut . . . before collapsing in the driver's seat . . . exhausted and drenched. For a long . . . long . . . long moment, Karen didn't move . . . in fact, couldn't move a single muscle. Finally, after catching her breath, she fumbled in her pocketbook, found the keys, and turned on the ignition.

"Thank you Lord!" she gratefully said, as the car started and she began to accelerate forward.

Even with the wipers noisily swiping away at full speed, the rain, pelting the windshield with tremendous volume, made it almost impossible for Karen to see the road as she drove off.

"I must be crazy to go out in this," she mumbled.

"The weather is even worse than I thought."

Karen couldn't have known. Not even the New England weathermen really knew . . . or paid any serious heed . . . to the tropical disturbance, reported by the Miami Bureau, lurking off the Northern coast of San Juan, Puerto Rico on Sunday. Even the follow-up bulletins on Monday that the storm seemed to be heading north-ward, aroused no concern to anyone. Why should they? After all, these disturbances typically would swing out to sea long before they hit the New England coastline. History was on their side. Was! But not this time, Because as fate would have it, a large high pressure system stalled over Nova Scotia and, as a consequence, this tropical depression was prevented from drifting seaward . . . instead the storm intensified . . . grew into a monstrous hurricane . . . hugged the coastline, picked up momentum, and roared up the Eastern seaboard to New England packing a deadly wallop.

No warning of eminent disaster would have been heard, even if Karen had faithfully listened to the radio all day. None was ever broadcasted. Everyone responsible seemed to be lulled into a com-placent mood by the routine, speculative reports from the Washing-ton, D.C. Weather Bureau that the disturbance was expected to weaken and dissipate rapidly during its voyage up the coast.

Poor Karen! . . . Poor innocent Karen. A victim of circum-stance, who now was heroically trying to drive cautiously along the highway to the Hartford Hospital, while frightened to death by the increasing ferociousness of the wind whose violent cyclonic agitation kept provoking even the large trees to courtesy and bow-with dancing branches randomly kissing the ground as they bent in tune to the strong buffeting gales. She was so astonished to see their leaves being stripped effortlessly off their out stretched branches . . . as easily as a strong breath blows apart a dandelion weed gone to seed . . . and was almost mesmerized by their helter-skelter flight in the heavens which created an eerie kaleidoscopic wonderland of color . . . before being driven by sheets of rain back down to earth to glaze the roads she was traveling on with layers that made their surfaces slipperier than if coated with thin ice.

No! Karen never did know that she timed her leaving for the hospital precisely with the arrival of the worst hurricane that had ever ripped across the Connecticut Valley. If she had any knowledge at all that it was coming, she never would have left, but would have taken the uncertain risk of a self delivery at home. However, fate now controlled her destiny as she was caught up in an unbelievable nightmare in which the storm's wrath continued to create havoc . . . not only for her, but for the entire Northeast.

The prolonged nightmare also came in the form of another strong contraction that had her groaning with pain as she gripped the steering wheel with such intensity her knuckles became white from the loss of blood circulation. While fighting this new spasm, she inadvertently crossed over her lane, and headed straight towards a huge truck coming in the opposite direction. Quickly swerving, hard to the right, then to the left, she narrowly avoided a head-on collision. Now, gripped by an unquenchable fear by this near miss and by the premonition that an accident was bound to happen during one of her labor pain seizures, she made up her mind to get off . . . and stay off, the congested main arteries.

Fortunately for her, her many trips to the hospital made her very familiar with the back roads where isolation could be assured . . . unfortunately . . . she was now using them . . . in spite of her phobia and the devastation being wrought all around her by the storm.

Bill felt very uneasy after talking to Karen. Something just wasn't right. Maybe it was the slight anxiety in her voice that he detected and failed to mention to her . . . maybe it was her eagerness to cut short their conversation, when every other time she would babble on for over a half hour . . . refusing even then to hang up. Whatever it was, it bothered him . . . so much so, he was tempted to call her back immediately . . . but didn't . . . deciding he was being foolish again. After all, she had assured him she was O.K. . . .

"And she has never lied to me," he told his doubting conscience.

None the less, this lingering doubt still nibbled and gnawed at his peace of mind . . . even an hour later as he tried to relax by turning on the radio. Within minutes his mild apprehension converted to one of sheer panic . . . as soon as the Augusta announcer interrupted the regularly scheduled program to present a news bulletin about a killer hurricane now tearing across Long Island and threatening the entire New England area.

Before the announcer had finished his statement, Bill had already jumped for the phone and, frantically, asked the hotel operator to dial his home number. Fearfully, he waited . . . and waited . . . as seconds expanded out to eternity. Finally, the operator came back on his line and apologetically said,

"I'm sorry Mr. Price . . . but we can't put your call through. The long distant circuits to Connecticut are temporarily out of order."

Bill was in a frenzy. He tried to calm himself with the belief that Karen was safe at home and sheltered from the storm. After all, he had just talked to her a little while ago. Although nothing could have been further from the truth, perhaps it was best that he didn't know the truth . . . At least not yet !

Bill might have eventually won control over his edgy emotions . . . might also have stayed in Augusta until morning . . . if Karen's acute shortness with him on the telephone didn't constantly haunt him.

"If something wasn't dreadfully wrong," he surmised, "She never would have acted like that." Then, as he restlessly paced the floor of his hotel room cogitating, a subconscious thought surfaced in the form of a wild, but correct assumption.

"It must have something to do with Jonathon!" he cried aloud.

Now nothing could restrain his emotional distress. He must go home . . . home to the woman he loved . . . home to Karen, who he intuitively felt needed him. So, in spite of the desk clerk's stern warnings to stay off the roads until the storm blew over, Bill quickly checked out of the hotel.

Although the weather was beginning to also deteriorate around him rapidly, he bravely defied the elements and headed his car towards Connecticut . . . and Karen.

3 B

The nerve wracking wind and torrential rain were very upsetting to Karen . . . but not nearly as much as the shortened time period between contractions, which she estimated now to be only fifteen minutes apart. Because of their increased frequency, she didn't dare travel as fast as she wanted to on the desolate country road winding its way from Cromwell to Hartford. Didn't dare . . . and couldn't have anyway since the five days of steady downpour prior to this hurricane had transformed the once smooth gravel surfaces into deep, undulating, sinuous tracks . . . peppered occasionally with deeper holes and pockets of debris.

Karen found herself locked into these dual rut tracks and being jostled and swayed continuously from side to side in unison with their skewed contours and very random motions, which were so reminiscent to her of the wild vertical and lateral gyrations that she use to experience during her childhood roller coaster rides.

Somehow, Karen persevered . . . Sometimes by praying . . . as debris, snapping from branches as easily as one can break match-wood, came hurtling at her . . . only to slam harmlessly off the steel body of her car . . . Sometimes by cursing . . . as the flooded muddy ruts slowed her momentum and threatened numerous times to leave her stranded in the mud . . . And, sometimes by crying out . . . as the contraction pains became more and more severe . . . more and more frequent.

Then suddenly, when she hit a deep pot hole that jarred both Jonathon and her to the raw bones, she did all three simultaneously . . . until the gush of amniotic fluid stopped running down her legs. Horrified at what was happening to her, she squirmed as if attempting to shut off the flow. Despite all her personal discomfort, she had enough presence of mind not to stop the car to relieve her distress for fear it would never start again. Her only thoughts were of Jonathon and making it to the hospital in time to save him. An urgency which was even more critical now that her water had burst. Yet, her hope was waning rapidly because of her snail's pace of forward progress.

"Still SEVEN miles to go," she cried dejectedly as emotional anguish ruptured her brute courage and determination.

Time was certainly her worst enemy. The lack of it . . . and these country roads would surely result in Jonathon's demise. With this realization, she lost all residual confidence in her ability to prevail and, suddenly, broke down and bawled uncontrollably . . . before screaming,

"I'll never make it! . . . I'll NEVER make it!"

Then, throwing all caution aside, she irritably jammed her foot down hard on the gas pedal and began accelerating. As Karen weaved swiftly along the rutted road, locked into tracks that traversed the narrow lane, she prayed that her forward passage wouldn't be blocked by another vehicle coming the other way. Karen had a premonition that that prayer might be answered.

"Who in their right mind would be out in weather like this?" she couldn't help but blurt out . . . followed with her own objective answer . . . a reiteration of what she expressed when she left her safe harbor at home.

"I must be crazy."

But there was no turning back now. She was trapped by her decision and had no alternative but to keep going.

Absentmindedly, she turned on the car's headlights to alleviate the strain of an early dusk caused by a sky blackened to opaqueness by the swirling hurricane clouds. The rays of diffused white light reflecting back from the sheets of rain had a hypnotic effect which soon made her feel drowsy. Worse yet, her far vision was blinded. As a consequence of both, she didn't see the huge oak branch that had blown down across the road in front of her . . . until suddenly it loomed as a death trap before her. At the last possible moment, Karen reacted instinctively again and jerked the steering wheel to the right with all her strength . . . and prayed. At first, there was an infinitesimal moment of delay without anything happening . . . then, the Studebaker menacingly leaned drastically to the left side threatening to tip over . . . before it obediently responded by pulling out of the rut track, swerved off the road, and started to plunge down a low inclined marshy slope.

Karen slammed on her brakes, and zigged and zagged skillfully to avoid ramming two large oak trees in her path, as she skidded to rest about 100 feet from the road's edge. Her heart pounded like a jack-hammer . . . even though she had miraculously escaped the immediate danger. Her head and chest, thrown forward onto the steering wheel, remained still for an anxious second before her body started to shake violently from fear. The type of chill-reaction one gets just before the onset of a very high fever.

Slowly . . . ever so slowly . . . she lifted her head . . . thankful that she and Jonathon were still alive. In time, she was able to calm herself sufficiently to stop the chills and to attempt to back the car out of the slime and onto the road again. But, the mud was like quicksand and the more she tried to extract herself by shifting gears and rocking the car . . . the deeper the tires sank into the muck. Although the effort was obviously futile, she didn't give it up until a series of rapid fire contractions seized her. The excruciating pain that followed told her what she didn't want to know. Jonathon was coming! His birth was going to be here . . . and now! Again she screamed . . . as she did many, many more times, under the agony of a delivery without medication. Somehow, she managed to elevate her feet and press them against the passenger door for leverage as she laid as flat as possible on the front seat. Then, grasping the steering wheel—as if it was a preserver thrown out to rescue someone drowning—she clung on for dear life . . . all the time straining and pushing with a herculean effort.

Over . . . and over again . . . she tried to expel Jonathon from her fully dilated cervix and lower birth canal in order to relieve the unbearable pressure that was torturing her internally. As she struggled, unsuccessfully, she couldn't help but recall the numerous births she had watched so routinely during her nursing career, and the superficial advice she offered to the expectant mothers in the delivery room as she tried to alleviate their concerns.

"It's easy," she would tell them. "Just push."

Now, she appreciated their suffering as never before. Now she knew first hand that no pain was greater than that experienced at child birth. Never again would she ever say,

"It's easy."

Karen continued to muster all the force her nearly exhausted body could provide to carry out Nature's miracle. All to no avail.

Then, in her darkest moment of despair, she felt that Jonathon's head was beginning to protrude from her stretched vagina. Tears of joy now joined those of intense pain as the ecstasy of his impending birth swept over her. With renewed energy, garnered from the adrenaline released by this expectation, she pushed . . . and stretched . . . and cried . . . as she bore down as never before. Finally . . . enduring one last . . . sustained contraction, she was rewarded with the expulsion of Jonathon.

Sheer exhilaration quickly absorbed all Karen's residual remnants of pain. And in spite of her still precarious state, her spirits soared with the thought of her accomplishment and the knowledge that she was now a mother. Waiting only long enough to restore a smidgen of lost energy, she gingerly sat up, rested her back against the door panel and, then, in true motherly fashion, reached down and, ever so carefully and adoringly, brought her crying baby to her bosom As she lovingly cuddled it, her lips tenderly kissed the top of the baby's bald head . . . over and over again.

Curiosity then overpowered all her emotions. She had to
know! Not wanting to be kept in suspense . . . even a moment longer
. . . her fingers slowly slid down along the baby's round body . . . and
ever so gently probed between its soft, puffy legs. Excitement
mounted to a crescendo pitch, then a loud "Ahhhhhh" exploded out
of her lungs with the same intense paroxysmal emotion as that
expressed by sky watchers when a fourth of July rocket suddenly
reveals all its inherent beauty of surprise.

"You ARE a Jonathon!" she exclaimed with unsuppressed
delight. "Your daddy is going to be so happy."

For long moments, in which the passage of time no longer
caused her any anguish, she continued to press Jonathon close to her
chest. Even when his cries subsided . . . and her adorning eyes
remained misty blue.

Finally, her nursing know-how took charge as she maneuvered herself carefully, reached into the glove compartment, removed the small emergency medical kit she always carried with her
and, then, very professionally, proceeded to sever and tie the umbilical cord. As soon as this necessary chore was completed to her
satisfaction, she proudly informed Jonathon,

"There! Even Dr. Brown couldn't have done it any better."

Karen, then, obsessed with the desire to hold Jonathon intimately . . . impulsively struggled out of her raincoat, removed her
sweater, unbuttoned her blouse and bra straps, and, cradled Jonathon
against her exposed warm breasts, while covering his body with the
oversized blue bunting she had knitted.

"Oh! Jonathon," she lullabied. "You'll soon outgrow this . . .
just you wait and see."

For the first time in hours, Karen relaxed completely as if she
didn't have a care in the world. Now she could even enjoy the fury of
the hurricane. Her imaginative mind began to translate the rhythmic
sounds of the rain bouncing off the metallic car roof into musical
chords . . . now the hard ominous beats of the Fifth symphony as the
deluge continued . . . now the soft notes of the Moonlight Sonata as

36

the storm temporarily abated. It was Nature's lullaby to her in a moment of peaceful bliss, and she couldn't help succumbing to its mystical charm . . .

And to her exhaustion. She fought bravely to stay awake . . . But, her resistance rapidly weakened. Soon, she too joined Jonathon in a well deserved deep sleep.

How long she actually slept wasn't to be measured in hours . . . Karen wasn't that lucky. Perhaps 10 minutes . . . certainly not more than 20 had elapsed before her eyes suddenly shocked wide open in total bewilderment . . . and a new, apprehensive wrinkle creased her sweating forehead as she clutched tightly to Jonathon. She moaned softly . . . a reflex reaction to the medium level contractions that were stimulating her uteri muscles once more . . . as she gasped, in disbelief, words she had uttered just this morning came back to haunt her.

"Oh . . . No! It can't be."

But it certainly was . . . as the next hard contraction removed all doubts from Karen's dazed mind, and painfully convinced her that she was about to deliver again. Quickly, but ever so carefully, she wrapped the blue bunting completely around Jonathon, lifted him over the front and placed him ever so gently onto the backseat. Then, she folded up her raincoat and propped it under him . . . just to be sure he couldn't fall off the edge of the seat.

Once again she raised her legs and pressed the soles of her feet hard against the passenger door . . . once again she suffered contraction after contraction in an effort to eject her second baby. Only this time, she somehow mustered superhuman courage and willpower to muffle her cries of agony in order not to awaken Jonathon. And while her face distortions clearly revealed her misery and immense pain . . . her larynx, was paralyzed into voluntary immobility and effectively silenced her screeching vocal cords.

Psychologically, Karen was now feeling a tremendous high . . . her euphoria being an understandable display of emotion for one enthusiastically waiting to be the mother of twins.

37

Physically, however, she was drained like a dish rag . . . with all her strength squeezed out of her . . . yet, in spite of it all, she was still resilient enough to tap the latent reservoirs of human energy that seems available to all expectant mothers, at moments like these, to fulfill Nature's insatiable demands during childbirth. Fortunately, the few short periods of quiet respite between contractions enabled her to recover sufficiently to persevere . . . until the deluge of pain suddenly ceased with the successful delivery of her second child. Calm now prevailed . . . not only due to the birth, but also due to the fact that the eye of the hurricane was passing overhead. As a consequence, the wind's howl that had reverberated through the shimmering trees soon reduced to soft whispers . . . as did the loud cries of her second born soon fade into faint whimpers by the soothing warmth of her bosom.

Once again Karen discovered she had given birth to a boy . . . once again she expertly performed the necessary surgery on the umbilical cord . . . and once again she improvised a blanket in which he was comfortably bundled. However, this time using her pink sweater. Then, extremely contented . . . and oblivious to any imminent danger . . . she decided the only sensible thing for her to do was to wait for help to arrive, which she optimistically believed would occur even before the storm waned. So with her head propped on the door arm, as a pillow, and with her second born cuddled next to her, Karen . . . deliriously happy . . . but also physically exhausted, closed her eyelids and fell quickly off to sleep.

3 C

The dilapidated Ford pickup truck heading towards the apple orchards of Amherst, Massachusetts that evening dutifully traced the dual rut tracks followed earlier by Karen. However, it didn't have to veer suddenly off the road at the sight of the fallen oak limb because without the driving rain to cloud the windshield with a blinding glare, its driver, Joe Walker had ample warning of the potential danger imposed by the obstacle in his path. Thus, Joe was able to deftly navigate the truck to the right in a semicircular sweep around the debris, catching a glimpse as he did of the disabled Studebaker when his reflecting lights beams revealed its presence.

Abruptly . . . Joe stopped. On a whim . . . on a spur of the moment reaction. Destitute from their long travel East, he wavered for only a brief second before convincing himself of the dire necessity of pilfering anything of value left in the empty car . . . anything that could be later sold to allow Sue and him to survive, yet, another day.

Before Sue realized what Joe was up to, he had already jumped out of the truck and, with long purposeful strides, headed straight for the stranded car. The going, however, was sloppy and slow as his worn cowboy boots sunk deep into the thick, molasses like mud to above his ankles. Because of the unusual effort required with each step . . . just to accomplish separation of his feet from the restraining suction force of the taffy-like ground surface, Joe was

39

really puffing wind by the time he reached the door handle on the driver's side. But his gasp of surprise upon opening Karen's Studebaker door was not from this over exertion . . . but from the unexpected shock of having a women's head drop out and come to rest with her neck bent slightly over the side edge of the front seat. Looking down, his startled brown eyes glued onto a pair of blue eyes frightened into confusion and puzzlement by his intrusion.

Both were petrified into momentary inactivity. God! If only they had remained so for a longer period of time. But, no they didn't. For a chain reaction of events was triggered when Joe reached over Karen's prostrated body for her pocketbook. Karen . . . erroneously believing that the intruder was trying to snatch her baby from her protective grasp . . . did what any mother would have done. She screamed! . . . But, the shrill had barely emitted from her bellowing lungs . . . when a frightened Joe Walker impulsively covered her screeching mouth with his left hand to quiet her.

Where was their logic? Joe should have known that with the exception of his wife, Sue, no one was within hearing distance of them. It wasn't necessary to suppress the shrieks. And Karen, traveling the isolated backroads for over an hour, should have realized how foolish it was to scream and expect anyone to hear or respond to her shrill cries. But . . . the reactions of people oftentimes defy logic . . . particularly in moments of a crisis.

What a pity. For there they were . . . one not wanting to be harmed, trying only to protect her young . . . and the other not wanting to harm.Just wanting to steal to survive. If only Karen hadn't tried to screech again when Joe relaxed his grip and started to lift his hand. If only Joe hadn't covered her mouth once again as soon as her cry escaped . . . if only he hadn't pressed down with all his might . . . Karen would not have been silenced for life! It really didn't matter whether or not he choked her to death . . . or, that he just broke her neck. The realty was . . . she was dead!

Joe's next reaction, however, was very predictable. Scared white . . . as if he had seen a ghost of equal color . . . he turned and bolted back to his truck. Shaking and whining uncontrollably, he began unloading his guilty conscience on an astonished Sue by incoherently blurting out in tears,

"I've KILLED her! . . . I . . . I didn't want to do it . . . but she wouldn't stop screaming. Oh, God . . . I didn't want to hurt her Sue . . . I've never hurt anyone in my lifetime. I just wanted her pocketbook."

Sue was mortally stunned into deathly silence . . . only her silence was the living kind that eventually heals itself. And, her mouth began the recovery process . . . first,by dropping open in utter disbelief . . . unable to speak or hardly catch a breath because she was now hyperventilating. HER Joe couldn't do anything like that. Not her sweet, lovable Joe. Not her mild tempered husband . . . that wouldn't harm a flea. But, there he was . . . grieving his act of violence . . . his wanton murder of another human being.

Suddenly, Joe was a stranger to her. Suddenly both heard a baby's wail above Joe's. Both began swiveling their heads around in amazement . . . trying to focus their ears onto the source of the crying.

Finally, Sue reacted by unlatching her door, sprang to the ground, and ran as fast as her legs could carry her through the muck to the victim's car. Meanwhile Joe, still in his own world of bewilderment and shock, remained sealed in the truck.Not wanting, under any circumstances, to ever return to the scene of his heinous crime. Not wanting to ever see the dead body again.

A very short time later, the baby's cries ceased . . . and Sue could be seen slowly returning towards the truck . . . rocking a small bundle in her folded arms. Joe starred perplexed as she climbed carefully back into the truck . . . now holding the precious bundle close to her chest.

"Oh, Joe," she lamented. "The poor woman must have just given birth to this baby. Look its still slimy wet, wrapped only in this blood spotted, pink sweater.

Joe's glance over to see it lasted only a fraction of a second.

41

Then, he quickly turned away, paled and nauseated at the sight of the little infant, whose mother he had just murdered.

"What are we going to do now, Joe?"

What options did they have? Joe knew he'd be hanged for murder, if they stayed around. No one would believe or care that it was unintentional. Anyway . . . the intent didn't really matter. The fact was he killed her. That was the only thing that really mattered.

"Put the baby back, Sue," he pleaded . . . "Leave it . . . and let's get the hell out of here!"

His plea, however, fell on deaf ears as she quickly retorted,

"I can't . . . I can't do that, Joe. I'll never do that. The baby will die if we leave it here. I won't let you murder the baby too, Joe by doing that. I won't . . . I just can't. Don't make me do it."

Joe really knew, deep down in his heart, that he couldn't abandon the baby either. So, as he turned the ignition key, started the truck, and put it into low gear, he compassionately said,

"Well then . . . Let's get as far away from here as we can . . . and fast . . . before anyone finds out what I did. We'll take the baby and raise it as our own, Sue. Maybe that way God will forgive me for what I''ve done . . . Oh . . . Sue . . . I feel so sick . . . so very, very sorry."

3 D

Even before the demonic hurricane had spent its full fury, emergency crews by the thousands were already mobilized and sent out on rescue missions. The formidable task confronting them was perilous beyond belief as the gust velocities, exceeding 100 miles per hour, continued to level and pile up homes in splintered array . . . Even structures that valiantly resisted being lifted by violent winds were blown apart, as if exploded by sticks of dynamite, by the spin-off miniature tornadoes that touched down throughout New England . . . And, all trees in their paths were uprooted and sucked out of their earthen nest . . . as easily as a vacuum cleaner devours dust . . . and, then, swept away, as readily as specks of dirt swiftly scatter under the spanking action of a straw broom.

The new run-off from the torrential rains . . . added to the volume already released from heaven's sluice gates during the past five days . . . flowed with terrifying speed over saturated grounds to quickly flood and engulf the low lands. While in the highlands, trickles turned into streams and streams into rivers which rose to record heights as they bubbled over vehemently. And, just as balloons burst when filled to excess . . . so too did dam after dam shatter, as if made out of untempered glass, due to the pressure of the mountainous water levels, that no longer could be restrained.

Karen was not alone in being an unwilling victim of this disastrous hurricane . . . over one hundred of just her Connecticut neighbors also breathed their last breath and were destroyed by the bloodthirsty winds and rampaging flood waters that unmercilessly entrapped them within their death webs.

Ironically, however, Karen might have been saved . . . if only! For less than an hour after she was killed, two State troopers, patrolling the backroads in search of anyone marooned, came upon her car. If only they hadn't pulled over and stopped, just a couple of miles down the road, to let a blue pickup truck pass, and if only they hadn't prolonged that rest stop for more than a half hour, chatting and sipping several cups of hot coffee from their bottomless thermos, they would have been the first ones to discover Karen and her twins . . . very much alive and very well indeed . . . and certainly most appreciative of the merciful assistance they would have afforded them.

However, the 'if only' of this world is not renegotiable. Instead, it always seems to dangle . . . like Diogenes' sword . . . to taunt those who wish things different. Who wish to reverse time's progression. When in truth, the die is irrevocably cast by the very passage of time. And the 'if only' . . . as a consequence, has already lost out. As Karen did, for example, by this final, sad twist of fate.

However, now that the policemen were aware of the disabled vehicle, they dutifully decided to check it out, even though they had already prematurely concluded that it was empty since no visible signs of life were evident. Parking at the edge of the road, they initiated a cursory investigation, without disembarking, by calling out with their small bullhorns, while simultaneously probing the thickly treed area with sweeping motions of their flashlights.

Like gyrating spotlights at a mobile carnival show, these white oscillating beams penetrated through the darkness and displayed weird streaks and blotches of diffused, reflected, and colored light throughout their intercepted space . . . painting an abstract picture that might resemble the random brush marks of a Piccaso-style artist . . . who was energetically portraying his creative work in a panoramic fashion using the atmosphere for his canvas.

Besides their sparkler-like display, these rays provided the officers with the desired strobic-like image recordings of the area, as the light reflected back from the various surfaces in their path through a translucent drizzle curtain.

Those from the rear window of the Studebaker revealed no body-like silhouettes to indicate occupancy . . . nor did those from the open side door infer anything unusual for an abandoned car. However, when the scanning beams were lowered to seat level, they briefly locked onto a woman's exposed head for a split second. As if in total disbelieve, the flashlight beams were purposely oscillated off . . . then refocused quickly back onto the dangling head to reconfirm the fact that the original sighting was not an optical illusion. The dual pair of wide-open Eddie Cantor eyes of the policemen vividly revealed their mutual shock.

Dumbfounded at first . . . they remained paralyzed for just a few seconds before bolting out of their car and running towards Karen's. They hadn't traversed more than fifty feet, at the most, when suddenly Jonathon started howling . . . with a burst of trip hammer wails, reminiscent of a screeching siren. Although mystified by what they were hearing, its net effect was to propel the State troopers forward even faster. Soon, the heart rendering tragedy was uncovered.

The officers quickly comprehended the gravity of this pitiful situation, and hastily jumped to their false conclusion, based on the massive blood pools under the victim's buttocks, that the deceased apparently died from a hemorrhage shortly after giving birth. Because of the critical need to obtain medical attention for the new born baby, they had, unfortunately, neglected to undertake even a superficial canvas of the area, searching for evidence that might lead then to any suspicion, what so ever, of a possible homicidal cause of death.

As a result, they failed to notice the dual sets of fresh footprints, one male and the other female, embedded in the thick mud, which emanated from just off the side of the road, went to the disabled car and, then, returned again to the origin, where deep grooved tracks made by a heavy vehicle, such as a truck, were now being washed away by the renewed onset of heavy rains from behind the eye of the storm. They also failed to close the mental loop of circumstantial evidence by ignoring the important link between the Ford pickup that they graciously allowed free passage, only a short while ago, and the present scene of distress.

For the official record, time was their alibi for these errors of omission. Lack of time just didn't allow them the liberty of dilly-dallying and engaging in traditional detailed inspection of the scene. The urgency of the mission of mercy facing them, with respect to the probably dead woman's baby,clearly dictated that time was of the essence . . . so they quickly grabbed a grey woolen blanket from the backseat of their cruiser, thoroughly wrapped it around the assumed corpse and, then, carefully placed it into the backseat of their vehicle.

With one of the policemen now timidly holding Jonathon . . . still crying and still bundled in his blue bunting, they rushed as fast as humanly possible, without regard to prevailing treacherous road conditions, to the Hartford Hospital in a noble effort to save the tiny child's life.

3 E

Fierce winds and hammer pounding rain soon turned the Maine road conditions from bad . . . to worse . . . to near impossible. Yet, Bill pressed on with a dogged determination to get home to Karen somehow. But, his confidence ebbed swiftly as he became both intimidated and humbled by the magnitude of Nature's wicked on-slaught, whose unharnessed weather lashed out constantly and toyed, challenged, and endangered him and his Lincoln as it swayed and arduously chugged along . . . mile after mile. What really scared Bill the most, however, wasn't the ferociousness of the storm, but the life threatening risk imposed by the massive flooding . . . whose waters at times climbed to running board level, and occasionally even higher, causing the Lincoln to cough, sputter and steam vio-lently as the high waters, lapping menacingly at its hot twelve cylinder engine, frantically tried to stall it out forever.

And,thus, by the time Bill reached Portsmouth, the situation, already dismal, became even more precarious . . . ever more intoler-able, as he now had to contend with detour after detour around impassible stretches of highway sealed shut by the unimpeded ava-lanche of water cascading freely into the coastal low lands. Bill astutely realized his only salvation was to head westward to the higher inland terrain, if he was to avoid being trapped or drowned on washed out roads . . . even though he knew that this move would add many hours onto his journey. However, as he correctly prophetized.

"Better hours late . . . than stranded for days."

Bill was too consumed with worry about Karen to stop and rest, even though his mind and body were numbed and exhausted from the extreme pressure of total concentration required to contend with the hazardous conditions confronting his almost every moment. The only break he allowed himself was a brief one when he tried, unsuccessfully again, to telephone Karen . . . hoping by some miracle the call would be completed. Just hearing her voice . . . just having her say "hello", and just knowing she was all right would have done wonders to lift the cloud of doom and depression that now obsessed him and drove him forward so unrelentlessly. After enduring the enveloping fatigue for hours, his strained eyelids became mere slits,which he incessantly rubbed vigorously and often just to keep their hairline cracks pried open.

"I need toothpicks," Bill now sadistically uttered.

"Just to prevent them from shutting."

Bill's first real hope of relief from the inclement weather came around one o'clock in the morning when he noticed that the distant southern horizon was no longer painted black by thick cumulus clouds. Instead, bright stars, embroidered on its periphery, peeked out and began winking at him.

With time, more and more twinkling stars polka dotted the sky, causing Bill to breathe more freely and to feel reassured that the hurricane had spent its fury locally and was moving out to the northeast. Suddenly . . . a full moon burst out from its hiding place behind the last of the rapidly moving cloud banks. As it majestically arched across the clearing heavens, Bill became mesmerized by its celestial brilliance and beauty, and momentarily found his thoughts flashing back to that unforgettable warm May evening when he proposed to Karen . . . remembering how the golden reflected light of the moon danced in her sensuous blue eyes as they laid on a soft, grassy, isolated knoll at the Cromwell Country Club. Bill blushed . . . something he hadn't done in years . . . as just recalling that night caused him to become aroused.

Day Broke . . . and with it came the first sunrise seen in New England in almost two weeks. However . . . with the daylight also came a vividly grotesque view of the vast devastation left in the wake of the killer storm. From his vantage point on the high roads, overlooking the valleys, Bill could see town upon town floating in great lakes of flood water . . . reminiscent of medieval castles surrounded by moats . . . with one exception. Instead of offering life protection for those contained within its environs, it proffered only misery, hardship, sickness and death for all those ensnared within.

From what his unbelieving eyes were witnessing, Bill conjectured that the property damage and loss of life had to be enormous in every community. This knowledge made him shudder with chilled fear over the fate of Karen.

Everywhere scores of tired men, women, and children were feverishly working to remove the silt and debris from their homesteads. Everywhere people were attempting to restore normalcy to the chaos that, in some instances, still jeopardized their lives. But Bill, selfishly, wasn't concerned about their plight. His only thoughts were of Karen and the miles yet to travel before reaching her.

Still the going was rough and slow . . . and many times his forward progress was brought to a complete halt as rescue crews, wielding axes and saws in their painstaking, heroic effort to clear the roads, forced Bill to endure long hours of delay. Delays which soon wore thin his patience and turned his temperament into one of quarrelsome belligerence expressed in angry outburst against exhausted, volunteer workers,

"What the hell is holding everything up? Can't you work any faster?"

But, as the day past, Bill overcame his fatigue, his short temper, as well as sundry other obstacles . . . as he struggled forward, refusing to let even the impossible deter him from his quest of getting home to Karen. And finally . . . about eleven o'clock that night . . . after thirty tedious hours of driving, he turned onto his driveway, climbed the winding gravel path up to his house, leaned forward and turned off the ignition to his faithful Lincoln Zephyr. He was home . . . Through guts, perseverance and mostly luck . . . he had accomplished the miracle.

"Thank God!" he acknowledged with a weary sigh. "Home at last."

Against all odds, he had made it. Now exuberant that he would soon be with Karen, he quickly disembarked, and hastily ran up the cobblestone path to his backdoor, all the time peering through the moonlit darkness to see if the hurricane had done any major damage to the premises.

Seeing none, Bill mistakenly conjectured,

"Karen must be safe and unharmed also."

Flinging open the door, which he noticed with slight dismay was unlatched, he excitedly announced his presence,

"Karen! . . . I'm home!"

Not hearing any reply, he repeated himself several times before assuming she must be sound asleep. When Bill tried flicking on the light switch, his luck ran out. The power was still down from the storm, and he almost fell down . . . tripping over the discarded umbrella which Bill kicked away without identifying. More cautious now, he gingerly felt his way through the kitchen and hall, climbed the circular staircase, and slowly walked into the master bedroom. No longer concerned about waking Karen, he loudly announced his presence.

"Honey . . . I'm home."

The vacuum silence was eerie . . . and Bill seemed stunned, as he deftly moved along the edge of the bed on her side, hoping that his searching hands would soon move over the contour of her pregnant body. Finding nothing, he anxiously leaned across the bed and frantically groped up and down his side. And then panicked when he didn't find her. Calling. Shouting. Screeching for her was all to no avail. A cold sweat left him trembling in fear as he moaned,

"Oh God . . . I knew it . . . I knew something was wrong!"

As Bill struggled to control himself, he fumbled in the night stand drawer, swiftly withdrew a small flashlight, and, then, hurriedly ran apprehensively from room to room, inspecting the house to determine if it had been broken into and Karen made a victim of foul play at the hands of an intruder.

However, he found nothing unusual that disturbed him . . . except for the phone being off the hook in the living room and the mangled umbrella in the kitchen. Perplexed, Bill mulled over these exceptions for a brief moment . . . before bolting outside . . . looking for Karen's Studebaker.

It was gone . . . where to he didn't know for sure . . . but he correctly speculated somewhere between his home and the hospital.

So without an another second of hesitation, and in spite of his total exhaustion, Bill leaped back into his car and headed out again to find Karen.

CHAPTER 4

Bedlam reigned in the main lobby of the Hartford Hospital with a noisy decibel level and busy commotion activity that mimicked New York's Grand Central Station at rush hour, even though it was well past midnight when Bill arrived. Scores of distraught people were scurrying about . . . some seeking help . . . others trying to help . . . but the majority of those present were anxiously inquiring about loved ones or close relatives that were victims of the storm. Without parallel, the aftermath of this hurricane catastrophe stretched the hospital's physical and human resources to its full capacity and well beyond.

Bill was just one of the many lost souls adrift in this troubled sea of humanity, as his tragic personal problem was mirrored many fold in the lives of those all around him . . . some of whom wept internally while trying courageously to portray an outward appearance of self control over pained emotions, no matter how much the endured suffering was wrenching at their hearts . . . while others cried out openly . . . unable to bear the burden of heartache without vocally releasing the pressure caused by their grief with pathetic sobs and wails of anguish.

But, no one present was really successful in camouflaging the telltale human stress that everyone obviously felt and visibly displayed in the form of deep tension wrinkles that warped the skin surfaces of their concerned brows.

Yet, through it all, the unsung heroes . . . the doctors and nurses . . . unselfishly labored away helping the needy . . . as they had been doing around the clock since the storm first struck. Perhaps, more than anyone else these weary souls craved relief from the debilitating effects of acute exhaustion. Still, they labored, uncompromisingly, to swiftly administer aid, comfort, and professional service, as calmly as possible, to the wounded and emotionally distraught . . . even though every one of them were literally dead on their feet.

And certainly Bill fitted the latter mold as he now weaved and pushed through the milling crowd . . . exhibiting a behavioral pattern abnormal to the gentlemanly mannerisms he otherwise always showed. Impudently, Bill ignored all the belligerent stares and harsh comments of irate individuals surrounding him They rightfully resented his aggressiveness and rudeness . . . as he continued to force his way through the stacked circles of people bunched together in front of the admissions desk.

Bill now acted as if possessed by a demon . . . and nothing on earth was going to stop him, or deter his resolve as he boldly wormed his way forward in quest of information about Karen.

Finally, as he now confronted the seated receptionist, he asked anxiously,

"Is my wife here?"

The clerk's puzzled look upward was followed by her searching reply.

"What's her name? It's impossible for me to help you unless I know her full name."

Bill, blushing with embarrassment at his neglectful oversight, quickly responded,

"Karen . . . Karen Price." And without being asked began to amplify by rambling on, "She's pregnant . . . eight and a half months pregnant. She wasn't home when I got back from my aborted business trip. I thought maybe the baby started to come prematurely and she rushed to the hospital . . . I'm going out of my mind trying to find her."

Then, in a desperate tone, he reiterated,

"Is she here?"

The desk clerk, who almost immediately started thumbing through the large stack of alphabetized "P" admittance cards, as soon as Bill mention the name, Price, found her card, pulled it out, and hurriedly scanned its brief contents . . . including the large typed notation which read,

'Please contact Dr. Jordan Brown immediately if Mr. William Price asks for his wife. DO NOT . . . UNDER ANY CIRCUMSTANCES . . . inform him about the subject's demise.'

The receptionist, disturbed by what she had just read, tried to cover her inner distress by forcing herself to smile compassionately, while pleasantly responding,

"Mr. Price . . . Doctor Brown is handling this case personally. I have instructions to contact him immediately in the event that you did arrive. He's still on duty . . . has been ever since the hurricane hit. Please be patient for a moment while I get hold of him."

For the first time in a long, long while Bill issued a strong sigh of relief. Karen IS here! That was such sweet music to his ears. At last he could allow himself to unwind, believing that his friend, Dr. Brown, was taking care of her.

"Good old Jordan," Bill thought thankfully, as he now heard the intercom ringing the doctor's code bells . . . followed by the message, repeated three times,

"Dr. Jordan Brown . . . Dr. Jordan Brown . . . please contact the admittance receptionist on line 6."

After the receptionist finished her paging of Dr. Brown, Bill asked in a concerned tone,

"By the way, how is my wife?

Fortunately, at that very moment, her desk phone rang and she was provided with the desired reprieve needed to trump-up an evasive answer. When she hung up, she avoided any definitive response to his previous question by immediately stating,

55

"Mr. Price . . . that was Dr. Brown . . . he'll be right down to see you."

"Great! . . . Thank you very much," Bill acknowledged appreciatively before pressing for a reply to his previous unanswered inquiry,

"But, . . . what about my wife? Is she O.K.?"

Pretending to carefully study again the contents of the card before reinserting it back into the middle of the pile, the admission's clerk looked straight into Bill's torpid eyes as she lied convincingly,

"I'm really sorry Mr. Price . . . I just don't know. As you can see, we are so swamped with people coming and going in this terrible emergency, we haven't had a chance to keep our patient's records up to date. But I'm sure that Dr. Brown will explain everything to you shortly. As I said, he's coming right down."

Then, hoping to avoid any further involvement on her part in this sad situation, she politely requested,

"Do you mind waiting for the doctor over there . . . near the elevator, so that I may take care of the next person? . . . Please!"

No . . . Bill didn't mind . . . he didn't mind at all. After the hell of not knowing anything for more than thirty six hours, another moment or two really didn't matter. Not now anyway. Not when he knew for sure she was here, and obviously in Dr. Brown's capable hands. So, he contented himself with the happy thought that he'd soon be with her . . . and maybe with Jonathon too.

"Damn," he snapped, slapping his forehead with the palm of his right hand, obviously mad at himself for neglecting to ask about the baby.

"I may already be a father . . . and not even know it."

With that pleasing speculative thought, a broad smile broke across his unshaven face as he positioned himself over by the down elevator door and calmly waited.

Meanwhile, Dr. Brown was disturbed. His mood was anything but jovial as he descended from the fifth floor. His mind was in a turmoil . . . trying to think of an appropriate way to break the tragic

56

news to Bill . . . knowing full well how devastated Bill was going to be over the loss of Karen.

Somehow . . . somehow he was expected to play God and temper the shock. But how? Words . . . regardless of language of origin . . . are hopelessly inadequate in expressing condolences even for doctors . . . or, perhaps, especially for doctors . . . in human traumas such as this.

How? Dr. Brown silently pondered over and over. How could he mitigate the blow . . . soften the impact of the weight of the universe that was about to collapse on Bill's shoulders? Without question Bill's whole life centered lately around Karen . . . and with her now gone, Jordan speculated there was a high probability that Bill might become an emotional cripple as soon as he learned the truth. No wonder Dr. Brown's confidence was mired at ebb tide.

Still searching for the magic words, Dr. Brown wondered just how long he could successful keep the truth from Bill . . . for that was what he concluded he had to do . . . both for Bill's mental and physical well being. While such a course of action was very unorthodox for a doctor . . . even controversial to the point that he might be rebuked by his peers he, nevertheless, decided to delay telling him . . . and thus postpone the truth . . . at least until some kind of crutch could be provided for Bill to lean on. Although he personally abhorred any deviousness, Jordan reasoned that if he had to play God . . . this time, at least, he was going to play him his own way.

Still he dreaded the inevitable . . . which kept getting ever closer . . . as the elevator now stopped at the lobby . . . and its doors slowly opened.

Bill sprang forward to meet Dr. Brown . . . with the same eagerness that a starved cat exhibits in leaping towards its master bringing it food. There was so much Bill wanted to know . . . and only Jordan could provide him with the desired input.

Both simultaneously greeted each other . . . Bill's tone being one of exhilaration in anticipation of the good news he was expecting . . . while Dr. Brown's was very much subdued . . . as he detested being the bearer of such bad tidings. And while aching internally for Bill . . . and for the departed Karen . . . he bravely contained his grief, at least at the moment of their meeting.

Bill, then, inundated the doctor with a battery of rapid fire inquires about his Karen . . . about Jonathon . . . about both, all at once.

"Bill . . . you've asked me more questions in 30 seconds than I can answer in 30 minutes. I know how anxious you are to know everything . . . and believe me . . . I understand. But come on . . . I want to show you something that I know is going to please you."

With that Dr. Brown took hold of Bill's arm at the elbow, gently steered him onto an up elevator, and pushed the button for the fourth floor . . . the maternity ward. All of a sudden, Dr. Brown's confidence began to return as he suddenly knew just precisely what sequence of actions and scenario to follow in his dictated role of playing God.

"First," he silently reassured himself again, "I've got to give him something tangible to hang onto . . . before I pull the floor out from under him. It's imperative that he now have a strong unbroken link with the living bond that existed between him and Karen . . . a part of both of them . . . conceived in love . . . that still remains alive."

As the elevator rose, Dr. Brown placed his right hand firmly on Bill's shoulder, and then patted it warmly while saying,

"Congratulations, Bill . . . You're a father!"

Spontaneously, Bill let out a howl of joy that loudly resonated off the walls of the elevator . . . with reverberations as clear and as refreshing as reflected sound waves, echoing off the chamber walls of a symphony hall . By the time that Bill recovered from his moment of intense elation, the doors of the elevator were already opening onto the floor of the maternity ward.

"Boy or girl?' he asked excitedly.

"A healthy . . . 7 pound boy."

"Jonathon!" Bill exclaimed. "OUR Jonathon after all."

58

As Bill was led down the wide, spit-polished corridor by Dr. Brown, his chest noticeably began to expand, and his floating gait took on an air of jubilation. When both finally stood in front of the glassed enclosed nursery, Dr. Brown nodded to the attending nurse, who apparently understood the cue because she immediately moved along the second row of bassinets, stopped aside one, picked up a tiny infant wrapped in a blue bunting, and cradled it in her arms . . . as she brought it over to the glass window, where it might be properly adored.

Bill's supreme happiness was so very apparent . . . and his reaction so very typical of first time fathers, as evidenced by his ever broadening grin and his predictable paternal request,

"May I hold him?"

Dr. Brown was hoping against hope for such an immediate positive response and, thus, without any hesitation gladly replied,

"Hospital regulations say no, Bill. But this is one time we're going to say to hell with the rules. Of course you may."

With that he pointed his curled index finger at the baby, and wiggled it back and forth in a motion recognized by the nurse as a sign for her to bring the baby to them. When she did, she offered it to Bill who initially was tentative, almost to the point of reluctance, about accepting him in his arms. However, encouraged by both the nurse and doctor, Bill soon reached out longingly, then proudly took him from her and instinctively cuddled his son . . . with the inherent confidence that grows exponentially in all new parents. It was obvious that Bill was infinitely pleased at what he and Karen had created and watched absolutely spellbound as the baby stretched his tiny arms and fingers to full extension, yawned, and opened drowsy eyes that Bill swore locked onto his.

"Look!" he rejoiced in uttering aloud, "He has Karen's blue eyes."

Dr. Brown pretended to notice for the first time that which he had already observed several times before . . . but played the Devil's advocate by commenting on the known medical fact,

59

"All babies have blue eyes when just born, Bill. We'll have to wait a few weeks to see what color his eyes will really be."

Bill stared down again at Jonathon for a brief moment, contemplating Jordan's remark, before raising his head and laughing jubilantly,

"They'll still be Karen's crystal blue!"

The nurse smiled . . . even Dr. Brown joined in the merriment with a wide ear to ear grin. But his gaiety quickly evaporated into a solemn posture when Bill casually asked,

"Speaking of Karen . . . when can I see her? She's all right . . . isn't she Jordan?"

Dr. Brown's reply wasn't exactly an untruth, although it was purposely misleading in its implication.

"Not yet Bill. She's sleeping . . . sleeping the sleep of the just . . . as they say."

Still trying to stall for more time, Dr. Brown, none the less, circuitously started to reveal Karen's fate, now that Bill had Jonathon to hang onto,

"Neither of us can comprehend what Karen went through the day the hurricane struck . . . with her having Jonathon prematurely as she did."

Bill, feeling extremely guilty because he was away at this critical time, immediately interrupted and said,

"Of all the times I should have been home with her . . . that was the one Jordan."

"Don't blame yourself Bill. No one had any inkling that the baby would come early. I certainly didn't expect it. Just like no one anticipated that the storm would strike . . . but it did. So many lost their lives needlessly because of it. Yet . . . your son was born. Nature's strange dichotomy . . . seeds of life and death . . . both taking and giving at the same time. Satan's and God's endless battle with humanity that makes us either victims or victors . . . and in some cases . . . both, simultaneously. A never ending evolution that none of us will ever fully understand . . . even though we may come to accept it."

Now at Dr. Brown's subtle hand signal, the nurse gently took Jonathon from Bill and returned him to his bassinet while Jordan, still conversing metaphorically, led Bill to the elevator on route to the doctor's fifth floor office.

"You've been holding onto something very special Bill . . . A treasure that is part of you . . . part of Karen. Always remember . . . Jonathon will carry both of you in him throughout his life, no matter what happens to either of you. He'll remain part of both of you in sundry ways . . . just as you saw Karen's blue eyes in him a few moments ago. No one will EVER take that bond away from you."

Bill was confused by Jordan's line of the discussion. And when the door to Dr. Brown's office door closed behind them, he stated bluntly,

"Jordan . . . what in the world are you trying to tell me. Ever since we saw Jonathon your conversation has vacillated between the beauty of life and the acceptance of . . . well for want of a better analogy . . . death. Frankly, I don't know why the philosophical lecture at this time. I just don't unders----"

Bill didn't finish his last thought because all at once his eyes bolted wide open with fright as he intuitively now understood completely. Uncontrollably he screamed out,

"Oh, God NO! . . . no . . . no . . . NO!"

Dr. Brown remained mute . . . experiencing the same deep, tortuous pain that now was ripping Bill apart.

Unashamedly . . . both of then broke down and cried . . . and cried . . . and cried . . . And as Jordan had expected . . . Bill soon became hysterical.

CHAPTER 5

When Bill slowly opened his eyes about two hours later, he found himself lying in a hospital bed, a needle dispensing the last drops of fluid from an I.V. container into a vein of his right arm, and Dr. Brown standing alongside of him reading his chart. Looking up confused, he inquisitively asked,

"Jordan . . . what happened? What am I doing here?"

"Relax Bill . . . We're just treating you with a very mild tranquilizer . . . for the shock you experienced after surmising the fate of Kar--"

"Oh, God!" Bill shouted out loudly as he now wailed anew . . . now remembering.

"Poor Karen. I just can't believe it. Tell me it's a bad dream Jordan. Oh, God . . . please tell me she is still alive. She had everything to live for. She was too young . . . too vibrant . . . too beautiful to die." Then, he began angrily lashing out at Dr. Brown, "Why couldn't you save her? You know how much I love her and need her. Why didn't you save her . . . instead of Jonathon ?"

This spontaneous outburst . . . against both Jordan and Jonathon . . . bounced harmless off compassionate Dr. Brown, who had been exposed to this type of reactionary emotional release many times before. But, it penetrated deeply into Bill's ear canals, echoed loudly within his distraught mind, wakened his conscience to the raw cruelty of his remark, and caused him to quickly react by slamming shut his fiery eyes, in utter disgust, as he meekly tried to apologize,

"Forgive me Jordan . . . I really didn't mean what I just said . . . I'm sure you did everything possible to save Karen."

"Bill . . . I understand completely. Believe me I do. There's absolutely nothing to forgive. But I do want you to know that Karen didn't have the baby here. She apparently self-delivered on a back-road, somewhere in Rocky Hill, probably while trying to get to the hospital.

"The police say her car got stuck in the mud when she drove off the road in order to avoid an obstacle in her path. When they brought her and Jonathon in, we tried exhaustively to revive her . . . believe me we tried! Tried for over an hour. But, she was gone . . . there was nothing any of us could do . She undoubtedly was already dead when the State Police found her. To be perfectly honest though, Bill, we don't know how she died . . . we only know we couldn't save her. Just Jonathon."

Bill frowned . . . before lashing out again, obviously perplexed and disturbed about something Dr. Brown had said.

"What do you mean you don't know how she died? Didn't she bleed to death or, have some other type of fatal delivery complication?"

Dr. Brown regretted that the conversation had focused in on Karen's demise so soon . . . a discussion that he had hope to put off for a day or so until Bill had more fully recovered. However, noting the agitated build up of stress in Bill's tone of chastisement, Jordan abruptly decided to speak frankly,

"We can't be sure, Bill. From the police report, the front seat of her car was soaked with blood. It certainly appears from that observation that she hemorrhaged. Probably did . . . that would seem to be the most logical cause.

"But if you ask, are we positive? The answer has to be no. That's why the police keep hounding us. They want to know if the death was due to natural causes . . . or if they are dealing with a homicide."

Bill commenced to shake violently, while the impact of that last remark began sinking into his dulled mind. When it finally did, he bolted straight up and shouted mournfully,

"Homicide? . . . Murder? Do you mean that someone killed my Karen?"

"Bill . . . please calm down. No one said she WAS! Or, was not murdered. That's only a very remote possibility. But until we inform the police as to the apparent cause of death, they're going to keep the file open . . . There's only one way that we're going to find that out for sure . . . and remove all doubt."

Dr. Brown suddenly realized what a deep quagmire he was about to get into . . . as soon as Bill asked curiously,

"How's that?"

Jordan paused . . . the explanative word perched on the tip of his tongue . . . Reluctant to spit it out, he swallowed hard, momentarily suppressing its release. Now, sighing deeply, he blurted out,

" An autopsy."

Bill, at first, seemed stunned by the utterance. Then, his face flushed red with anger . . . Bill was visibly pissed . . . at the doctor . . . at the whole world. The mere mention of the word autopsy triggered a repulsive reaction that almost caused him to throw up.

"Autopsy!" he bellowed, in vehement protest. "On my Karen! . . . You want to slice her up . . . cut out her beautiful heart . . . mutilate her lovely body. Are you insane Jordan? In God's name what for . . .?"

"So we'll know positively," injected Dr. Brown defensively.

"Who gives a shit!" retorted Bill, using exclamatory language quite foreign to his normal vocabulary . . . but quite indicative of his intense mental anguish and distraught state of mind. "She's dead isn't she?

"Will your goddamned autopsy bring her back to life? Will

65

that make her well again so that she can open her pretty blue eyes and say to me, "Hi, Bill darling . . . have you seen Jonathon yet?"

At the conclusion of this short tirade, Bill broke down and wept profusely.

"Bill! Control yourself," pleaded Dr. Brown. "I know you're upset . . . but for now why don't you just think about it."

"No. Never! No autopsy ever. I'll never let anyone butcher her. Let her sleep! Please let her sleep in peace without being disturbed again. You . . . yourself . . . said she was sleeping the sleep of the just . . . Well, Goddamn it then . . . just let her sleep."

"But Bill . . . suppose someone did murder her. Don't you want him brought to Justice? Don't you want revenge?"

"Revenge! That's one reason I don't want to know. Do you think I'd ever have a moment's peace if I knew some savage destroyed my precious Karen? I'd spend the rest of my life searching for him, until I found him. Then, I'd tear him to shreds . . . one ounce of flesh at a time.

"What kind of miserable life would Jonathon have when he finds out his mother was murdered . . . and his father was a murderer. It would cripple him psychologically . . . just as I'm crippled now over the lost of Karen . . . No! No autopsy. I won't permit it."

Now looking straight into Dr. Brown's eyes, he pleaded passionately,

"Jordan . . . Please! Can't you just say Karen hemorrhaged? . . . And let it be done at that. Let the matter rest. For God's sake Jordan . . . PLEASE! . . . For Jonathon . . . For me . . . Even for the bastard that killed her, if she was really murdered. Don't put us all through hell . . . every day of our lives. I couldn't live with it, Jordan.

"Can't you just put on the death certificate that she died of natural causes? That's all I ask. That's all my fragile mind will accept. Please Jordan! Don't make it any harder to bear than it already is. Just say that she hemorrhaged . . . please!"

Dr. Brown, listening intently, stood both motionless and

speechless for several minutes as he contemplated his obligation . . . not only to Bill . . . to Karen . . . but also to society . . . and to his own personal integrity as a doctor before announcing softly,

"There'll be no autopsy on Karen, Bill. You have my word on that."

Bill's eyes welled with tears of relief as he whispered gratefully,

"Thank you Jordan," now followed immediately by his unexpected request.

"Please take me to Karen . . . I want to see her now."

The hospital morgue was situated down in the basement in a large cement-block room, painted white, located approximately 300 feet along the left corridor leading away from the cafeteria. As Dr. Brown's and Bill's footsteps now echoed in the dingily lit hollow chamber, Bill couldn't help but recall that only twenty months ago, he and Karen were happily sipping coffee in that cafeteria at the beginning moments of their life together . . . with tomorrows that promised fairy tale joy and contentment. And now, as he came to see her in death, he felt cheated . . . because life without Karen would be no life at all.

As Jordan started to push open the swinging wooden doors, at the entrance to the morgue, he asked in a soft church voice,

"Are you sure you want to do this now, Bill?"

Without hesitation, Bill responded,

"I Must!"

With their exception, the room was devoid of the living, but otherwise occupied with about ten bodies, neatly laid out in orderly array on wooden slabs, covered completely with white sheets. The undeniable stench of death permeated the heavy atmosphere, in spite of constant gyrations of two large ceiling fans nobly attempting to exchange foul air for fair through an elaborate sheet metal duct system.

"Mostly yesterday's flood victims," Dr. Brown offered without being asked. "They'll be moved out shortly to the funeral parlors

67

for embalmment, as soon as the nearest kin make arrangements later this morning." Then, getting more tense, he added,

"Karen lies over there in the refrigerated vault, We were waiting for approval to conduct . . ."

Quickly cutting himself off before finishing so as not to resurface the painful discussions of a short time ago, he began anew,

"She'll only be kept here until I sign the certificate in the morning."

Dr. Brown hesitantly waited in front of the vault, reluctant to open it, hoping that Bill might change his mind. But now found himself doing so because of Bill's determined emotional plea,

"Please open it!"

Slowly . . . ever so slowly . . . Dr. Brown slid out the slab, which cantilevered so that the head was furthest from the wall cavity. Then . . . even more slowly . . . and carefully . . . he began folding back the white cover sheet.

Bill trembled . . . not in response to the cool draft emanating from the cold vault . . . but from the chills of remorse that racked his quivering, jellyfish-like frame as first her head . . . then, her body became visible.

Bill forced each tentative step over to the slab, as if his feet were weighted with concrete. Once aside the slab, he gazed at Karen . . . So dead . . . and yet so angelic in appearance, dressed in a white hospital smock with her long taffy blonde hair draped in front over her breasts, culminating at her waist where her clasped hands rested in a prayer-like arrangement.

"A Madonna still . . . even in death." Bill thought, unable to suppress the tears streaming down his wet whiskered cheeks, or, the scream of "Oh, God NO!" that surged suddenly out of his voice box.

Then, leaning over, Bill gently cupped her face in the palms of his trembling hands, and longingly kissed her cold lips ever so tenderly while quietly whispering.

"Oh! Karen . . . Oh! my darling Karen!" just before collapsing onto the floor.

CHAPTER 6

Bill was hopelessly crushed by Karen's death and, quickly, became a basket case over her loss. Nothing could free his tormented mind from the guilt of not being with Karen in her critical hour of need. Erroneously, he felt that he . . . and he alone . . . was responsible for her demise. Whatever the cause! And the mental torture of this self-inflicted burden was so unrelenting and so unbearable, he soon exhibited outward signs of being brain dead . . . just as surely as if he had been laid to rest along with Karen . . . Only his living crypt encased his body with a sinister gloom of deep depression, instead of the colorful floral blanket bouquets that adorned Karen's ornate casket at her funeral.

"She'd still be alive today if I hadn't made that trip," he wailed as his hands shook violently, while holding a photograph of Karen that was now saturated with his tears.

He became both judge and jury. And, convicted himself for her death . . .

Then, sentenced himself to the lifelong punishment that this guilt would always bring him.

He became so unbalanced by her loss, his motivation and will to live drained, incessantly, from his weakened body, which rapidly wasted away from lack of needed rest and proper nourishment. Not only did he now portray the tragic image of an emaciated zombie . . . a victim truly of the living dead, but his deranged mind

... cracking under the unyielding pressure of self guilt began to foster suicidal thoughts.

Only thoughts of Jonathon rewove the thread of life into his dead body. Only Jonathon . . . his unbroken link to Karen . . . was his savior from the suicide he often contemplated and surely would have executed if it hadn't been for him. But because of Jonathon, Bill's broken mind slowly began to mend and recover over the dreary months that followed.

Painfully, Bill discovered that life goes on . . . even when all happiness and purpose has been dissipated from it. Life does go on . . . and, somehow, one continues to endure, in spite of the vacuum. At first, only from hour to hour . . . then, only from day to day. But, Bill also learned that time, in all its passing, never really heals all wounds. At best, it sometimes just stitches a permanent scar that forever entraps the misery and lonely strife inside a lamenting heart, which in his case stopped beating and feeling when Karen died.

Yet, solely for Jonathon's sake Bill went on . . . even though inwardly . . . he continued to cry in anguish for relief from the agony of no longer having her.

Bill had to start over. But, he knew it couldn't be in Cromwell where he was constantly reminded of Karen . . . her personal touch . . . the wonderful life they were building together. Not in Cromwell. Anywhere else! Not there, but in some new environment . . . where the reminiscent thoughts of Karen might someday fade and not dominate his present or future.

So at the end of December, Bill tearfully sold his home, continued to leave Jonathon under the temporary care of his elderly parents, who took him back to their residence in Worcester, Massachusetts, and moved away.

Boston was an easy choice for him to make. After all, this historic capital stood tall as one of the Nation's richest financial centers . . . teeming with powerful banks and industrial entrepreneurs. But, more than that, it possessed an environment conducive to the strong cultural and educational growth that he wanted Jonathon to absorb.

Bill considered himself very fortunate in quickly finding just the perfect home. One exquisitely furnished. And, one purchased for a fraction of its real value due to the lingering cancer of the economic depression. A home far away from all the noisy, congested, narrow-lane streets of the metropolis . . . one away from the claustrophobic monotony of the row houses of Beacon Hill. One set out among the sprawling, prestigious mansions that skirted the circumference of the city limits where Jonathon, as he grew older, could frolic freely within the confines of a magnificently treed, spacious five acre estate.

Their new home was a classic English Tudor, artistically brushed onto the brow of a rolling landscape, surrounded by the natural shade umbrella of numerous massive chestnuts, walnuts, and elms . . . all idyllically secluded by the privacy of a shoulder-high, hand-laid, brown stone wall that ran unbroken for two thousand feet along its peripheral boundary, except for a small gap between which two huge iron gates provided the only entrance to a graciously winding driveway, terraced with hundreds of low-cut rosebush hedges, that promised to preview an exterior highlighted in a fertile garden-like atmosphere in the summertime.

As soon as Bill arrived in Boston, even before settling in, he started looking for someone who could satisfy his housekeeping and nanny needs, so that he could be permanently reunited with Jonathon.

However, the first two weeks of January passed without any success. His ads in the Boston papers resulted only in interviews with a handful of candidates, who according to Bill's rigid standards were totally unqualified.

Understandably, Bill was now very discouraged as he sat reading in the library while waiting for the last scheduled applicant of the day, . . . doubting that he would have any luck in the near future of discovering just the right person. One capable of meeting his very special requirements and expectations for the position.

The musical chimes of the front door bell indicated that this latest candidate was at least prompt . . . a characteristic he identified with very appreciatively. Opening the door, Bill came face to face with a comely, fair-skinned woman, approximately 5'6" in height, having auburn hair that was swept up and hidden under a blue ribboned bonnet that blended very nicely with her navy blue woolen overcoat.

As her lively green eyes smiled at him from behind an attractive pair of horned-rimmed glasses, Bill couldn't deny that her appearance was certainly neat and proper . . . even though he had already prejudged her . . . deciding on the spur of the moment to reject her because of her young age, which he estimated to be no more than 27 years . . . much too young for the matronly person he had in mind for the job. His next advertisement would correct this apparent omission of detail on his part.

"Good Afternoon," she said in a crisp tone, saturated with an undeniable Irish accent. "I'm Cathy O'Connor. I've come to interview for the service job you advertised in the Boston Globe."

Even though Bill's mind was negatively made up, he felt obliged to be courteous and go through the pretense of considering her.

"Please come in. My name is William Price. May I take your coat, Mrs. O'Connor?"

"Miss," she politely corrected, Bill . . . while removing both her topcoat and hat which he took and placed into the vestibule closet.

"Sorry," Bill offered apologetically for his mistake."I just naturally assumed an attractive person of your age would be married. Come. Let's sit in the living room where we can discuss the position and your qualifications."

As they moved out of the marbled tiled entry foyer, through an opened glass paneled doorway, and stepped down onto a plush

Chinese oriental rug that almost embossed the entire surface of the highly polished mosaic oak floor, Cathy caught herself silently releasing a deep sigh of wonderment, as she viewed the beauty of the almost square, spacious living room adorned with a ponderous, hand-split stone fireplace centrally located on the far wall.

A unique cathedral-type mahogany, hand-hewn beamed ceiling expanded overhead, which lorded over several large windows, each impressively dressed with antique satin drapes, And, directly in front of her, at eye level, an array of cut velvet couches and lounging chairs that seemed to reach out with promised comfort, as they reflected the homey warmth now oozing from a roaring log fire . . . whose tongues of dancing flames crackled their own hypnotic glowing welcome.

Cathy was so stunned by the eloquence of the surroundings that her fully dilated eyes were now perceiving, she found herself day dreaming of how wonderful it would be to live and work in a mansion such as this.

"Won't you please be seated," Bill offered, pointing to a large three-cushioned sofa by the fireplace.

Then after she sat, he proceed to relax his frame into a black leathered, easy chair facing her . . . before beginning,

"Now then," he said, "As stated in my ad, I'm looking for someone, or a married couple, who on a full time basis will live-in, take charge of running this home, and, more importantly, provide loving care for my four month old son."

Cathy's unasked question about Mrs. Price was soon answered by Bill's delayed follow up remark, which was tearfully expressed,

"My dear wife died in childbirth . . . and."

Bill had to pause briefly to recapture his lost composure . . . then bravely continued,

"This position will be very demanding and, under the circumstances, ideally requires a person who has a special combination of qualifications. You see, I've had no experience yet in being a

73

father and wouldn't know where to begin in taking care of my son, Jonathon, or this house."

Now that his lowered brown eyes were no longer misty, he looked directly into Cathy's and inquired,

"Did you bring your resume and references with you?"

Without hesitating, Cathy fumbled for a few seconds inside her black patent leather bag, removed several folded sheets of paper, and handed them to Bill who had gotten up and stepped over to accept them. Bill returned to his recliner, sat again, and commence at once to study the contents of the documents.

"I was right!" he exclaimed silently. "Only 25 . . . much too young."

As he scanned through the rest of her credentials, however, Bill couldn't help but be deeply impressed. Three years working for Dr. and Mrs. Bernard, caring for their household and two children . . . and almost five years with Attorney and Mrs. Rogers and their three youngsters. Both references spoke highly of her competency, loyalty, innate intelligence, and remarkable way with children.

"Almost the perfect candidate," Bill thought as he caught himself wavering in his previously set opinion. But, once again staring directly at Cathy, he said,

"Well, Miss O'Connor . . . everything seems to be excellent . . . except . . . "

"Except?" Cathy interrupted quizzically.

"Frankly . . . you are much younger than the nanny I had envisioned for Jonathon."

Cathy bit down hard on her lower lip, for a brief moment, in an attempt to suppress her obvious anger but, her effort failed.

"Why . . . Mr. Price? Were just you looking for someone to grandmother your child . . . rather than mother him? Believe me, I've changed more bottoms, washed and hung more diapers in my short lifetime than the whole city of Boston unfurls flags on the fourth of July . . . My training started when I was eight because I was the oldest in a prolific Irish family that grew to be three brothers and two sisters before I left for my first nanny position when I was only seventeen."

She paused again . . . but this time only to catch her breath before continuing,

"Your son will soon be darting around here with the vigor and speed of a yearling. Do you really think an older . . . more matronly, grandmother type will be able to keep up with him then? And . . . still possess enough residual patience and energy to do the housework."

"I'm sorry, Mr. Price if my youth, as you so unkindly put it, voids all my natural abilities to be a good housekeeper . . . and more importantly to be an even better governess for your son . . . because of my love for children."

Having now completed her soft spoken, controlled tirade, she then promptly picked herself up, walked over to the hall closet, withdrew her hat first, which she plunked awkwardly on her head, and then reached for her coat, which she started to put on before Bill, who had been caught off-guard, by Cathy's blunt remarks, could respond.

"Wait. Please wait Miss O'Connor . . . Please come back."

But Cathy continued to don her garment until Bill walked towards her and pleaded,

"You have to forgive my impudence . . . my stupidity. You are absolutely right. An older person is not really what we need for this home or for Jonathon. I must have been blinded by sight not to realize that my late wife would now be exactly your age and would have managed everything quite nicely.

"You obviously have all the experience necessary to do more than an adequate job. The work will be exhausting . . . and does require a person with your apparent drive and vitality. I certainly like your references.

"And I must confess, I also like your spunk and your righteous display of pride for your past accomplishments. It shows the type of character that I want Jonathon to possess . . . and from your actions a few moments ago, I know you are going to be a great teacher for us both. Jonathon will be in good hands under your care . . . I'm convinced of that now.

"You see . . . he means everything to me . . . he's all I have that really matters. So if I portrayed an immature prejudice about age for the position, it was because I was only thinking of what's best for him . . . when in reality, in my naivete, you would be a better judge of that . . . than I would be, I'm sure."

Cathy absorbed every word, and liked what she heard and what she saw in this thin, but, still handsome gentleman, who was man enough to immediately admit to a mistake and right a wrong in his judgment of her.

"Apparently, I have already put my big foot in my mouth where we're concerned, but if you'll forgive me and want to reconsider, I would like to give it a try.

"The job is yours if you want it . . . but."

"Not again . . . Mr. Price," injected Cathy, fully expecting yet another frivolous reason for her rejection.

Bill was amazed at her quickness in hanging on to a word and to snap back with an appropriate retort.

"No," he interjected, "But, I was just going to add that you must give me at least two months notice if you decide to leave me. Because if you do accept, on this weekend we'll pick up my son, who is now staying with my mother . . . And once we do that, I'll really be completely at your mercy."

Relieved at last, Cathy unequivocally stated,

"Don't you worry about that Mr. Price. I don't think that's ever going to be a problem with us unless you ask me to leave. And, then, all I want to know is why."

"Consider it a deal Miss O'Connor . . . or may I call you Cathy?"

"Please do, Mr. Price."

"Call me Bill, Cathy"

Even though she had never done so before, and knew it was

highly unusual for a person of her station to refer to an employer by his first name, she felt instinctively that in this instance it not only was a good omen, but it seemed natural that she should do so. Therefore, without hesitation she replied,

"Well then . . . please do, Bill. And now, if you'll help me, I have my bags ready to be unloaded from the taxi waiting in your driveway. As you can readily see, I am confident of my capabilities . . . and aggressive about getting something I want. And, I do want this job."

With a nodding of his head, which seemed to again reflect his continued amazement, yet approval, Bill reiterated,

"Just as I said, Cathy, I certainly do like your spunk . . . Now then, let's go get your bags so I can show you the rest of the house and your room."

6 B

Bill was up before the crack of dawn on Saturday . . . long before the alarm, set for seven, went off . . . long before the morning sun had a chance to filter through lacy bedroom curtains to flash dance on sleepy eyelids. Jonathon was coming home today! And for the first time since before Karen's death, Bill felt a twinge of excitement that even his remorse could not suppress.

Quickly, he showered, shaved, and dressed as his eagerness to start out for Worcester and Jonathon propelled him forward. Now ready, he stood in front of Cathy's closed bedroom door and knocked. A knock that he had to repeat several times, while simultaneously calling out,

"Cathy . . . Cathy are you awake?"

Snuggled peacefully under a down puff, Cathy, who had been sound asleep, reacted ever so slowly to Bill's disturbance. First, by blinking startled eyes, then by stretching arms languidly towards the high ceiling, as she yawned sleepily. Finally, after another series of knocks, followed by the same repetitious calling of her name, she rewarded Bill with a muffled acknowledgement that he sought.

"Uh huh . . . I'm up Bill . . . I'm sorry, I didn't hear my alarm go off. I must have overslept. What time is it?"

Bill glanced down at his wrist watch and blushed beet red, as he responded sheepishly in a low voice,

"Five thirty."

78

So softly in fact that, at Cathy's request, he had to repeat it in a louder tone.

"Five thirty! No wonder I'm still groggy. I thought you told me to set the alarm for seven?"

"I did. But, I just couldn't sleep a moment longer. Do you mind if we start for Worcester a little earlier?"

Cathy admired the way Bill treated her as an equal in his requests . . . never as just his servant.

"Not at all. Just give me ten minutes to wash and dress and I'll be right down to make your breakfast before we leave."

Bill certainly was in a mood to eat that morning . . . his adrenal glands activated hunger pangs that finally were being properly nourished.

"We'll have those cheeks filled out in no time," Cathy impulsively chuckled as Bill dove into his second batch of pancakes.

"And probably my stomach too," Bill answered with a straight face. "Your cooking seems to have stimulated my appetite again."

"Thanks for the compliment, Bill. However, I really think Jonathon is the one that deserves all the credit this time. Your enthusiasm today reminds me of a child about to receive a lollipop."

"Oh, Cathy! You just can't imagine how happy I am to be bringing Jonathon back home where he belongs. It's a whole new world opening up for me."

For some reason, Cathy felt as if a whole new world was awakening for her, also. And because of Bill, she eagerly looked forward to the trip and to her future role of mothering Jonathon.

The sunrise that particular morning was rather spectacular, as the near eastern horizon's cirrostratus clouds were ablaze with a reddish atmospheric radiance that gave one the illusion that the Boston harbor must be burning and the heavens above had caught on fire. Cathy, awed, kept looking backwards periodically over her shoulder at the glowing sky as they headed west, out of the city, towards Worcester.

79

Bill was not immune either to Nature's display as he now muttered the legendary seafarer's prediction that usually accompanies its sight,

"Red sky in the morning . . . Sailors take warning."

"Now don't go and spoil it all, Bill. It's absolutely magnificent!"

And it remained so during the entire trip, as the only foul weather encountered along the way were light snow flurries that painted the countryside a renewed, bright, fresh appearance that mirrored Bill's present emotional attitude.

For the moment at least, memories of Karen were temporarily suppressed as Bill watched Cathy's child-like delight in absorbing both the sunrise and the scenery. In fact, he couldn't resist the urge to say,

"Looks as if you are enjoying your lollipop too."

Both smiled broadly. And Cathy seemed especially pleased at this occurrence because it was the first time since meeting Bill that he had done so.

However, from that moment on, Bill's spirits began to ebb noticeably. For the more he glanced over at Cathy, the more he reminisced about Karen and her travels with him. He felt himself slipping backwards again . . . both in time and in mood, as his conscience kept whipping him in denial of the smidgen of pleasure he was now experiencing while watching Cathy.

The hurt became so bad, he finally just kept his eyes focused on the road ahead, refusing any temptation to glance again at Cathy and share her exhilaration.

Cathy noted the mood change in Bill but, while ignorant of its cause, decided not to draw attention to its presence. Intuitively, however, she suspected that his sombrousness must be associated with his wife's passing.

"The bond between them must have been strong and beautiful," she thought to herself with a twinge of envy that seemed to startle her, particularly in light of the fact she had never experienced this emotion before.

Still awash in all the memories of trips past, Bill suddenly stated out of the blue,

"Oh, by the way Cathy . . . every month I have to travel for two weeks on company business.

"My next trip is in mid-February. Will you be able to handle the house and Jonathon alone while I'm gone?"

Cathy snatched this opportunity to perk Bill up, and to dispel any worries he might have in this regard by replying confidently,

"No problem at all Bill. I'm use to being on my own. And I'm sure everything will be just fine. In fact, the way time flies when you have a little baby to mother and a big house to take care of, I probably won't even know you're gone . . . until you return."

Bill knew Cathy was joshing but, none the less, was relieved by her retort, and by the fact that they were now driving up a narrow macadam driveway and parking alongside a traditional, wooden shingled bungalow .

"Well, Cathy . . . here we are. The old homestead where I was born. My parents have lived in this house from the time they got married, over thirty five years ago. I've offered to buy them a new, bigger home in the country a hundred times, but they love this place, even though it is quite simple.

"They say they aren't moving until the good lord takes them. Both of them can be a little obstinate at times . . . especially my mother. So if I show a streak of stubbornness now and then, you'll know where it came from. But, they mean well, in spite of their opinionated and sometimes old fashion ways.

"They're Yankee stock and have developed their own roots. I've stopped trying to dig them up or change them in any way."

Bill's mother, who was awakened by a call from Bill and alerted to an early arrival, was anxiously watching at the window and, upon seeing them approach, quickly rushed to the front door and waved a hearty welcome.

"You'll like my mother," Bill said while waving back. "And, I just know she's going to like you."

But Bill was so wrong . . . again. For as soon as they entered the home and began removing their overcoats, he immediately recognized a sudden stiffening of his mother's posture . . . and a slight cocking of her right eyebrow . . . both give away signs that she always unconsciously exhibited whenever disturbed about something. But about what? It wasn't long before Bill had the answer.

"Mother. I would like you to meet Cathy O'Connor . . . Jonathon's governess."

Cathy had already gone through close scrutiny and first impression analysis by his mother's detailed eye scan of her, which noted with dismay . . . even before her coat was removed . . . the bare fourth finger of her left hand. The absence of any tell-tale ring had precipitated her unfriendly mood, and the adverse direction of the conversation that followed,

"You're not married, yet, Cathy?" she stated bluntly.

Cathy was completely taken back by this initial, unfriendly greeting, but soon recovered and answered honestly, and politely,

"No . . . Mrs. Price. Not yet."

"Oh! . . . then, you must be going steady and expect to be engaged soon?" was her cool retort.

Cathy bit down hard on her lower lip in anticipation of a confrontation about to transpire. And in spite of her brewing Irish temper and feisty nature that normally dictated a vocal response . . . she didn't reply . . . she just bit down harder. Hard enough to cut her lip.

Meanwhile Bill, who also was visible upset by his mother's surprising third-degree inquiry into Cathy's personal life, reacted immediately,

"Mother! I don't understand. Is something bothering you?"

"Yes. There certainly is Bill. When you called the other day and told me you finally found someone to care for Jonathon, I naturally assumed that she would be married . . . or widowed. Not young and single! Good Lord . . . whatever were you thinking? Do you realize what your neighbors will say? What a heyday Boston gossipers will have whispering about the two of you living together! How could you be so naive and so foolish . . . so blind to the scandal talk that will circulate . . . regardless of whether or not there's any truth to it?

"Cathy, undoubtedly, is very capable. And I'm sure she's a very fine person. But, it just doesn't look right to me . . . and I'm your mother. What do you think it will look to others? No! I don't like it, and I'm sure your father won't either. You can't allow this, Bill. For your sake . . . Jonathon's sake . . . even Cathy's sake . . . you just can't permit this to happen."

Bill was dumbfounded. Dumbfounded and angrier than he had been in years at hearing his mother's brief morality lecture. It never entered his innocent mind that he would have to contend with this biased consideration. His only objection to Cathy, initially, was her youth. Never that they might become victims of malicious rumors. Obviously hurt by his mother's remarks, no matter how well intended, he lashed out adamantly,

"To hell with the bias crowd mother! I hired Cathy because, in my mind, she's the right person to care for Jonathon. Nothing will change my mind about that unless, and until, she proves my intuition to be wrong. Now, let's not argue about it anymore . . . today or ever again. Let's just drop the subject. Let that be the end of it."

Even though this line of discussion was cut short . . . the fragile thread of a happy mood that had weaved back into Bill's life, stemming from the anticipation of seeing Jonathon was badly frayed. And, in spite of all effort to ignore the morning's event, the hangover tensions of the episode lingered and considerably dampened his excitement of once again holding his son, Jonathon.

Consequently, Bill decided not to prolong his stay in Worcester, and after a brief snack at noontime, quickly packed the car with

Jonathon's belongings and headed back to Boston with his son and Cathy.

Throughout the return trip, Bill's mood remained quiet and somber, while Jonathon, wrapped inside the blue bunting knitted by Karen, contentedly slept, cuddled in Cathy's arms. Bill fought off the tears . . . internally lamenting the fact that it wasn't Karen that was now holding Jonathon motherly close . . . but almost a perfect stranger. He felt cheated . . . for this moment really should have belonged to just him and Karen.

Cathy's utterance, "I guess you were right after all about the 'red sky' omen," suddenly awoke Bill, engrossed in his own self-pity, to the realization that he had selfishly neglected any consideration of Cathy's feelings. He hastily tried to atone for his oversight by saying,

"I'm sorry Cathy for being such a dull traveling companion. But I seem to be mired in a sea of depression . . . have been ever since losing Karen. I certainly owe you an apology for not being in brighter spirits. Also, for my mother's uncalled reaction towards you."

"No you don't Bill . . . on either account. I understand what you must be going through with the lost of your wife, and I really do understand what your mother was implying.

"In fact, I've been thinking about what she said ever since it happened. Maybe it would be best for you and Jonathon if I did leave . . . I'm willing to do so as soon as you find someone else that is more suitable."

"Cathy . . . I've been watching you with Jonathon. You do have a way with children And I can see that Jonathon is going to get all the motherly love that Karen would have given him . . . I want you to stay Cathy . . . even if the local tongues start wagging."

Cathy was buoyed to the heavens by his remark for the last thing in the world she wanted was to leave Jonathon, who she knew needed her, or to leave Bill, for whom she already felt a strange attachment.

"Bring on the wags then. They will soon find out they're no match for my Irish temper."

Bill's tentative smile did a lot to blow away the gloomy clouds that had stalled over them since their arrival in Worcester. But, he surprised himself even more when he impulsively asked,

"Cathy, how come a pretty woman with all your wit and charm never got married?"

Cathy didn't bite her lip this time. This time she just looked directly into Bill's brown, magnetic eyes and without a moment's hesitation, truthfully responded,

"I just never met anyone before that I really loved."

Bill noticed Cathy's mild blush, and the teasing sparkle in her smiling eyes, as he slowly nodded knowingly . . . after all . . . he once felt exactly the same way . . . until he met Karen.

6 C

Meanwhile, down in the deep South near the apex of the Florida peninsula, just below Miami, Joe and Sue were still on the run in their continued exodus from the dastardly crime committed in Connecticut. For months, their day to day existence had been a living hell ... an unbelievable nightmare that tormented and haunted every waking moment since the tragic event.

Joe's paranoia about being caught by the law, and Sue's moral schizophrenia, over being an accomplice to the murder and kidnapping of the victim's new born child, was driving them both to the brink of psychotic behavior.

"They know I did it!" Joe would cry out over and over again. "They're after me. They're going to hang me."

Convinced that his fantasied law-hunters were constantly pursuing and closing in on him, he resorted to every conceivable trick to camouflaged their presence as they fearfully zigged and zagged southward, behaving much like a cunning fox, who desperately tries to throw off the baying hounds from its scent of prey. Consequently, like gypsies, they never stopped in any one place for more than a couple of days ... And then only when absolutely necessary to work an odd job, here and there, to get the cash needed for food and fuel before rapidly moving on to yet another unknown destination. Being so destitute, they couldn't afford to waste money on lodgings, so instead, crawled each night onto a make-shift bed created in the back of their open pick-up truck, one poorly sheltered from the elements of bad weather by a crudely hung canopy, fabricated out of tattered sheets of canvas scrounged along the way.

Only upon reaching the warmer soils of lower Georgia and Florida were they finally allowed the comfort of sleeping on the grassy ground, sometimes under a blanket of discarded newspapers when it was chilly or, other times, just under the stars when it was warm enough.

Through it all, Sue faithfully tended to the baby's needs with the same passion of motherly love that possessed her to steal the child in the first place, even though heartbroken over her inability to nurse him and provide his trembling lips with the mother's milk that he wailed for constantly. But, unpasteurized milk, pilfered from grazing cows in the open fields, had to suffice as his primary source of nutrition, while her dry nipples could only serve to pacify his insatiable desire to suck, despite his frustration and failure to drain anything of substance from her soft, warm breasts . . . except love.

But Steve survived . . . And Steve, who Sue named after her late brother, was the only ray of sunshine enabling her to endure the grueling hardships of each miserable day . . . for Joe's fright quickly turned him into a bitter, weak, and incoherent man, who babbled constantly in tirades against a world that stacked the cards of life against him, climaxed by his unintentional murder of Steve's mother.

Thus, in reality, Sue had two babies that she had to comfort with her patience and affection. But while Steve's baby cries kept diminishing with time and care, Joe's whimpering tears steadily increased, reducing him to a hopelessly scared coward that no longer functioned in the manly capacity that was so desperately needed at this time . . .

Now, as they stood together at the road's end, watching and listening to the pounding surf of the Atlantic's incoming tide, Sue could take it no longer and started to plea,

"Joe . . . We've got to stop running. This is no way to exist

. . . We're worse off now than we've ever been. At least out west, we still had a roof over our heads and weren't being chased by the police. Oh, Joe! Why did we ever leave? Joe . . . Why did we ever leave?"

Then sobbing uncontrollably, she stated bluntly,

"We've got to give ourselves up . . . it's the only way that makes any sense."

"I won't! Never!" Joe objected vehemently. "They're not going to hang me at the end of a rope, or put me to death in the electric chair. Is that what you want them to do to me, Sue? Is it?"

"No! Of course not Joe. You must know I don't want anything to happen to you. But we've got to stay in one place long enough to pull ourselves together and not be afraid of our shadows and our tomorrows . . . like we are now. We've got to chance giving ourselves up . . . tell them it was unintentional . . . Tell them you just panicked and didn't mean to do it. They'll believe you. They won't hang you Joe. Let's give ourselves up!"

"Never! We can't take that chance. Look what they did to Bruno Hauptmann when they caught him for allegedly kidnapping and killing the Lindbergh baby. They electrocuted him . . . just like that," he said, snapping his fingers quickly. "And he claimed he was innocent! I know I'm guilty of murder . . . And we're both guilty of kidnapping. I'll hang for sure, Sue if they ever catch me. God only knows how long you'll be sentenced to prison. Do you want to rot away in the penitentiary, with the rats, for the rest of your life?"

Sue squirmed . . . almost as if she could feel the rodents nibbling at her feet. She shuddered, before responding,

"What are we going to do then? Run until our legs come off. Or, until we drop dead from starvation. Or, fright! We've got to do something before we both go insane from fear. We must stop here and now . . . We've got to for our sake and for Steve's sake. He deserves more . . . even if we don't. Maybe . . . maybe, we should leave him at a home for orphans. Oh, Joe! . . . I didn't mean that . . . I love him as if he was our own. I could never leave him . . . or you. I'd rather die first."

"We'll stop soon, Sue. Just as soon as we get to Cuba . . . Out of this country . . . so that they can't come after us. We're almost there Sue . . . Just a little while longer. I don't want to be hanged. I want to live and breath the fresh air.

"Not the smelly rot from inside a prison's death cell."

Sue wanted to live also. Free from fear . . . free from an endless life in prison. Cuba was just over the horizon. Maybe Cuba would bring them both the freedom they now cherished.

"But," mused Sue pensively, "Even if we do gain our physical freedom by escaping to Cuba . . . I just wonder if we'll ever obtain our psychological freedom for what we both have done?"

CHAPTER 7

As Spring approached, earth shattering events on the European and Asian Continents rapidly cascaded the World into a series of escalated bloody conflicts, whose untold miseries soon dwarfed the most tragic hardships attributable to the mundane effects of either poverty or draught. The resulting chaos soon affected the lives of all of its generation . . . with no exceptions. Some . . . like Sue, Cathy, and Bill . . . more than others. But, not even young Jonathon or Steve were immune from its ultimate consequences.

For Satin's warlords, Hitler, Mussolini, Hirohito, and Stalin, having previously dressed and polished their military toys for war, now were ready by March of '39 to begin their parade of conquests to the cadence of their rumbling death drums, whose loudly resounding, rhythmic ra-ta-ta- machine gun beats swiftly martialled and sucked all civilized Nations on their Continents into reluctantly joining the never ending march of a doomed mankind into the foreboding abyss of World War II.

However, across the thousands of miles of vast quiescent seas, in isolation prone America, the death tunes of these distant war drums invariably fell on deaf ears, reverberating only as dampened whispers of calamity in its freedom minded people, who preferred listening to the lively, musical beats of their own peaceful marching bands.

For everyone loves a parade. Particularly in Boston . . .

particularly when celebrating St. Patrick's day, and more particularly when you're Cathy O'Connor.

Then, even if your name is William Price, there is no way that you're going to miss the swinging of the shillelagh . . . or, the wearing of the green. Not on March 17th, when Cathy zealously informs you,

"Come on Bill . . . we're going to watch . . . Jonathon will love it."

How could Bill refuse? Cathy had quickly learned that Bill's Achilles' heel was Jonathon. And since this fresh air outing was supposedly for Jonathon's benefit, Bill enthusiastically agreed.

When they arrived downtown, Bill was absolutely flabbergasted by the size of the crowd lining the sidewalks along the parade route, so enormous in fact, it created an illusion in his mind that everyone in Boston was either Irish, or directly related to the 'blarney stone'. As expected in a jubilant celebration such as this, the blaring fife and drum corps, the many decorated floats, the endless stream of marching dignitaries and everyday people assured this special spectacle a carnival-like atmosphere . . . most understandably boisterous, merry, and colorful with countless green banners and green balloons fluttering proudly in the seasonably cool, on-shore March breeze that is traditionally Boston.

Bill couldn't help but notice that Cathy was enjoying herself immensely as she spontaneously joined with the jovial crowd in singing "When Irish Eyes Are Smiling", in the same sweet, soprano voice that quickly lulled Jonathon to sleep whenever she sang the soft, lilting refrains of the "Too-ra -loo-ra- loo-ral . . . Too-ra -loo-ra-li" . . . lullaby.

He also observed, with interest, how her pretty green eyes . . . so appropriate for the occasion . . . reflected her present happiness, and appeared just as sunny and bright as the fun filled day. Her joyous mood was certainly contagious. And even Jonathon, seated in his stroller, was cooing and gooing with apparent delight at the noisy goings-on.

But, when Bill reached down, picked up Jonathon, and moved forward a couple of steps so that both might get a better view of the parade, Cathy's very happy mood inexplicably became subdued. She caught herself watching Bill as he held his son in his arms, close to his chest, gently cupping Jonathon's tiny right hand in his so as to playfully wave it at the passing paraders. She was watching and admiring his fatherly devotion, as well as his handsome facial features, now that she had fed him back to good health.

She liked what she saw . . . and liked how she felt about him very much, confessing to herself that during the last two months a strange need had developed within her that she now longed to have Bill fulfill. However, she realized, pessimistically, that there was little hope of that happening, especially since Bill always seemed so oblivious of her, except as Jonathon's nursemaid.

A twinge of jealousy piqued at her conscience, causing her to ashamedly look away. Jealous . . . not only of Jonathon for commanding all of Bill's attention . . . but also of the late Karen for the love she must have shared with Bill, and the way, even after death she still possessed him. And while confessing, she also admitted how much she had missed him in February when he was away on his business trip. And with the next one coming up on Monday . . . how she was going to miss him even more.

It was while wondering if Bill would ever allow himself to love again that she became sad and pensive, having concluded that probably no woman would ever replace Karen in his heart. She was so preoccupied with these thoughts, she almost failed to hear Bill's concerned remark,

"Suddenly . . . you're awfully quiet Cathy. Is anything wrong?"

Determined to hide the truth, she nonchalantly replied,

"Oh, I was just thinking, Bill, how much Jonathon is going to miss you when you leave on Monday."

"You must be a mind reader, Cathy . . . I was also thinking how much I was going to miss him. It's getting more difficult for me to go away and leave him . . . but if everything works out as I think it will, I won't be making these monthly trips much longer."

Cathy's curious ears perked up and she inquisitively sought the reason,

"Why . . . are you getting promoted?"

Bill smiled . . . pleased that she thought so highly of his talents.

"No, Cathy. That's not it. I've been extremely fortunate lately with my investments in the stock market . . . and if my hunch is right about commodity futures, I'll be a millionaire several times over before the year's out. If that happens . . . I'll be spending full time at home with Jonathon and only work, whenever the spirit moves me."

Bill didn't hear Cathy's internal happy sigh, nor notice that she crossed her fingers behind her back to make a wish. What he did hear though was Cathy's cheerful exclamation,

"Bill! . . . that will be just wonderful for Jonathon and . . . "

Somehow she was successful in trapping the "me" just before it escaped . . . substituting in its place . . . "you". Then, reaching over to tickle Jonathon's chin, she added,

"We better go now before Jonathon gets a chill. Anyway, its time for me to start cooking my corn beef and cabbage special that I've planned for this evening's meal . . . You do like corn beef and cabbage . . . don't you?"

"I have a feeling I better . . . unless I want to risk losing Jonathon's terrific governess," Bill said, as both he and Cathy began laughing, simultaneously.

Then . . . as the weeks rolled over into months, Cathy's strange attraction for Bill continued to intensify . . . so much so she found herself longing to be held and caressed by him, as tenderly and as lovingly as he did Jonathon. If only he would reach out to her, whisper her name, and tell her he needed her . . . she long ago had decided she would rush into his open arms . . . eagerly giving herself to him . . . no matter the consequences or lack of commitment on his part. But he didn't!

Her yearnings grew into an emotional addiction, whose desire could be only satisfied by the intimacy of his touch . . . his manly embrace. Cathy had never felt this way before about anyone . . . and realized to her surprise, she had now fallen hopelessly in love . . . with Bill possessing her every thought . . . whether he was standing by her side, just watching, as she cuddled Jonathon . . . or miles away on one of his monthly business trips.

"Surely, he must need a woman's physical self . . . if not her love," she often frustratingly uttered silently, while secretly harboring her passionate urge to hold him sensually.

There were so many times, after tucking Jonathon in for the night, while they were both sharing a peaceful evening together either reading or listening to classical music on the radio, that she almost poured out her heart to the man she now worshipped. Almost . . . but never did . . . out of fear his rejection would result in her termination from the two people she adored so much. And now knew she no longer could live without . . . Jonathon and Bill!

"How could this be happening to me?" She asked herself a thousand times. "I feel like a lovesick calf. If only he would say one little word of encouragement . . . I'd be the happiest woman alive. Just one word! Just one word to prove that he desires me."

Cathy waited in vain. For Bill maintained his outer shell of indifference toward her . . . even though at times she thought she detected signs that revealed how much he long to possess her too . . . as she unequivocally did him. For example, by the way his soft brown eyes would light up tantalizingly when her presence couldn't be denied as she passed Jonathon into his arms and their warm hands touched, or their bodies rubbed slightly as they came into momentary . . . but innocent contact. She swore that it wasn't just an illusion . . . or was it?

"Why do his eyes say one thing . . . only to be contradicted by what his voice is telling me," she wondered, speculating that his aloofness might be a charade contrived to cover his true feelings for her . . . "Why does he hold back? Why can't he throw abandonment to the winds and put his arms around me?" But Cathy really knew why.

Cathy always blamed Karen! Karen's living presence . . . even in death . . . for keeping the man Cathy loved and adored from loving her. No wonder she found herself growing to hate Karen . . . whose memory was so totally ingrained in Bill's lonely mind, she doubted that he would ever allow romantic feelings for anyone else to surface.

Unfortunately, Cathy seemed to be so right . . . for as the months continued their slow turnover, Bill steadfastly refused to provide pining Cathy with the slightest encouragement of whether or not he cared for her. Not even a single word of encouragement . . . Only, from time to time, the frequent exchanges of teasing eye conversations that always conflicted with his stoic spoken words.

"It all must be just a figment of my imagination," she now resignedly believed.

By February of '40, nothing had really changed . . . except Bill's success in the Commodities Future Market far exceeded even his fondest expectations . . . his profits, totaling in the millions, now enabled him to implement his early retirement.

Consequently, Bill's mood was joyous as he started packing for what was to be his last business trip away from Jonathon . . . when suddenly Cathy called to him from the vestibule hallway downstairs,

"Bill . . . there's a Mr. Edwards that would like to speak to you."

Bill wasn't expecting any visitors . . . and certainly didn't personally know a Mr. Edwards as one of his neighbors or clients. Therefore, while drifting down the circular staircase, his curiosity motivated his unusual action of leaning his head over the outer railing in an attempt to catch an early glimpse of this stranger, who he noted was distinguishedly dressed in an opened, black overcoat, covering a pin-striped gray woolen suit, and who vigorously was smoking a hand-carved hickory pipe, whose distinctive Havana tobacco aroma already had permeated to Bill's nostrils, even though he still had ten more steps to descend before reaching the level of the first floor.

Their greetings were mutually friendly, with the usual hand-shakes . . . and quick dispense of the traditional coat removal ritual.

Now as Bill led his visitor into the library, he inquisitively asked,

"Well . . . Mr. Edwards . . . what can I do for you?"

Instead of any immediate response, Bill was too flab-bergasted watching Mr. Edwards take it upon himself . . . first to close and . . . then, to lock the library's heavy mahogany door.

"I hope you don't mind," he offered apologetically," What we have to discuss is not only extremely urgent . . . but it's also extremely confidential."

Bill, perplexed, could only blurt out, "Just who are you? . . . And what's this all about?"

"I work for the government."

"Oh, I get it. You're interested in having my company bid on an insurance package for Uncle Sam."

"No! Mr. Price . . . nothing as trivial as that."

"What then? Why don't you get right to the point."

"Well, Mr. Price . . . you might say I'm here on a recruiting mission. Yes, that sums it up exactly," replied Mr. Edwards while slowly inhaling a long, deep puff before bellowing out three perfect smoke rings that dissipated only a few feet from Bill's resting place, after encircling a small marble bust of Teddy Roosevelt anchored on the end table near the fireplace.

"Recruiting for a mission that offers no monetary reward, may be extremely dangerous, but is vital to the security of our country."

"Are you serious?" Bill asked completely dumbfounded and baffled.

"Never have been more, I regret to say. I'm sure you're well aware of what's happening overseas with that mad-man Hitler on the rampage in Europe . . . Britain and France will prove to be no match for Germany's powerful, mechanized, well oiled war machine. And although there happens to be a lull in the fighting over there right now, undoubtedly, Germany will strike out again soon and complete its conquest of the European Continent."

Now, after a brief moment so as to give proper emphasis to his next remarks, Mr. Edwards continued,

"We don't have much time! If our mission is to be successful at all, it must be started soon. That's why I'm here. I came on the overnight train from Washington, D. C. for only one purpose . . . to recruit you . . . We have to know . . . and soon . . . if you will join us."

"But Why me? . . . For God sake Why me? I have no training in military operations. My line is insurance. Are you sure you have the right Price? . . . I'm William Price."

"You're the Price we're looking for to help us. Your assumption is incorrect . . . this is not a military activity . . . it's got something to do with counterintelligence."

"Good Lord!" Bill gasped. "Now I know you have the wrong man . . . I've had no training whatsoever in espionage work. I wouldn't know how to begin to carry out a spy mission. I told you before . . . I'm just an insurance executive. One that's about to retire after I take my last swing around New England starting today."

"You're the man we want all right . . . you've got just the cover we need to pull it off . . . Someone like you . . . so innocent . . . so free of suspect. Bright . . . intelligent . . . with the charisma that inspires the unswerving allegiance and devotion required to get the job done.

"Believe me Mr. Price . . . we've checked you out thoroughly ever since the chairman of your corporation was consulted for likely candidates . . . and spit out your name without hesitation

98

saying, 'He's your man!' Our follow-up investigations of you convinced us too that he was right. You are the perfect recruit. May I take the liberty of turning your question around and of asking . . . why not you Mr. Price?"

"I've already told you . . . I have absolutely no experience in counterintelligence . . . I'd be greener than a shamrock on St. Patrick's day . . . besides you haven't even told me yet what it is you expect me to do."

"Ironically, Mr. Price . . . until you say you will work for the service . . . and a unequivocal yes, without reservation, we aren't able to even give you the code name for the operation, never mind the intimate details."

"And you expect me to make a decision . . . not having the vaguest idea of what I'm getting myself into . . . except its for the good of the country?"

"Unfortunately, you MUST! We have to appeal to your patriotism and realization that we wouldn't be asking if it wasn't imperative for us to do so. And believe me . . . time is of the essence! We need to know your answer right away in order to properly prepare the groundwork for your three months overseas journey."

"Three months!"

"Maybe . . . more."

"I can't do it then . . . even if it's only for a month I won't do it. I have a young son . . . only 16 months old that I have to worry about . . . a motherless, 16 month old son I might add."

"We know . . . Mr. Price . . . We know all about that . . . and."

"My God!" Bill interrupted rudely, "Is there anything about me you don't know?"

Then, he wondered silently behind a slight blush . . . "What about my feelings for Cathy? Are they aware of those also?"

Bill felt his left eyelid twitch, a nervous reaction brought on from believing his mind was being read by ESP, when Mr. Edwards stated bluntly,

"We have to know everything Mr. Price!.That's the only way we have a chance of succeeding in this planned operation with a minimum loss of . . . " He was going to say 'life', but abruptly refrained so as not to unduly alarm Bill, at this time. The sentence was completed by his utterance, "mission objectives."

Then, after a short . . . deliberate pause . . . he continued,

"If your son is truly your primary concern Mr. Price, I have no doubt at all that you will say YES! . . . because if we fail in our mission, our security will be gravely jeopardized. And when we get into this war . . . and we certainly will Mr. Price . . . I can promise you that!

"Maybe in a year . . . no more than two . . . countless sons will be lost needlessly. One's that might otherwise have been saved by our success in this contemplated operation. Even your infant son won't be able to escape the horror that we envision will occur if we fail."

Bill's head reeled in confusion."It's damned if I do . . . and damned if I don't," he muttered quietly . . . before shouting loudly, "I can't make a decision like this without giving it considerable more thought. I just can't give you an answer on the spur of the moment. Especially, when all I've got to go on if I do agree . . . is that it maybe dangerous."

"Mr. Price . . . If I said 'maybe' before, I stand corrected . . . Not maybe . . . will be! But just as necessary to undertake as your inhaling your next breath. We need your prompt answer. However, if you insist, we can wait, at the most, a couple of days. But no longer. And if you say 'yes', we'll start your orientation and training in less than two weeks. Right after you return on February 26th from this last scheduled trip of yours."

Bill blushed. Then, was possessed by an uncomfortable feeling that his personal life was surely an open book in their hands . . . he almost . . . but didn't ask . . . if they also knew who might have killed Karen.

100

"As soon as you make up your mind, call me," Mr. Edwards said, quickly handing Bill a business card, blank except for a telephone number scribed on it with red ink. "Because of the sensitivity of this matter, the only message I want you to give is . . . 'This is Mr. Price. My answer is' . . . you supply the yes or no. Then, hang up. Nothing more . . . nothing less. If it's yes . . . and I pray that it will be, you won't have to do anything further until I contact you here when you return. We'll take it from there."

"And if it's NO!"

"Then, God help us all Mr. Price if we can't find a suitable replacement . . . and fail in our mission."

Drawing one long, last, deep puff before snuffing out his pipe, Mr. Edwards then concluded,

"Say nothing to anyone about my visit . . . or what little I've been able to tell you. A leak could be fatal . . . in more ways than one."

Bill churned this last statement over in his bewildered mind with considerable discomfort, wondering if what was said was an implied threat on his life, or a dire warning related only to the future consequence of the mission. He never did resolve this conflict . . . and certainly wasn't about to ask Mr. Edwards for a clarification. With the discussion now ended, Mr. Edwards left after a cordial exchange of handshakes that replicated their initial greeting.

Solemnly, Bill climbed back upstairs to resume his packing, already deeply immersed in thought and internal debate over his impending decision. Cathy's mood, on the other hand, was filled with acute apprehension as she finally garnered up enough courage to follow Bill upstairs and asked him to read a poem she had written. Bill, who was genuinely surprised by her request since he was unaware of her artistic inclination for poetry, immediately stopped what he was doing, and commenced to read. The first time with scanning curiosity . . . the second time . . . very slowly and deliberately . . . as if trying to commit its contents to memory. For as he read . . . and reread,

OUR EYES SPEAK SO DIFFERENTLY

Have you ever noticed
When I converse with you
Our Eyes speak truths
Our lips dare not reveal

And since there's no immorality
In what eyes do
They take certain liberties
Our lips must conceal

They laugh—they smile
They dance—they sing
Reflecting hidden emotions
From love's mystical spring

They romantically touch and caress
Since lips must be held apart
As love's rhythmic melody flows
Through eyes to our hearts

All innocence is lost
There are no pretenses
For eyes receive their impulse
From within the soul

And unconsciously betray
Our most intimate senses
By expressing inner feelings
That cannot be told

Since unspoken words
Need never be denied
Our eyes speak so differently
Then words replied

And contrary to what our voices echo
And seem to say
We listen in silence
To what our eyes portray

Bill discovered that he could personally identify with every single word that she had so astutely . . . so honestly . . . so very beautifully expressed.

"She has read my mind!" he said . . . "My thoughts . . . mirror exactly these that she has so perfectly captured in rhyme."

Now for the first time Bill admitted to himself . . . the undeniable depth of his emotional feelings for Cathy. Even though she had been Jonathon's nanny for only a year, he now looked upon her as if she was the real mother of his child. And through this psuedo-parental bond, he had not only grown more dependent upon her but, emotionally had fallen in love with her.

A love never to be declared to her or anyone else. One he never would allow to be consummated . . . no matter how strong his passionate desires for her.

"My God!", his conscience berated him. "How could you ever love anyone but Karen? Have you forgotten her already?"

Bill guiltily strived to atone for his sinful feelings by silently swearing,

"Karen . . . I promise you . . . I never will break our marriage vow . . . even if you are sleeping the eternal sleep. A sleep I would be sharing with you now . . . if it wasn't for Jonathon."

And so hypocritically, Bill denounced the existence of any romantic bond between him and Cathy. It was wrong! . . . At least in Bill's mind it was very wrong. And that's all that mattered! Therefore, he had no alternative but to immediately disassociate himself from Cathy's amorous overture . . . a tempting overture that he nevertheless wished he was emotionally free to accept . . . and also wished he had enough courage to initiate.

But life always demands uncompromising decisions be made

in the present . . . ones that forevermore affects one's future. And when Bill tipped the scale irrevocably against Cathy by deciding to severe the emotional bond of love that obviously was beginning to fuse them together, he consciously shut out forever all physically and spiritually links with any woman . . . except his departed Karen.

Having done so, Bill concluded reluctantly that Cathy's let down must be curt and expressed without feeling . . . so as to leave no doubt in her mind that her love for him was a misdirected fantasy.

"I have to be blunt, cold, and cruel . . . to the one person in this world, besides Jonathon, that I want so longingly to be gentle, warm and loving."

His mind made up, Bill hoped he could lie convincingly . . . because if Cathy challenged his bluff . . . his false facade would rapidly crumble.

And, as a consequence, he knew he would unconditionally yield to her . . . not only accepting . . . but willingly give to her the love that both of them frustratingly craved.

"How can I be strong . . . when I feel so weak? How can I lie . . . when I ache to tell her the truth? My God! If only this was another time. But right now there's just too much on my mind."

So both he and Cathy lost out when Bill handed the poem back to her, while tersely saying,

"Cathy it certainly isn't an Elizabeth Barrett Browning masterpiece. However, it probably is the first poem you've ever written and, does have some merit. But, I'm really no judge of romantic poetry . . . particularly since I can't identify with the theme that you're trying to express. If you keep working at your hobby . . . who knows . . . someday you may become famous."

With that he turned his back towards her and continued packing, saving Cathy the embarrassment of having Bill see her green eyes misting profusely. Cathy, who had abruptly stopped listening to Bill's comments as soon as she heard his words 'I can't identify' wanted to crawl into a hole and hide . . . she wanted to burst out crying . . . right then and there . . . but, somehow, miraculously managed to dam her sea of tears . . . at least until Bill departed on his trip, after which she broke down weeping and moaning for hours,

"Oh! How could I have made such a fool of myself? I'm so humiliated, I can't bear to look Bill straight in the eye ever again. He must think I'm so childish . . . so immature . . . so undeserving of his love anyway . . . which I now know will never be mine. Why did I have to fall for someone already committed for life to someone else . . . someone dead? Yet, someone so alive in his thoughts."

Cathy was understandably depressed as she pondered her hopeless predicament,

"I can't stay on. Not now . . . knowing he doesn't care. It's impossible for me to be so close to him everyday and yet be denied!

"His rejection hurts so much . . . I could die . . . I've got to leave.

"My Irish pride won't let me stay and beg him to respond to my needs. I have no choice . . . but to go . . . and I guess . . . the sooner the better. I'll tell him the moment he returns. I only pray I can hold together, when I do, without bawling like a baby."

Cathy's noble intentions surely would have been kept, and her promise to terminate fulfilled if fate hadn't intervened and deprived her of even this opportunity.

Once again Bill was in turmoil as he drove the New England highways, this time heading for Augusta, Maine. What was to be a very happy occasion . . . one filled with pleasant expectations over retiring, had now turned into a nightmare of indecision concerning Mr. Edwards' visit. As he drove northeastward, Bill constantly debated with himself, weighing the pros and cons of his unresolved internal dilemma,

"If it just meant being away from Jonathon for a month, I probably would say yes . . . even though I don't want to leave him for that length of time. But what about the consequences to both of us if the mission fails . . . or God forbid, I get badly maimed or even killed? Who's going to look after my son then? It's tragic enough he lost his mother . . . if anything happens to me, he'd be an orphan! That's too great a price to pay . . . too great a sacrifice to make.

"And for what? Damn it . . . I don't even know what for. No! I won't do it. It's too risky. How the hell could Mr. Edwards ever think, for one moment, that I would say yes? The Government may think they know everything about me . . . but they don't really know me at all . . . not the me that now only yearns to be with Jonathon as much as I can . . . not the me that yearns for relief from the guilt of not being with Karen in her hour of need.

"Do they really think, under the circumstances, I'd leave Jonathon for three months? Suppose something happens to him while I'm gone. Do they really expect me to live with that guilt too? Isn't It bad enough I have to live every day with the mental torture of Karen's death. Living with a guilt that will never set me free!

"My answer must be no! That should end it. But will it?"

To his uncomfortable surprise, Bill now found himself arguing vehemently in favor of the Government's request.

"Mr. Edwards did stress the absolute urgency of the mission . . . of a successful mission! And if they failed . . . the awesome consequences that would result. Not only for me and Jonathon . . . but for all civilized mankind. It's incomprehensible to me that anything could be that important, or be so earthshaking in its impact. But he certainly implied as much.

"God! If I only knew what it was all about. Then, maybe, I could make a rational . . . if not an intelligent decision. One that won't leave me with still more guilt to live with than the burden I already carry. Because if I say no . . . and, as a result, something happens to Jonathon . . . that guilt will kill me anyway . . . only the agony of his death would be even more painful and unbearable than Karen's."

And so . . . on and on it went . . . mile after mile . . . as Bill kept mulling the problem over in his mind without resolution. It wasn't until a day and a half later while registering at the same hotel that he stayed in when the killer hurricane struck . . . the night Karen needlessly died . . . that his troubled mind snapped to a final decision.

Having done so, Bill quickly dialed the number given to him by Mr. Edwards, gave his terse answer as instructed, hung up, and almost immediately began regretting what he had just done.

The next day, right after breakfast, Bill instructed his office to cancel all of his remaining scheduled appointments for his trip, checked out of the hotel, and hastily departed for home, where upon his arrival he told Cathy he had to talk to her, simultaneously with her announcement,

"Bill I have to speak to you."

However, Bill didn't hear, or simply chose to ignore Cathy's request because he continued with his dialogue without pausing,

"Something has just come up . . . an unusual opportunity that I just couldn't say no to. It means I'll be traveling for an extended period of time, maybe for three months or more . . . I really don't know for sure just how long it will be."

"On business?" injected Cathy curiously . . . as she now tried to orient her thinking in light of Bill's sudden return and uncharacteristic, impetuous, behavior.

"Not exactly . . . just an unplanned vacation. Just something I have to do for my own peace of mind. And since I know I can depend on you to handle everything here at home, I won't have to worry about Jonathon while I'm gone.

"Thank God he cottons to you like a mother . . . that's what makes it possible for me to even leave at all. I hope you don't mind Cathy . . . I'm committed to go . . . and, frankly, I wouldn't know which way to turn if you told me you couldn't . . . or wouldn't do it. You will won't you?" he pleaded.

A thousand thoughts raced through Cathy's mind as she tried to understand the motivation for Bill's sudden desire to take an extended vacation . . . but the only one her jealous mind could accept was that Bill wanted to go away with someone he had just met . . . or else someone he had been seeing secretly on his regular business trips.

"That explains why he's so distant towards me!" she unwittingly convinced herself. "And all this time I blamed it on Karen."

Even before she had a chance to reply directly to his last question, Bill inquisitively asked another,

"By the way Cathy, I'm sorry I was so rude as to interrupt you when I first came in . . . what was it you wanted to tell me?"

Although her words . . . those well rehearsed words now hung back bitterly in her throat, aching more than ever to be expressed, she dutifully suppressed them . . . by biting down hard on her lip . . . until they were properly transformed into a harmless lie,

"Nothing of importance Bill . . . really"

Frantically, she groped for yet another untruth . . . an untruth now being uttered out of necessity . . . or perhaps only out of a spurned woman's need for reprisal,

"I was just wondering if you would mind my having visitors now and then. And, as to your going, don't worry, I can manage quite nicely while you're gone, but I'm sure Jonathon will miss you. So I hope for his sake, you won't stay away too long."

"Not a moment more than necessary, Cathy . . . I can promised you that," Bill replied with wrinkled brow, all the time wondering who it was that Cathy wanted to have visit with her!

CHAPTER 8

The loud shrill of the steam locomotive's screeching whistle, spasmodically belching out its warning signal in long and short asthmatic gasps, constantly woke Bill from a much needed sleep as the Liverpool-to-London Over Nighter, now roaring blindly across the fog shrouded countryside . . . continued to race through numerous ungated crossings with reckless abandonment.

The agitated driver seemed oblivious to the prevailing zero-ceiling adverse weather condition as he perilously tried to make up for the two hour departure delay experienced at the Riverside Station in Liverpool. Time that was irretrievably lost because massive quantities of war material and hundreds of Canadian Army troops, in transit to the Allied front in Europe, had to be loaded onto this special passenger-freight train.

Restlessly, Bill continued tossing and turning. His weary body refused to succumb to his insomnia, correctly anticipating being shakened awake anew by, yet, another annoying blast. Finally, in frustration, Bill buried his face deep into his crumpled pillow, clutched the underside of its ends, with the palm of each hand, and pressed them over his ringing ears in a futile attempt to drown out the irritating noise that prevented him from getting any sustained sleep. Since this new endeavor also proved unsuccessful, he reluctantly lifted his very drowsy head off the mattress of the hard bunk, and, labored strenuously to raise his tired upper torso into a sitting position.

Although his surroundings were pitch black, Bill somehow managed, with a single grasping effort, to flick on the overhead night-lamp. Then, after his blinking brown eyes adjusted slowly to the light's glare, he groped awkwardly for his wrist watch which had been conveniently placed within arms length on a small metallic shelf located next to his berth compartment.

"Damn! 3 A.M.," Bill disgustingly observed as he flipped the light switch off, "I'll never get any sleep tonight."

But it wasn't only the whistle noises that were bothering Bill. Although he refused to acknowledge the real truth, fear . . . a steadily increasing fearfulness began to dangle his already jittery nerves. And, understandably so, for the closer he got to London, the more and more anxious he became. Why shouldn't he be frightened and nervous?

"Even seasoned espionage agents would be queasy," he reasoned defensively.

And he was certainly right on that score. Because in the exceedingly dangerous world of espionage activities,even the hard core pros lack immunity from the gnawing feelings of self-doubt, insecurity, and apprehension.

They are always aware of its inherent dangers . . . always in dread of that one unexpected catastrophic moment when any carefully planned cover could be blown away Thereby, exposing their fragile lives to a calamitous fate.

It's living hell for anyone to navigate in a world of the unknown. Even if the navigator is a 'Columbus' on a maiden voyage of discovery, or an ordinary patriotic citizen, naive like Bill, who couldn't suppress an inner consternation that 'his' was a mission doomed to failure. Doomed . . . not only because of his own overwhelming inadequacies as a counterintelligence agent but, doomed by the one in a million chance that anyone could ever succeed under the rapidly deteriorating conditions now facing him.

"Even if there wasn't a war on over here, it still would be an impossible mission," Bill dejectedly thought as he raised the black

110

shade that covered his small plate-glass compartment window, and stared blankly out into a gray sea of eerie mist that prevented him from obtaining the slightest glimpse of England's magical topography of constantly changing scenes of rolling hills, hamlets, big cities and fascinating countryside, even though the moon, high above the thickened blanket of soupy fog on this chilly night of travel, was nearly full.

As the repetitive cycle of the clackety-clack clamor, emanating from the rails of the train's wheels as they periodically rotated over minute expansion gaps in the steel tracks, droned on and on for mile after mile, Bill's despondent mind gradually yielded to its hypnotic overtures.

He relaxed, as if in a mesmerized state. Slowly, his thoughts drifted backward in time and began recalling the unlikely sequence of events of the past few weeks that somehow catapulted him from his safe haven in Boston to the brink of danger that lay ahead . . . His memory scan commenced, chronologically, with that afternoon when he informed Cathy about his having to leave.

"I know she thought I was taking a pleasure trip . . . And with another woman! . . . I could read the hurt in her blurred green eyes. God, if only I could have told her the real reason, she would have understood and not have retaliated by asking permission to invite someone over while I'm gone. I'm going to lose her . . .

"And I've no one to blame but myself. For some reason, I seem to want to have it both ways . . . I don't want anyone else to have her . . . yet, I just can't bring myself to tell her how much I care. I feel like a prisoner locked-up in my own body! Unable to allow myself the emotional freedom I need to ever love again . . . without guilt. It's no wonder she's trying to get on with her life.

"How can I blame her for now wanting to develop a meaningful relationship with someone else . . . someone that can give her the love she rightfully deserves?"

Bill now lapsed into silence, jealously meditating the unhappy thought of Cathy being embraced by another man.

111

"It shouldn't bother me . . . but it does. After all, I was the one that rejected her . . . by refusing her . . . indirectly . . . but brusquely . . . when I belittled her poem and denied that I had any romantic interest in her. What a liar I am!

"Yet . . . if she was here with me now, I doubt that I would act any differently, nor tell her how much my body aches for her . . . or how much I really want her . . . how much I need her. I can't tell her. Not with my conscience constantly torturing me and saying that I must be faithful to Karen.

"However, I probably won't have to worry about that much longer. Not if my Cathy rebounds into someone else's arms while I'm away . . . and certainly not if anything fatal happens to me on this mission . . . as I feel it might."

That latter, bleak thought sent a sudden cold shiver down Bill's spine, causing him to reach quickly for a woolen bunk blanket and, then, to wrap it snugly around his fear-chilled body.

"At least, I've adequately provided for Jonathon and her as best I know how with the money I made in the Commodities Market," he reflected confidently.

And indeed he had! For during Bill's last days at home, he frantically spent hours with his lawyer and banker, making out his will and setting up various financial trusts for Jonathon and Cathy. In his will, he requested that Cathy become executrix of his estate . . . and, more importantly, pleaded with her to adopt Jonathon.

Vividly, he now remembered his last moments before leaving . . . his insatiable embrace of Jonathon . . . his passionate plea to Cathy,

"Take good care of him while I'm gone."

And his impulsive desire to hold her in his arms and kiss her, which he now regretted suppressing with his last words,

"And yourself too."

Bill broke his nostalgic recall to glance again at his watch, which, in the darkened light, could barely be seen as ticking slowly past 4 A.M. Then, disgustedly, he stared out the window at the

112

opaque shadows of a passing town made almost invisible . . . not only by the impenetrable low hanging pea soup fog but, also, by a mandated blackout curfew that had been just imposed that very week throughout Great Britain because of the expectation of renewed air-raid attacks by Germany's dreaded Luftwaffe bombers.

Only his blurred facial image reflected back from the mirrored window. Its monotonous silhouette precipitated again, Bill's flashback of thoughts . . . this time to when he next met Mr. Edwards . . . It was on the morning of February 28th, at 9:50 A.M. upon his arrival at the Union Station, in Washington, D.C . . .

By prearranged instructions, no words were exchanged between them until Bill's bags were placed into the trunk of a waiting car, and they had departed for a destination as yet not revealed to him. Then, Mr. Edwards broke the ice and warmly spoke out,

"Welcome aboard, Bill. I can't tell you how glad we are you decided to join us."

"You bastards! You really do know me. You knew I couldn't refuse if the safety of my son was involved. You knew just how to intimidate me . . . to make me say 'Yes'. Whatever this is all about . . . it better be as important as you say . . . or I'm going to be really pissed!"

"Just hang on for a few more minutes, Bill . . . until we arrive at 1600 Pennsylvania Avenue for our conference. There's a select group of people I want you to meet. After you hear what they have to say about this mission, I guarantee you'll comprehend the significance of what we're trying to do . . . and why! I can assure you, you're not going to be 'pissed' as you put it. On a scale of 1 to 10 . . . this ranks at 1000 . . . maybe more. But judge for yourself. There'll be no more beating around the bush, once we get there. Let them explain. Then, you can tell me if we're making a mountain out of a molehill."

It never dawned on Bill that the address previously mentioned by Mr. Edwards was that of the White House . . . at least not until they drove up to its guarded rear iron gates, were permitted

immediate entrance upon the utterance of a softly whispered pass-
word that Bill could not hear, and were parked in a macadam
driveway, adjacent to the semicircular South portico.

"As you can see, it's real important. Bill! Maybe now you
can begin to appreciate just how much."

Bill was at a total loss for words . . . and so meekly . . . and
obediently disembarked to follow Mr. Edwards through an exterior
central door, whose long corridor led them directly into a large
conference room. Inside, already seated around a large oval table,
were a civilian and three military personnel.

Each rose and shook hands with Bill as they were introduced
by Mr. Edwards, starting sequentially with General E. M. Watson,
who Bill vaguely recalled was appointed Aide to President Roosevelt, Colonel K. F. Adamson of the Army Ordinance Department,
Commander G. C. Hoover of the Navy Bureau of Ordnance, and Dr.
L. J. Briggs, Chairman of the Advisory Committee on Uranium.

"Jesus!" Bill murmured under his breath to himself. "What
in hell am I doing in the same room with all these important people?"

But, that wasn't the half of it . . . for no sooner had these
salutatory introductions been completed . . . when a side door to the
conference room, one marked 'PRIVATE—NO ADMITTANCE
ALLOWED' . . . slowly opened and in wheeled the President,
Franklin D. Roosevelt, whose buoyant, dynamic, gregarious, and
friendly personality quickly surfaced.

Bill understood immediately why this man enjoyed such
enormous popularity with the masses. His lightness of mood was a
welcome contrast to the somber, almost stern profiles projected by
everyone else around him.

"So Bill! You're our man of the hour! I wanted to meet you
personally and wish you good luck. General Watson and the boys
will brief you on my mission. Just remember . . . I'm counting on

you to get back safe and sound . . . and on time for you to vote for me again in this year's election."

And with that, he smiled his broadest political grin, took a short puff through his favorite silver-plated cigarette holder on his smoldering butt, wheeled his chair 180 degrees around, and left with his right hand fluttering in a very friendly goodbye jester.

Overwhelmed and, obviously, stunned by the President's appearance and performance, Bill, now, absolutely amazed, looked over to Mr. Edwards, whose returned nod and eye blink seemed to be saying,

"There, I told you so. Are you starting to believe me now?" General Watson's serious tone brought the situation back to reality when he initiated his fairly long discourse,

"As you must have surmised already, Bill . . . your oversea's mission is a mission for the President! One whose consequences may affect civilized mankind for centuries to come. Its been code-named "ADAM" . . . which is an acronym coggered up to stand for Atomic Destruction Annihilates Mankind."

Bill's wrinkled brow, a cue immediately picked up by General Watson, inferred a complete lack of understanding.

"What we're talking about Bill are bombs that potentially will have more than 2000 times the blast power of the largest ones available in our arsenal today, or, for that matter, ever conceived on any of our drawing boards. Ones that can destroy whole cities and wipe out millions of people, instead of just a city block with limited casualties.

"Ever since the German scientists, Hahn and Strassmann, demonstrated a couple of years ago that the uranium atom could be successfully split . . . all hell has broken loose over here with our top weapons experts . . . as well as those in France, England, and even Russia.

"This discovery is big! It's hard to imagine the enormous destructive power the ultimate nuclear weapon will possess.

115

"However, we speculate it will be more than enough to change all methods of warfare . . . and the outcome of a war overnight for whichever country that first succeeds in its development."

Bill was beginning to understand the big picture, and, as a consequence, his mind absorbed General Watson's continuing dialogue more receptively.

"That's why the Russians are frightened to death about the German triumph. They dread German technology almost as much as we respect it. Stalin has read Hitler's 'Mein Kampf' . . . he's not stupid. He realizes Hitler has Russia on his hit list and that Germany will attack them someday . . . in spite of the non-aggression pact both have just signed. However, the Soviets don't know when it will come! If the Germans had the atomic bomb today . . . God only knows who they would strike tomorrow."

General Watson paused, but only long enough to clear his raspy throat, and to swallow a sip of water,

"Our intelligence tells us the Germans already have initiated a large secret project to expedite the development of this atom bomb. Naturally, we don't want to be caught with our pants down. That's why the President personally authorized us to start our own secret research in this area last August . . . as soon as he received a letter from the world-reknown physicist, Dr. Albert Einstein, urging him to do so without delay.

"Our Advisory Committee on Uranium, chaired by Briggs, is our cover for that program. Both Colonel Adamson and Commander Hoover are members of that committee, and one of their recommendations is the reason why you're here with us today. But before I get sidetracked into that, let me get back to the President. He realizes that a project of the scope necessary to produce atomic bombs . . . if its feasible to make them at all . . . is going to costs hundreds of millions of dollars . . . maybe as much as a billion."

Bill's sudden gasp at the mention of a billion dollars didn't surprise General Watson. In fact, it appeared to be just the response he anticipated,

"Exactly the reaction of the President! How can he, in clear conscience, commit to a project of that magnitude when our country still has not fully recovered from the present disastrous depression? Why should he even contemplate it . . . when our country is at peace . . . and the war zone actually thousands of miles away? Well, for one thing, the President feels certain, as many of us do, that America is soon going to be drawn into this thing . . . if not in Europe . . . almost certainly in the Asian arena against the Japanese tyrant.

"Therefore, there really is no alternative . . . He's concluded that we've got to have it! Regardless of its cost . . . His only indecision concerns whether the next President . . . the one who will be elected this fall . . . will allow the work to continue or will shut it down for economical reasons, thereby jeopardizing the security of all freedom loving people because of a lack of vision, or courage to bite the required financial bullet. That's one big reason why he has convinced himself to run for an unprecedented third term, in spite of the fact his health is starting to fail him."

Again General Watson paused for a brief moment before passionately declaring,

"Our country must have the atomic bomb first! And the country needs President Roosevelt at the helm so that 'ADAM' won't be scuttled."

As if to further justify the need for this awesome death bomb, General Watson felt compelled to add,

"With that maniac Hitler in control of our destiny, what choice do we have but beat him to the punch? If he had it now . . . he'd cremate the world. Look what he's doing to the Jews . . . threatening to persecute an entire race because of his personal bias. Who's next? The Russians. Then who? Maybe us . . . even though we're really trying to remain neutral. But, surely you must know that this tyrant doesn't respect neutrality or weakness. He's the type of bully you have to pulverize with power! An atomic bomb is the only deterrent that he'll respect . . . the only weapon that can wipe out his Blitzkrieg type of warfare . . . just like that!"

117

With those harsh last words, the General snapped his large thumb across the fingers of his right hand with a loud, resounding pop to emphatically drive home the point.

"Bill . . . You may think we're a little hysterical . . . but, I can assure you, if we are . . . we're not alone in our hysteria. The Russians are also paranoid about this atomic fission discovery. They have their scientists feverously working around the clock to unravel the secrets of spontaneous fission so that they may begin manufacture of the atomic bomb. And what they can't discover for themselves . . . you can rest assure, they'll steal from others! Our covert sources inside the Russian intelligence service have informed us that they have already launched a major industrial espionage effort . . . under their code-named 'CANDY'.

"We aren't sure whose running the U.S. operation, but we suspect Vassili Zarubin, who is Chief of Soviet Intelligence over here. Nor do we know, yet, who their "Candy man' is, the traitor picked out to supply them with our nuclear secrets . . . except the name Gold keeps coming up. But if its not Gold, it'll be someone else . . . it's almost impossible to stop them from enticing some of our most trusted scientists . . . those who believe in Russia's brand of ideology . . . those misguided souls who wouldn't blink an eyelash about betraying us. Can't say that I blame the Soviets for trying to steal technology. We're doing the same thing. They're running scared! So are we! But, for different reasons.

"We want the bomb first in order to protect the freedom of the World. Once we have it . . . no one will dare provoke or attack us. It will be our ultimate deterrent weapon for preventing war . . . Like Teddy Roosevelt once advised, 'Speak softly, but be ready to wield a big stick.'

"Of course, Bill, you know we'd only use it in dire emergencies . . . and then only against military targets. Never against the civilian populations of even unfriendly Nations. It's consequences are just too horrendous for that!"

General Watson's vehement denial of its use against civilians—whether friend or foe—was allowed to be fully absorbed by Bill, as the General intended it should be by his deliberate stalling action of pausing to sip the last swallow of water from his now emptied glass.

"On the other hand, we all know that Hitler wants it for only one purpose. Conquest! And the annihilation of all humanity that stands in his way of world domination by the Germans. And the Soviets? Who knows what Stalin would do with it, if Russia manages to get it before we do.

"But, first things first. We believe our biggest threat is from the Germans . . . not the Russians, who lack the technical where-withal to develop it as rapidly as either the Germans or us. Germany's our real menace. And that's where you come in Bill!"

Bill's whole body tensed-up as soon as his name was mentioned in the implied context of what he now perceived was going to be his role in an extremely dangerous mission. His head instinctively swiveled to face General Watson, like a directional radar antenna rotating to seek out its strongest input signal, and his shoulders leaned forward in order that his perked ears would be focused closer to the source of General Watson's rhetoric . . . so as not to miss a single syllable of the forthcoming exposition.

Understandably nervous and apprehensive, microscopic beads of sweat started to trickle through Bill's frightened skin pores from his brow down to the tip of his toes as he waited impatiently for the General to speak again.

General Watson didn't disappoint him, as he now succinctly . . . but very nonchalantly stated the objective . . . almost as calmly as if he was describing a spy mission that simply entailed going down to the corner drug store to steal a pack of cigarettes,

"We have to know what the Germans have accomplished lately . . . and what their Master Plan is for developing the atomic bomb. Your mission is to bring that information back to us."

119

Bill couldn't believe what his reticent ears had just relayed to his panicked brain. But, his snappy retort quickly conveyed his personal misgivings about the mission,

"Just how in the world do you expect me to accomplish that miracle?"

"Blake Edwards is the guy that going to explain 'just how' to you in great detail later, but very briefly I can say that you'll be overseas shortly on a combined vacation and business trip which will take you first to Liverpool . . . then to Copenhagen on the trumped-up pretense of closing out some risky insurance accounts for your company, before you visit briefly with your demised wife's parents in Oslo, Norway on your return trip to the States."

"So THAT'S why me," Bill thought under his breath, seemingly enlightened. "They're using poor dead Karen as part of my cover for being there."

His reminiscing now about Karen and soon having to relive her death with her parents upset Bill immensely . . . enough for him to temporarily lose concentration, and as a consequence, nearly miss General Watson's extremely important disclosure. This revelation almost deceived Bill, for a moment, into believing that maybe . . . just maybe he had a chance of making it, after all.

"We have a contact in Germany who has been leaking military secrets to us and the Allies . . . a highly placed officer in the Abwehr, the German Intelligence Service, headquartered in Berlin One working right under the Fuehrer's nose as chief assistant to Admiral Canaris. His name is Colonel Hans Oster. This man is an impetuous, imprudent German that hates Hitler more than the Jews do.

"Fortunately, the Abwehr has direct access to Germany's Master Plan for Atomic Bomb Development, and the Colonel has agreed to funnel a copy of this invaluable document to us . The place and date has already been set for the pick-up. For some reason, unknown to us, he has instructed that the transfer must take place in Copenhagen on the evening of the 9th of April."

Anticipating Bill's certain quest for more specifics, the General was quick to add,

"Now, as I said before, Blake is going to fill you in on these details, and anything else that is pertinent for you to know . . . including all the necessary data on your contact point and the rendezvous code you will be using."

Then, General Watson abruptly stopped his dissertation . . . hesitating for a few seconds, as if somewhat reluctant to spit out whatever it was that dwelled on his very disturbed mind . . . something that needed to be said, in spite of all its unpleasant implications. After clearing his throat repeatedly with a low, dry cough, he muttered slowly,

"There is just one thing I feel compelled to add, Bill. Since this mission is authorized by the President . . . it goes without saying that it must be kept secret . . . top secret. Thus, absolutely no one . . . I repeat . . . no one is to know about it. And remember . . . since we are a neutral country . . . we can't admit to conducting espionage activities against the Germans . . . or anyone else for that matter.

"Therefore, if you happen to get caught, we'll deny til hell freezes over that this mission ever existed . . . or, for that matter, any knowledge of you or your part in it. To put it bluntly, once you leave Blake in England . . . you're completely on your own! I think you get the message. Bill . . . without my belaboring the point any further."

Then, in what appeared to be almost an after thought, he sputtered,

"Good Luck! We're all depending on you."

And with those ominous sounding words of warning and encouragement, the meeting was quickly adjourned.

However, continuously for the next two and a half weeks, Blake Edwards and Bill were almost inseparable as they constantly went over the minute details of the mission . . . time and time again . . . first in Washington, as Bill learned the ABC's of counterintelligence operations and, then, reiterated on the high seas, as the

Ville D'Anvers crossed the turbulent Atlantic and docked safely at Liverpool.

Blake and Bill departed company on the 22nd of March at the railroad station with Blake's last words of advice,

"Bill . . . I know you'll be able to cope with all the external dangers that will confront you. But, remember . . . don't become a victim to the internal pressures that can make you lose faith in yourself and your belief that you can accomplish this mission.

"And, just one other thing . You may think you are doing this just for Jonathon. But, in reality, everyone in our free society is depending on you not to fail."

CHAPTER 9

The mid-afternoon flight from London to Copenhagen on Thursday, April 4th, aboard the Danish Airlines, while extremely tense because of the ever present possibility of attack by German warplanes, nevertheless, proved uneventful . . . a fact that not only drew a big sigh of relief from Bill upon landing at Kastrup Airport on Amager Island, located 6 ½ miles from the center of Copenhagen, but, understandably, now provoked his pressure-release prayer,

"Thank God!"

But then, it was just as Blake had told him during his many briefings,

"Both the British and German intelligence chiefs realize the useful purpose that these flights to neutral countries play.

"After all, both sides want to provide a means of convenient safe passage for their own undercover agents, those who periodically smuggle themselves, and vital espionage secrets to their respective homelands.

"The neutrals forge the perfect link, thus serving as a conduit which indirectly connect the warring nations to each other. Both sides conveniently look the other way and allow air travel to neutral countries in Europe to continue unmolested."

Whatever the reason, Bill really didn't give a damn at this moment . . . as he successfully hailed a taxi. He was preoccupied with the thought that in just five day after first picking up Germany's

Master Plan for Atomic Bomb Development, he'd be leaving Denmark. Then, after a brief stay in Oslo visiting Karen's parents, he would be flying back home, via London and Lisbon to Jonathon and to Cathy. Yes . . . to Cathy. For Bill had decided one thing for certain during this trip . . . if his luck held out and he got home safely, he was going to ask Cathy to marry him. He was going to bury the guilt complex and really start over!

Bill's bilingual cab driver, Stig Hansen, beamed with a desire to please . . . a characteristic routinely exhibited by the amiable, unpretentious Danish people. And, after quickly introducing himself, Hansen began an unsolicited discourse to acquaint this, obviously, first time tourist to Denmark's historic capital .

"We're a proud and patriotic people," he noted, pointing to a group of small children at the airport's exit gate waving little red flags with white crosses, miniatures of the Danneborg, the National banner.

"But, we treasure the friendship of our foreign guests as we do our own next-door neighbors. And why not? We're a tiny nation that has learned to live in peace with ourselves and those around us. We want for nothing . . . we have everything."

Then, pointing to the surrounding landscape, Hansen boastfully added,

"See for yourself the beauty of our land," he said, motioning with his right hand to emphasize a countryside now traversed through long stretches of strawberry farms being readied for late spring picking.

"And the beauty of our architecture," he offered as they crossed over the outer bridge from Amager Island into Christianshavn, one of the oldest quarters of Copenhagen.

"There . . . on your right . . . is the infamous Vor Frelsers Kirke . . . Our Saviour's Church . . . with its beautiful green and gold spired tower, and its legendary winding spiral staircase which uniquely wraps around the tower's exterior."

Bill's head pivoted instantly, and his dilated brown eyes focused on it with more than a tourist's curiosity,

"So that's where the 'drop' is to take place!" he silently murmured to himself. "At the apex of that long staircase . . . which seems to end in nothingness . . . next to the staff supporting a golden globe, atop which Blake told me stands a life-sized figure in gold leaf of the Compassionate Christ."

Bill couldn't help but wonder if this particular meeting place was selected because of its religious overtone and spiritual significance . . . at a time when the world was being harassed and overrun by Satin's followers.

"Just how high was that tower?" asked Bill as they now proceeded across the Knipplesbro drawbridge and, then, onto Borsgade leading into the heart of Copenhagen.

"Oh . . . about three hundred feet," Hansen replied nonchalantly. "You'll have an unforgettable experience if you decide to climb those stairs to its pinnacle. Believe me! The cyclorama view of Copenhagen is absolutely breathtaking."

"Oh . . . I'm sure it must be," Bill chuckled. "Especially, if you're out of condition as I am."

Hansen laughed . . . in the tradition of all fun loving Danes that enjoy a good retort.

Then, as Hansen deftly maneuvered his vehicle sharply to the right onto Holmens Kanal, and left again into Kongens Nytorv Square, his fluttering index finger pointed to a magnificent palace-like, five story building coming into view through the front windshield.

"There's the d'Angleterre . . . you couldn't have chosen a finer hotel . . . besides being the most deluxe in all of Denmark, my father-in- law happens to be its Director. I'm sure his personal attentiveness will make you feel as if you're at home . . . away from home . . . in no time."

Bill was indeed impressed, as he alighted from the now stationary cab, by the regal charm of the hotel, which stretched for an entire block on one of Copenhagen's most beautiful squares, and by its promised old-fashioned elegance as revealed by its aristocratic design and a broad canopied sidewalk terrace that added a gaiety and distinction unsurpassed in his experience as a traveler.

However, he didn't kid himself either . . . he knew that the only reason this particular lodging place was booked for him was because of its nearness to the 'drop' site, which he estimated to be no more than 1500 yards away. Close enough to walk alone to in less than 20 minutes on the evening of the 9th.

"If you'd like a guided tour of our captivating city, I would be honored to personally show you around," Hansen offered just before departing.

"All you have to do is ask for me at the desk. My father-in-law knows all my hang outs and hang ups . . . he'll have me at your service in a jiffy."

"I'll may take you up on that starting tomorrow," Bill hollered back to the moving cab as he entered d'Angleterre's spacious lobby, walked briskly up to the check-in counter, and waited patiently while another tall, brown haired, thirty-five-year old civilian was just completing his registration.

"And how long do you plan to stay with us, Mr. Bergmann?" asked an impeccably dressed, 5' 5", rather plump, grey-haired man standing behind the wide semi-circular, highly polished mahogany counter.

"Only a few days this time . . . but much longer on my next visit . . . I can promise you that," he replied with a grin, before being escorted towards his room by one of the ever present bellhops.

As soon as he was out of hearing range, the desk host, who Bill assumed was Hansen's father-in-law, abruptly commented,

"Now there's a German officer if I ever saw one."

Bill's ears perked up and, unconsciously, his head swiveled half-circle to stare again at the departed Bergmann, while his keen mind mulled the wild thought that, maybe, Bergmann was his contact man.

"What makes you suspect that?" Bill inquired curiously, as he turned his head slowly back towards the registration desk. "He looks like an ordinary civilian to me."

"I can see you've had no military training. Just look at his gait . . . his rigid posture . . . his physical shape. Exchange those fancy civilian clothes for a hated Nazi uniform and you have at least a Major. "And I might add, my intuition in these matters is rarely wrong. For example, unless I miss my guess, you ARE a business man . . . in spite of your excellent build. Its just the way you come across to me, a man in my late fifties who has registered thousands of strangers of all races and professions into this grand hotel. Now then . . . how can I help you?"

Bill was speechless for a brief moment, but recovered quickly to respond,

"I'm William Price. I believe you have a room for me until the 10th."

"Oh . . . yes . . . of course, Mr. Price. Please let me introduce myself. I'm Johan Cilborg . . . at your service day or night. In fact, you can count on all of us here to make your stay as pleasant and as memorable as possible."

Bill wasn't so sure just how pleasant everything would turn out . . . but he had to agree it was certainly going to be memorable. Especially for a business man who unwittingly was playing the unrehearsed role of an espionage agent.

"I'll bet Johan can see right through my thin veiled facade also," Bill wagered with himself as he left for his room.

Before that day was out, Bill began hearing distressing rumors, circulating fast and furiously amongst the hotel personnel and guests, that Denmark was going to be invaded by Germany on April 9th. Ironically, the same day as that set for his clandestine meeting to pick up the Master Plans. Normally, Bill put little credence in gossip tales, but this particular one had a special authentic ring to it because of the privileged secret information Gen. Watson's gave him during the Washington briefing.

This rumor source was Captain Kjolsen, Denmark's Naval Attache in Berlin, who had just rushed home to report to his government that an anti-Hitler officer high in the Abwehr had leaked secret intelligence about the forthcoming invasion. But, his warning cry, like a voice in the wilderness, went unheeded. For Kjolsen's passionate plea for immediate defensive action was adamantly rebuked by his superiors, who summarily dismissed the input as an obvious fabrication, steadfastly refusing to accept the hypothesis that anyone in Hitler's trusted Abwehr would ever be disloyal to him.

"You really expect us to believe that the Fuhrer has surrounded himself with traitors in the Abwehr, his most prestigious intelligence and counterintelligence service. In the Abwehr? Of all the unlikely places! How naive can you be to propose that disloyal German officers would risk their lives by leaking even one operational war secret to us?"

So in spite of Kjolsen's exhaustive insistence to the contrary, the King's cabinet members responded,

"Poppycock!"

But Bill knew differently! For he suspected the high ranking officer supplying information on the invasion was none other than Maj. Gen. Hans Oster, the man who Gen. Watson said had promised to deliver a copy of Germany's atomic bomb plans to the United States.

What Bill wouldn't have given for the opportunity to compare notes with Kjolsen so as to confirm this, so that he might rationalize the significance that the date chosen for the pick up was exactly the same as that of the rumored invasion. Was that just coincidence? Or, was that also planned?

"Does it mean my mission has to be aborted or not?" Bill nervously asked himself a thousand times.

But, since all contacts with Blake had terminated when Bill left Liverpool, he had no way finding out the answer to this or, any other question. As Gen. Watson had warned him, he was on his own now. And God help him if he made a mistake in judgment or, in execution.

Bill was facing a dilemma! And had less than five days to decide his final course of action . . . either to get out of Copenhagen before it was too late . . . or go ahead as planned, discounting all rumors as a deliberate disinformation ploy of the Germans. Try as he might though, he couldn't make himself believe the latter. Not if Maj. Gen Hans Oster was really the one tolling the warning bell for the Danes.

And even though Bill's pondering went on for hours, the ultimate determination seemed impossible for him to make.

"I'm a coward if I run," Bill thought. "But, I'm a damn fool to stay and try to go through with this mission if the Germans really are going to attack," he concluded . . . just before dropping off to sleep that night, totally bewildered.

When morning broke, the sun suddenly filtered brightly through the delicate white-laced curtains, embellishing two large bedroom windows, and silently trumpeted-in the beginning of a new day.

And as Bill opened his eyes . . . refreshed and alert . . . to the soft, warming movements of the sun dance reveille, he was thankful that his confused mind had finally cleared and, no longer was paralyzed by indecision.

Every available moment between now and his anointed hour of rendezvous, Bill decided would be used to enhance his chances of success and survival.

What better way to start than to become familiar with every nook and cranny of Copenhagen, so as to facilitate his escape movements in the event of an unforeseen crisis.

His early morning call to Hansen had already set this action into motion. And since he was determined to find out what Bergmann's real purpose was in visiting Copenhagen at this time, Bill decided that Hansen's unsuspecting assistance would have to be solicited also in this effort. Especially since sleuthing was just as foreign to Bill's repertoire of experience as espionage.

After devouring a hearty Danish breakfast, consisting of an assortment of home-made breads, a selection of delicious cheeses, a boiled egg, and a cup of hot brewed coffee, Bill, sauntered into the Lobby at 9 A.M., and informally greeted his garrulous, 5'7" guide, who was waiting for him.

"All set, Stig."

"As I said yesterday, it's my honor. I have our bicycles parked right outside."

"Bicycles! Are you kidding?"

Hansen's blue eyes smiled, giving away the fact that he was quite pleased at surprising Bill as to their mode of transportation.

"You told me when you called this morning, you wanted to get to know Copenhagen, like you know the back of your hand. Well . . . you can't get that feeling for it driving around in the back of my cab. I say we do it the old-fashioned Danish way!"

Bill hesitated for only a moment before responding positively, having admitted to himself that Hansen's logic was hard to dispute.

"O.K. Let's go. But you'll have to give me a few minutes to practice . . . at least until I'm sure of my balance. I haven't been on a bike since my college days."

"No problem . . . I'll just wait while you give it a whirl."

At first, Bill felt awkward as he amateurishly pedaled the bike up and down in front of the d'Angleterre Hotel for almost twenty minutes. Finally, however, his mastery of the two wheeler returned, sufficiently so at least for him to state with a shallow degree of confidence,

"I guess I'm as ready as I'm ever going to be. Which way are we heading?"

"Over there to the center of Kongens Nytorv Square by the base of the equestrian statue of Christian V. We'll use that as our reference point until you become more familiar with Copenhagen's bewildering jumble of winding streets and unexpected canals. You'll soon find that the inner city is a complex maze that will have you wandering around in circles . . . unless you keep your wits about you and try not to get too rattled."

Having pedaled over to their benchmark, Hansen continued his oratory,

"Before we start . . . just orient yourself by looking around this Square. From here you can see the d'Angleterre right across the street to our west, and the famous Kongelige teeter (Royal Theater) . . . not more than 500 feet to our south.

"That beige building over there to the east is the Charlottenborg Palace which once belong to Queen Charlotte Amalie, but is now our Royal Academy of Art.

"And directly down Nyhavn still to our east is the picturesque New Port canal which splits the street into a right and left hand side . . . On the right are charming little homes occupied by painters, dancers and actors, while on the left are numerous cafes and rooming houses for dock workers and sailors.

"As you might guess, the four blocks that stretch down from here to the harbor are quite lively at night, and more times than not, peppered with scores of harmless street fights and short-lived brawls."

After a brief pause to catch a much needed breath, Hansen continued,

"And at the far end of Nyhan is the departure point for the ferry to Malmo, Sweden, which is less than 30 miles across the Sound. It leaves precisely at 2 P.M. everyday."

Bill eagerly stored that fact into the instant recall channels of his brain since it represented an immediate escape hatch for him in the event the mission had to be aborted.

"Now, if we turn 180 degrees around that wide street in front of us, heading north is called Bredgade. I thought we'd begin our cook's tour today pedaling on it since it leads to both the scenic Amalienborg Palace, where the King and Queen reside during our

131

hard Nordic winter months and, also, to the Kastellet (Citadel), the principal fortress of our city.''

Bill liked that idea very much because he had seen Bergmann hailing a cab and heading off in that direction, not more than fifteen minutes ago, while he was practicing his cycling.

"The swallowtail flag is flapping in the breeze!" Hansen announced cheerfully, brushing blond hair out of his smarting eyes . . . as they pedaled under the huge colonaded entrance to the Amalienborg Palace grounds. "That means the Royal family has not left yet for their summer home in North Zealand. If we're lucky we just might catch a glimpse of them through the windows of the Palace.''

"Which Palace?" inquired Bill, as they stopped and dismounted at the foot of the high-pedestal equestrian statue of Frederik V in the center of the square. "All four look nearly identical to me.''

And indeed they did . . . not by accident . . . but by a direct mandate from Frederik V, who in 1750, when the French-style rococo mansions were built by four noblemen, ordained that the same architects must be employed and, the same basic design adhered to.

Looking out towards the harbor, through the wide open space between two adjacent palaces, Bill watched in awe as two huge collier ships sailed by. Hansen,astutely observing Bill's focus of attention, gladly offered,

"Those are German ships, Bill, bringing coal to Copenhagen. They'll be docking about a mile north of here at Langelinie in the next hour or so.If you like, we can go down to the wharf later and see them unload.''

"No, Stig. I'd rather not. I was hoping we'd use the time this afternoon exploring the inner City," Bill replied, while visually scanning the grounds, trying to see if Bergmann was anywhere around. He wasn't . . . which led Bill to conclude that whatever Bergmann's interests were in his visit to Copenhagen, the Amalienborg quarter wasn't high on his priority list.

132

"Tourist normally flock like pigeons to this court at noon-time, Bill, anxious to see the ceremonial changing of the Royal Guards that occurs here daily whenever the Queen is in residence, as she is today.

"It's tradition! A bit of regal-pagentry dating back to the eighteenth century that I just know you'll enjoy viewing . . . as much as we Danes always do.

"Where else can you watch thirty-six Guardsmen, dressed in deep, sky-blue uniforms and towering black bearskin busbies, parade, salute and flash swords to the rousing martial tempo music that loudly emanates from the fifes and drums, trumpets and clarinets of a thirty-one piece band that always proceeds the Guards on their march."

"Sounds great, Stig. But it's only 10:00 A.M. . . . "

"I know! Just enough time for us to cycle up Bredgade and see the Citadel, and then come back here, before the show starts. The fortress is only about a third of a mile up the road."

However, they never did return to Amalienborg to watch the colorful ceremony. For when Bill and Hansen arrived at the Citadel, Bill immediately noticed Bergmann being escorted around the grounds by a Danish sergeant. From the gist of the conversation that Bill was able to overhear as they passed by, Bergmann seemed unusually interested in knowing all the details about the ancient fortress, whose strategic location guaranteed Copenhagen's protection against any attack by sea.

"That's just like my drinking buddy, Truelsen," Hansen stated spontaneously. "He gets so bored with the monotony of the daily guard routine, he welcomes the opportunity to give a personal tour to any visitor that shows even the slightest curiosity about the place. And, from what I can see . . . he's out-doing himself this time."

Bill came to the same conclusion as he continued, as inconspicuously as possible, to observe the movements of Bergmann and his sergeant host. Movements which, in the hour that followed,

133

included visits to the General Staff headquarters, the barracks housing the Guards Regiment, the communication center, and the storage arsenal. It wasn't long before Hansen became aware of Bill's unusual intrigue with the civilian visitor . . . and while not commenting about it . . . nevertheless, became somewhat curious as to the reason why.

"That German civilian, Bergmann, is certainly getting his money's worth out of your friend Truelsen's tour today, Stig."

"He sure is, Bill. Tonight, when Truelsen and I are making our rounds of the local bars, I plan to kid him about that. After all, with these invasion rumors flying about, you'd think he'd be more discrete and not give the country store away."

Hansen's smile indicated that he was only jesting, apparently not concerned in the least about any rumors . However, Bill was of the opposite opinion, and more scared than ever. Why else would Bergmann be so intently interested in the Citadel? Why else indeed!

Instead of returning to Amalienborg Palace, Bill almost surprised Hansen by taking him up on his previous offer to see the colliers unload at Langelinie.

Almost . . . only because Hansen also heard Bergmann asking Truelsen for directions on how to get to the docking area . . . and quickly realized that Bill's innocent actions were actually a cover for his tailing Bergmann. For what reason, he again didn't know and, again didn't ask . . . because Danish people have a fetish about minding there own business.

Crossing back over the two rings of moats which isolated the Citadel from the surrounding park land, they steered their bicycles along Esplanaden onto Langelinie Promenade, which weaved gracefully along the seaside all the way from the Citadel to the wharf area where foreign countries moored their ships.

At Hansen's insistence, however, they stopped once on their short journey to admire the beauty and serenity of a bronze, life-size statue, which replicated the famous fairy tale illustration of the Little Mermaid of Hans Christian Andersen.

"It's a shame the world can't be as serene as that,"Bill remarked woefully as he longingly stared at the peaceful statue, perched atop two large granite boulders, wistfully gazing across the sparkling blue waters of the harbor. "But,then, that really would be a fairy tale wouldn't it, Stig!"

Hansen avoided a verbal response, choosing instead just to slowly nod his head several times in agreement. Although he had known Bill for a total of only a few hours, he already felt a deep bond of attachment developing between him and this sensitive American whose apparent love of life's real purpose mirrored that of his own.

When they finally arrived at the dock area, Hansen noted in amazement,

"That's odd. With the two German colliers now pulling into their slips, there'll be a total of four German coal ships tied up at Langelinie Pier."

"Is that so unusual?"Bill asked with a wrinkled brow, fully anticipating Hansen's worrisome reply,

"Sure is! . . . Hardly ever do we see more than two here at any one time. Especially since Germany has been on the war path. And more particularly in springtime, when our need for coal supplies greatly diminishes."

Then, staring at the ships already docked, Hansen exclaimed,

"Well, I'll be damned! Those colliers tied to the docks are just lazily rocking in the water. Doesn't seem as if there has been any effort to unload them."

"You've got to be mistaken, Stig. Their cargo must have been put ashore already, and they're getting ready to lift anchor."

"No chance, Bill. Don't you see how low their hulls sit in the water? The coal must still be on board. Just like Bergmann is. Can you see him standing over by the railing on the starboard bow conversing with that officer, who I assume is the Captain?"

Bill had certainly noticed and had already concluded, based on Hansen's astute observation, that something was definitely amiss which could only mean trouble for both him and Copenhagen.

135

"This couldn't have anything to do with those invasion rumors . . . could it, Stig?"

Now Hansen's thirty-year old brow wrinkled deeply, before slowly clearing, as he seemed to force a smile while calmly saying,

"I think we're letting our imaginations run away with us, Bill. I still don't believe that the Germans will attack on the 9th, or any other day for that matter. Come on! Before we both get paranoid and start complaining like 'Chicken Little' that the 'sky is falling'. Let's go grab a bite to eat and drown our thirst with a couple of jugs of Pilsner beer. I know just the place."

As grave as the situation was becoming in Bill's mind, he couldn't keep from joining in the laughter . . . when he sponta-neously retorted,

"I'm sure you do!"

Meanwhile, a jovial Bergmann was being dutifully escorted below deck by the coal vessel's captain, who proudly boasted in German,

"With the new arrivals today, Major Bergmann, we now have more than 2000 soldiers ready and waiting to seize Copenhagen!"

"Good! The gullible Danes have fallen for our Trojan-horse trick . . . just as I thought they would. Before daybreak on Tuesday morning, I'll be back with my panzer battalion aboard the troopship Hansestadt Danzig.

"Then, all of us will pour ashore to capture Copenhagen before the Danish people wake and sit down for breakfast."

"Then you expect an easy time of it, Major!"

"Yes! I certainly do. I've just finished reconnoitering the Citadel and, now know first hand the state of their inadequate defenses, and the caliber of their lackadaisical fighting men, who seem to have no appetite for combat. I can assure you Copenhagen will fall quickly. Copenhagen will be ours on Tuesday!"

On that confident note, Maj. Bergmann spent the rest of the afternoon visiting with the thousands of troops hidden below deck in the holds of the elaborately modified cargo areas of the four collier ships, personally assuring Germany's elite surprise attack force that little or no resistance would be encountered by them when they stormed ashore with him on the 9th. Needless to say, with this good news exuding so convincingly from Maj. Bergmann's trusted lips, everyone's moral on board the invasion ships rapidly elevated exponentially to an euphoric state!

During their break for lunch, which unexpectedly stretched into two hours, Hansen introduced Bill several times to an old Danish custom of gulping down an icy cold glass of their National firewater drink, called 'snaps', followed immediately with a foaming beer chaser. Under these spirited circumstances, Bill quickly became light headed, and soon felt as if his body was teetering in air, not unlike the wobbly motions of a freely floating helium balloon. And now uncontrollably giddy, he lifted yet another full glass to his wide opened lips, chugalugged its contents, before gasping with an unmistakable slur,

"This 'snaps' really knocks your socks off, doesn't it, Stig?"

As a result of their extended pause for food and drink, and certainly more of the latter, their afternoon exploration of the picturesque, southern half of Copenhagen's inner city was undertaken in a new, carefree atmosphere of fun and comradery. One that continued unchanged . . . well into the early hours of the morning as Hansen took special pride in giving his new found friend an expansive taste of Copenhagen's exciting night life.

Miserable was the only word that adequately described how Bill felt when he woke up late on Saturday morning, the 6th . . . Not only did his weary leg muscles ache but, his spinning head also pained from an enormous hangover that refused to succumb an inch, even to the popular muti-asprin remedy. When he finally did venture out that early afternoon, he walked alone, politely declining Hansen's kind offer to pick up where they left off yesterday.

And at least this time, when he returned to the d'Angeleterre about 10 P.M., he was only tired . . . not exhausted . . . and only

137

thirsty for a cold glass of water . . . not bordering on the brink of being foolishly inebriated again with 'snaps', beer, and the world famous Danish liqueur, Cherry Heering.

Having completed his reconnaissance of Copenhagen on Saturday, so that he felt thoroughly familiar with her network of streets and canals, Bill promised to himself that he would now relax and devote what little time remained until Tuesday's pick-up to a variety of the pleasurable sightseeing activities that tourists to this lovely Danish capital normally enjoyed.

However, Johan's innocent, informative remark just before noon on Sunday suddenly shattered Bill's short-lived vow. And, unfortunately, also served as a catalyst that now triggered a sequence of events catapulting Bill's temporarily suppressed anxiety up to a resonating amplitude.

"Now we have two German civilian business men with us. Kurt Muller's the second! He arrived earlier this morning by train, claiming to be a botany professor interested in the research being conducted in his specialty at the University of Copenhagen.

"Although he has a professor's sophistication and knowledge, his bearing and mannerisms still lead me to the same conclusion. He's strictly military! And most likely a officer with a higher rank than Bergmann! But then, you can judge for yourself Bill, he's parading into the lobby now with Bergmann."

Bill's glance over to see the new comer was slow and casual, despite his impatience to observe Muller. Now, seeing the two together, walking so rigidly upright and unconsciously stepping forward in unison, undoubtedly out of force of habit from extensive military training, was enough to convince Bill that Johan was absolutely right in his intuitive assessment.

And by the way Bergmann seemed to be kowtowing to Muller, there was no question either that Muller possessed the higher rank, whether it be business or military.

"Jesus!" Bill blasphemed in frustration. "Too bad we can't listen in on their conversation. Then, we wouldn't have to speculate as to who they really are, or why they're here in Copenhagen. We'd know for sure . . . wouldn't we, Johan?"

"Wouldn't do you any good, Bill . . . Even if you were a fly on Muller's lapel. Unless, of course, you 'Specken Sie Deutch'! Because from the few guttural sounds that I've been able to detect, their intensive discussion is being carried out in German."

When Bill saw both Germans stop suddenly. Not more than 15 feet away from them. And detected Bergmann flipping his right wrist so that his index finger momentarily pointed in their direction . . . his rapid heart beat froze with fear,

"They're on to me," he speculated to himself."That's why they're here. It has nothing to do with any invasion bullshit!"

Bergmann, however, wasn't at all interested in Bill. In fact . . . as he now walked over to the registration desk, he completely ignored Bill and, instead, hastily addressed Johan,

"Something has just come up Mr. Cilborg which necessitates my returning to Berlin immediately. So if you will kindly prepare my bill, I'll be right down to pay as soon as I pack my luggage."

Bergmann's unscheduled departure from Copenhagen settled one thing in Bill's mind. Bergmann wasn't the contact man from Germany who would meet him at the drop site on Tuesday. But, if not him. Who? Bill still hadn't the faintest idea, and strongly doubted now that he would find out until the final witching hour.

Tension mounted to an unbearable level for Bill on Monday. Edgy and extremely nervous, he couldn't help remark,

"If I'm this way now, I'll be a jellyfish by the time the drop occurs tomorrow evening."

Knowing he had to do something to relieve his strain, Bill gladly took Johan's casual suggestion and attended the opening night performance held at the Royal Theater. Under more normal circumstances, Bill would have enjoyed the gala performance of 'The Merry Wives of Windsor", staged in such magnificent surroundings . . . and with the thrill of watching it in the presence of King Christian X and the Queen, who sat in the Royal box. But, somehow on this occasion, the jovial mood exhibited by the King disturbed Bill. He thought it ludicrous that the King was oblivious to the imminent danger now facing his country.

Nor could he believe the whispered conversations overheard amongst the audience that . . . just that evening . . . the King, at the Royal table, had dismissed once again the threat that Germany was about to invade his Nation, with an unconscionable rebuttal,

"I really don't believe that. It's still poppycock!"

Bill couldn't help but feel he was witnessing an 'Alice in Wonderland' naivete.

"It's a fantasy world of make believe," he conjectured, while cringing over what he perceived to be a historical misjudgment of impending calamity.

So while the King may have been in a confident and happy mood, Bill certainly was not. A fact readily discernible by Johan, who immediately addressed Bill as he sulked into the lobby upon his return from the Palace Theater.

"You seem to be very troubled tonight Bill"

"Does it show that much. I guess there are somethings a person just can't hide. I'm both depressed . . . and astonished at the same time."

"About what? If you don't mind my prying."

"About the Danes! Everything indicates that Germany will attack tomorrow morning. Yet . . . everybody just seems to turn a deaf ear to these warnings. I confess. I don't really understand the Danish people. Why doesn't someone sound an alarm before it's too late?

"Everyone here is so relaxed . . . at least that's the way it seems so to me. Aren't you terrified at the thought that when the sun rises tomorrow, Hitler's assault troops may be blasting their way into Copenhagen?"

"Don't worry Bill. Hitler is just playing a cat and mouse game of psychological warfare with these rumored threats of invading us and Norway.

140

"Just a bluffing game to confuse the Allies and cover up his real intention of sweeping around the Maginot Line and occupying the Netherlands in order to execute his planned thrust into France.

"There's no reason for him to move northward against both a weak Denmark and Norway . . . Not when he risks the chance of losing the golden opportunity that now knocks on his Western front."

In spite of these reassuring words, Bill was far from convinced.

"What about those two so called German business men. First, Bergmann . . . and, now, Muller! Although Bergmann left two days ago . . . while he was here . . . he certainly had a uncanny interest in the Citadel and the port district. You said yourself he probably was a German officer.

"Well, I agree with you now! I believe he was sent here on an advanced reconnaissance mission . . . he came . . . he saw . . . and then left in a hell of a hurry. Almost as if he had to report back his personal observations immediately.

"However, the final straw . . . the one that removed any lingering doubt that I had was the manner in which Muller quizzed me at dinner last night. I've been out with hundreds of business men, and have never been so intently grilled on matters that had nothing at all to do with business."

Just recalling that evening meal was enough to resurface Bill's uneasy feeling that Muller obviously suspects him of being a spy!

"These rumors of an imminent attack tomorrow . . . not only have me worried . . . they have me scared because I think they are real. Yet, everyone in Denmark seems to pooh pooh the possibility and go on acting as if nothing out of the ordinary was happening.

"Either you're all a lot braver than I am . . . or you're . . . " Bill stopped short . . . because he almost was going to say 'stupid'. And he knew that wasn't the case, even though in this irrational moment he certainly felt it was.

141

"Or, you're cowards."

"We're neither brave nor cowards Bill . . . just practical. We know if Hitler decides to attack us we'd be gobbled up faster than a turkey can peck up a grain of seed. Just remember . . . we're not isolated from the rest of the world by two huge oceans as America is. Berlin is only 250 miles away from us . . . your nearest city is over three thousand miles away from the war zone.

"But that doesn't mean we embrace the Nazis, or the communists for that matter. Danish people hate them both with a vengeance. But history has taught us to be realistic . . . not reckless or fool hearty. At best . . . we could only put up a meager resistance with our untrained, ill equipped militia force of 15,000 men, against an enemy whose panzar units would cut through us like a hot knife through butter.

"No! Fighting would be to no avail. We'd be overwhelmed in no time.

Johan now reflected for a moment . . . before continuing,

"But don't get me wrong, Bill. Inwardly we also tremble with fear over the uncertainty . . . as you do. However, we must show our contempt for war the only way we know how. By looking at it's reality straight in the eye . . . and pretending it's a bad dream . . . a nightmare that we all must and will live through as we did in the first World War, and as our descendants did before that in times of adversity. That's why we have adopted the laissez-faire attitude of 'tomorrow will bring what tomorrow will' for the Danish people.

"And somehow . . . we will manage to cope with our destiny.

"Even if we are invaded tomorrow by the Germans . . . we'll survive somehow because of the freedom that burns in our hearts . . . an inner freedom and lust for life that a gives us the real courage to stay proud Danes forever.

"So, Bill, while we might be leery about Hitler's Third Reich, we can contain our despair and concern because we've also have learned that tomorrow's problems will fade. Just like each today always fades into our yesterdays."

What more could Bill say after that moving discourse by Johan? Since he had nothing further to add to the conversation, he just politely excuse himself and said "good night."

But, while Bill, around 11 P.M., was still nervously pacing the carpeted floor of his bedroom, unable to sleep, Muller, who had gone to the house of Renthe-Fink, the German Minister to Denmark, was just completing a coded call to corps headquarters in Hamburg relating that the harbor was ice-free and the Danes had not taken the initiative to bolster the Capital's defenses.

Then, in conclusion, he bragged,

"Everything can proceed . . . exactly as planned."

Now turning to Renthe-Fink, he instructed him to deliver an ultimatum at 4:15 A.M. to the Danish government to surrender unconditionally to Germany. Renthe-Fink was shocked, completely unaware that his country was really going to invade Denmark.

"But General Muller, he protested vehemently,

"These are peace loving, defenseless people. Must we shed their blood too? Is there no other way?"

"No! Our troopship Hansestadt Danzig is already docking at Langelinie Pier next to our four colliers, whose holds are loaded with assault troops and war materiel. We are scheduled to initiate the attack at 4 A.M.

"It is up to you to convince the Danes to capitulate immediately if they want to stop the bloodshed."

With that he left, but not before snapping his right hand to his forehead and saluting, while clicking his heels together and proudly shouting,

"Heil Hitler!"

It was a night of unbearable anguish for Bill, who was too keyed up to fall sleep. And why not. For as he watched the minute hand tick pass midnight, he realized that D-day had finally arrived for him.

"Today . . . at sunset . . . it will be all over. One way or the other!" he whispered with a sigh of relief, which only momentarily camouflaged the premonition of doom that remained harbored deep in his subconscious mind.

Bill was still wide awake at 3:30 A.M., when a very fast moving thunderstorm bolted across Copenhagen,ominously skewing streaks of lightning from the undercarriage of its dark cumulus clouds as it rapidly passed toward the eastern horizon. Then, about an hour after the roar of its thunderclaps faded into soft whimpers . . . not unlike the faint echoes of distant fireworks, Bill began to doze off. Suddenly, he was shocked awake when his alert ears detected a new, more menacing sound filtering through his open window. The unmistakable crack of a gun shot!

What Bill had dreaded was now fact!

Denmark was being invaded by the Germans with simultaneously timed attacks against Jutland, the strategic island of Fyn, and Copenhagen. By land, sea and air, the Germans had launched a massive, coordinated offensive, deploying two Army divisions, three motorized gun battalions, a motorized rifle brigade with Mark 1 and Mark 11 tanks, two batteries of heavy artillery, and three armored trains. .

So, in spite of the advanced warnings, leaked from within the Abwehr, which predicted to the day . . . almost to the very minute . . . the time of the invasion, now underway. Denmark was a country caught completely off-guard by the sneak attack. Pitifully, it was about to pay the piper for its failings. And worse yet, Bill was about to face the consequence of this stupid neglect . . . as Maj. Bergmann, just before sunrise, eagerly gave the order to his combat ready German troops hidden in the holds of four merchant ships and aboard the Hansestadt Danzig to disembarked and seize the Capital.

CHAPTER 10

Only two Danish sentries were on duty when the German troops cautiously crept up to the Citadel's unlocked iron-picketed gate a few moments before 5 A.M . . . And of these two, one was sound asleep in a far corner of the stone blockhouse, his lifeless body sprawled into a wooden, straight back chair, with his weary head awkwardly draped backward over its upper rung, tentatively supported by cupped hands anchored tightly to his outstretched pillow-folded arms. Both of his long, lanky legs, bent at the knees, were appropriately elevated so that their calves and heels rested firmly on the top surface of an old metal desk.

The other one, Sergeant Truelsen, having heard a suspicious noise, grabbed a rifle from the wall-mounted arsenal rack, stepped quickly outside, and peered anxiously into the darkness, while nervously twitching his tense finger on the trigger of his rifle.

Then, hearing a twig snap, he hastily lifted his old rifle to the ready position.

Suddenly, as a mass of shadowy figures began emerging out of the low, lingering morning mist, Truelsen courageously shouted,

"Halt! Who goes there?"

Truelsen's cry of alarm never reached the ears of the tired souls of the seventy-man Danish garrison that still laid fast asleep in their barracks. But, most unfortunately, it did provoke the firing of a single shot from the cocked pistol of an approaching Ger-

145

man officer, who by this time stood less than fifteen feet away from him.

It was the shot of a marksman. One that, as intended, unerringly blew off the front lobe of Truelsen's brain after penetrating his skull, right between his startled eyes. Frightened eyes that stared in disbelief, for a brief instant, before being blinded forever by a massive gush of death's blood, immediately after recognizing his assailant as being none other than the civilian, Bergmann, who Truelsen befriended and, so graciously, had escorted around the Citadel's grounds just four short days ago.

Mercifully, Truelsen's perked ears lacked sufficient impulse-time before death to audibly register Bergmann's derogatory blast, expelled, simultaneously,with the death bullet,

"You stupid fool!"

As fate would have it, Truelsen was the only casualty, on either side, in the surprise take-over of the Citadel. A tribute, in no small way, to the excellence of the reconnaissance mission previously conducted by Maj. Bergmann with the able help of his self-appointed naive guide, who now laid dead, face-down in his own small pool of blood, still pathetically clutching onto his unfired musket. Unfired because of frozen hands, first immobilized by the curse of fright, now paralyzed forever by the stiffness of death's rigor mortis.

Although Bergmann's blitzkrieg attack resulted in swift conquest of Copenhagen's fortress, it failed by ten minutes in the capture of Gen. W.W. Prior, Commander-in-Chief of the Danish Army, who had hastily departed from the Citadel only moments earlier to attend an emergency meeting of the Danish cabinet at the King's Palace in Amalienborg Square to discuss Germany's arrogant demand for immediate capitulation.

Before leaving the fortress General Prior reacted urgently by dutifully calling-to-arms the guards at Amalienborg, as well as mobilizing all fighting units throughout Denmark to resist any attack by the Germans.

All except one! That one exception was his very own garrison, the soldiers of which, as a consequence, peacefully slumbered on, total unaware of the eminent danger now facing them and their Nation.

How this oversight could have occur, can only be attributed to human error . . . human failing. Perhaps, the type of character failing that might be expected of a new recruit, operating under the stress of a rapidly unfolding crisis. But not, however, the type of omission that ever should be made by an Army's Commander-in-Chief. Yet, somehow it did happen.

And, as a result of this unforgivable blunder, not only did the Citadel's defense die without a chance to fight, but so too did poor, heroic Truelsen, whose prostrated body now was suffering the ultimate humiliation of being trampled into the mud by the heavy, black combat boots of the on-rushing assault troops as they poured, without any resistance, through the open wrought iron gates to quickly secure the sleeping soldiers and the fortress for their Fatherland, before moving out in mass to attack the Palace.

Bill heard the constant din of rifle shots ringing out from the direction of Amalienborg Square, and correctly surmised that the King's Palace must be under siege.

But thankfully he was spared witnessing the confusion and turmoil that prevailed therein, as King Christian and his Cabinet ministers debated the dire and rather hopeless situation confronting Denmark.

Like Bill, the seventy-year-old King appeared shattered by the rapidly unfolding events, And like Bill, his body also commenced to tremble uncontrollably while both Bill's and the King's panicky minds wrestled with making momentous decisions. For Bill,it was whether to stay, or abort the mission. For King Christian. it was whether to surrender meekly, or continue to fight on bravely in what was obviously a lost cause.

Then, just as the sun's rays lifted above the horizon, hundreds . . . upon hundreds of German bombers, zoomed menacingly low over the Capital to darkened Copenhagen's just brightened sky. Their trajectory was so low, in fact, Bill, looking up out of his open window, had no trouble in identifying the dreaded Luftwaffe insignia painted on the aircraft, as they rumbled directly overhead and blanketed the blue heaven from horizon to horizon.

So low, in fact, their combined engines' decibel roar was absolutely deafening!

And worse yet, the sum of all the bombers' extremely high, cumulative noise intensity was causing Bill such excruciating pain, he, out of desperation for relief, abruptly raised the palms of his hands to his tender ears. It was a futile effort. One that failed to shield his resonating drums from the nerve-shattering, high decibel pressure waves, emanating from these passing bombers.

Hitler was right! He knew the very presence of the Luftwaffe bombers would be intimidating. And within moments of their timely arrival, King Christian tossed up his arms in despair, acquiesced, and surrendered his country to the Germans without further struggle.

Thus, a most remarkable military feat had been accomplished! In less than two hours, Hitler had succeeded in his conquest of yet another nation!

Bill was absolutely stunned when he heard the despondent King Christian, at 6:20A.M., sadly broadcasting to all Danish military units and citizens that Denmark had capitulated to the Germans. How, he wondered, could any country lose a war in only two hours? All of a sudden, Bill understood what Johan was trying to preach to him the night before. All of a sudden, Bill had a first-hand, bird's eye view of the awesome power of Hitler's untamed war machine.

"My God! he exclaimed in awe. "No wonder our President wants the atom bomb first! Even with it, I'm not sure anyone can ever beat this madman's Army . . . Without it, I know they can't!"

Like King Christian, Bill now also made his irrevocable decision. However, his wasn't one of giving up passively . . . in spite of the impossible odds for success. He wasn't going to run away. He would stay and try to complete his mission, even if it meant dying in the attempt.

"Everyone certainly will live in tyranny if that psychopathic bully wins the war. And that's a fate Jonathon's not going to have to face. Not if I can do anything about it."

But, while Bill mulled over this latest crisis in a depressed mood, Bergmann joyfully reveled in the uncanny accuracy of his earlier prediction. The Capital, Copenhagen, and all of Denmark were indeed under complete control of the German occupation forces by the time most Danes awoke and sat down to their traditional hearty breakfast. Just as he boasted it would be.

Almost all of Copenhagen's inhabitants were numbed with total disbelief. Reluctantly. Despairingly. They accepted the reality of their uncertain future calmly and without challenge. All that is . . . except Stig Hansen. For around 8 A.M that morning when normalcy once again reigned in the Capital, in a quid pro quo arrangement as decreed by the Fuehrer, his concern for the safety of his bosom buddy led him to the Citadel to personally check out the rumor that one of its Danish guards had been killed.

Upon his arrival, Hansen saw scores of German's military troops inside the closed gate, nonchalantly milling about the grounds. Some were cajoling with each other, while others boisterously sang their favorite Nazi songs. Although he despised the Germans, it wasn't that particular scene that Hansen found so vile and disgusting.

What made him flush beet-red with anger was seeing the mangled body of a Danish soldier just outside the locked iron gate, lying prone in a dried-up puddle of blood.

"You dirty bastards!" he cried out. "Don't you show any respect for the dead? Can't you, at least, bring the dead soldier's body inside the fortress? If it was one of your own you wouldn't leave it discarded there . . . as if it was a piece of trash!"

Gloomily, he walked slowly over to the dead soldier, knelt

down by his side and, ever so gently, turned him over . . . while his taut lips began whispering a silent prayer of remorse.

But, upon discovering that the top of the guard's forehead was blown off, he recoiled in horror, and his startled blue eyes almost bulged out of their sockets.

"Oh, my God!" he pathetically exclaimed.

The inhumanity of this grotesque sight caused Hansen to immediately start dry-heaving. Followed . . . as soon as he recognized the corpse to be his best buddy, Truelsen . . . by him throwing up violently! For several moments, he wrenched out his gizzards . . . unable to make himself stop until the incessant gurgitations drained his stomach of all minuscule fluids and bile.

When the full impact of this very sad and tragic situation finally registered, Hansen went totally berserk. Forcing himself to an upright position, he staggered over to the locked gate, and defiantly commenced shouting obscenities, while belligerently shaking his clenched fists, and spitting disparagingly at the alarmed German soldiers around him.

"You murderers!" he bellowed. "You filthy swine! You no good German bastards!"

If he had possessed a gun, he would have used it by now to exact a small measure of revenge for the loss of the life of his close friend. But, if he had . . . most certainly he would be lying dead also . . . cut down by a heavy barrage of rifle shots that were almost fired at him anyway. And, undoubtedly would have been, if a German officer hadn't stepped forward, quickly intervened, by brusquely commanding loudly to his agitated troops,

"Hold your fire men! He's unarmed and harmless."

Then, an annoyed Maj. Bergmann marched swiftly over to the gate, glared sternly into Hansen's tear-filled eyes, and castigated him, in no uncertain terms.

"Stop provoking my troops. Or, I'll let them shoot you!"

"Why did they kill my friend?" Hansen growled. "Why? His old gun wasn't even loaded!"

150

"Ha!" Bergmann snickered. "Then, he was a bigger fool than I thought he was. I certainly didn't know that when I killed him . . . but, it wouldn't have made any difference anyway.

"One dead soldier, more or less, won't weigh heavily on my conscience. Not when you consider the mountains of corpses that will be joining him before the World's conquest by our Fuehrer is completed.

Pausing only long enough to peer sternly again at Hansen, he bellowed,

"Now . . . Get the hell out of here before I place you under arrest! "

Then, to emphasize the sincerity of the threat he was about to utter, he reached to his waist, placed his fingers around the exposed handle of his revolver, lifted the cocked pistol slowly out of his holster, and menacingly added,

"Or, before I loose my patience and kill you also!"

With these last words still reverberating bitterly in his smarting ears, Hansen mounted his bicycle, and wheeled briskly away. But, as his temper continued to flare unabated within, he made a vow, on the body of poor dead Truelsen, that he would have an 'eye for an eye', even if he had to fight alone against these German murderers!.

Later that afternoon both Gen. Muller and Maj. Bergmann pompously returned to the Hotel d'Angleterre. This time, however, they didn't bother to register. This time, they just arrogantly commandeered the top two floors of the building for their German occupational headquarters. Naturally, as victors, Muller and Bergmann also enjoyed the spoils of their conquest, including the comforts of adjoining luxury suites immediately adjacent to Bill's.

CHAPTER 11

Bill's luck wasn't all bad. Today, he still seemed to be blessed with the luck of the Irish, since the German's didn't declare martial law, or even evoke a dusk to dawn curfew, after their invasion . . . he still had the freedom of movement needed to keep his 8:00 P.M. rendezvous with his, as yet, unknown contact.

However, as he prepared to leave his room, he became extremely tense. As, indeed, anyone in his shoes would . . . considering the unpredictable territory about to be charted in his quest to obtain a copy of Germany's Master Plan for the Atomic Bomb Development. Also, he was chilled with goose-pimples that suddenly erupted and prickled his nervous body. Bill quickly slipped on a woolen argyle sweater, uttering, in self denial of his fright,

"The evenings are cool in Copenhagen due to the on-shore breeze."

Flipping his wrist and observing the time, Bill was now aware that he had only forty five minutes to make it to the 'drop' site. But, just enough time, he reasoned, to stroll leisurely to his destination, and to climb the outer spiral stairs to the top of the 300 foot church tower.

Now . . . approaching his door to leave, Bill abruptly stopped in his tracks when someone knocked.

"Who the hell can that be?" he muttered angrily. "Don't tell me things are starting to go wrong already."

Bill felt trapped in a no-win situation. Time . . . really the lack of time . . . prevented him from just ignoring the knock and waiting out the intruder. He had to leave . . . and leave now.

Besides, pretending he wasn't there wouldn't work, particularly if the caller was either Bergmann or Muller. Both of them saw him enter his room as they returned to theirs after dinner.

"If I don't answer and it's either of them. I'll be under suspect for sure."

Having decided he had no other choice, Bill moved forward apprehensively and swung the door open. To his surprise . . . and relief . . . it was not the Germans. It was Hansen. A depressed and tearful Hansen, greeting Bill with the tragic news,

"They've killed Truelsen!"

But Bill already knew. Confirmation of rumors sweep through Copenhagen even faster than the rumors themselves. And while words never come easy in sorrowful moments like this, Bill readily appreciated the extent of Hansen's loss and said sincerely,

"I'm sorry, Stig. I'm truly . . . very sorry."

Beyond that Bill was torn. He didn't want to be rude to Hansen, yet, he couldn't afford to take the time to console him at length. His urgent commitment gave him no option but to be curt, thus, he said impatiently,

"I must go out for an hour or two, Stig. So I can't talk to you now. Why don't you stay here . . . mix yourself a drink . . . and wait until I get back. When I do, we can discuss it further."

And with that Bill closed the door behind a mystified Hansen . . . who having shook his head dejectedly, astutely observed,

"That's not like Bill. Something serious must be the matter . . . otherwise he would have treated me with more compassion."

Meanwhile, Bill was proceeding down the long tapestry-walled corridor leading to the exiting staircase, totally unaware that as soon as the noise of his closing door had faded, the German officer in the adjacent suite quickly opened his and discretely began duplicating his footsteps.

154

Not expecting to be followed, Bill neglected to use a circuitous route on his trek to Vor Frelsers Kirke as strongly urged by Edwards during his training sessions. Instead, he sauntered directly towards the church at a pace purposely set so as not to garner the attention of the German soldiers patrolling the streets of Denmark, who were under orders to arrest anyone suspicious.

Bill was noticed, however. And since the streets were almost desolate, the German soldiers gave this lone American tourist long stares, wrinkled brows and raised eyebrows anyway. But, in spite of their curiosity and close scrutiny, Bill was allowed to pass without incident and eventually arrived safely at the iron gate entrance to Our Saviour's Church.

Now, for the first time, Bill exhibited sufficient concern to swivel his head in various directions to make certain that no one was monitoring his actions. Falsely reassured that everything was all right, he quickly moved through the gate, through the short courtyard, and began his arduous climb up the external spiral staircase.

And so did the German officer . . . who having successfully tracked him without being detected was now only 100 yards behind.

Even though twilight had descended on Copenhagen, there still was enough residual luminescence from the soft glow of the city's lights for Bill to get a phenomenal panoramic view of its beauty as he rotated upward on his climb.

The spellbinding sight was so impressive, he couldn't help but reminisce, painfully,

"If Karen was alive today, she'd be so exhilarated seeing this."

As Bill thought about Karen again, tears of remorse ran down his cheeks. As they always did whenever she came into his mind.

Now, puffing more strenuously . . . as he rose higher and higher on what he perceived to be almost a vertical climb for altitude, Bill was forced to pause often, making several stops to catch his breath . . . as did the German officer.

But despite his physical exhaustion, he pressed upward unrelentlessly, with the German officer now only fifty yards behind.

Finally, he reached the top. And none too soon ... as his strength was drained to a level that long ago would have read empty, if it was on a gasoline gauge. Anxiously, he looked around for his contact. To no avail. No one was anywhere in sight causing him to despondently utter in disgust,

"All for nothing. All the worrying. All the effort. And What for? Nothing! Damn it! The German invasion must have scared off my contact."

Then, when contemplating what his next move should be, Bill remembered the forgotten specifics of his secret instructions . . . 'next to the staff supporting the golden globe, atop which stands the life-size figure of the Compassionate Christ'.

"How could I be so damn stupid as to forget anything as important as that?" Bill asked himself, as he quickly walked over and stood directly underneath the statue of Christ.

However, to his chagrin, no one was there either.

Suddenly, out of the dark shadows from behind a massive three foot diameter marble column, appeared a tall German officer with his drawn pistol cocked and pointed directly at Bill's heart.

"So Mr. Price. We meet again!"

Bill was frightened . . . by the gun . . . and by the voice that he immediately recognized to be Muller's. And when his dilated eyes confirmed Muller's presence as he came vividly into view, Bill's heart skipped a beat . . . before accelerating rapidly to panic levels.

"There's no doubt that I'm going to be killed," he thought . . . wondering if Jonathon or Cathy would miss him.

"Well . . . look who's here. It is 'Adam' Price. Isn't it?" Muller asked inquisitively.

Bill sighed deeply with enormous relief, as he now realized from the cue Muller gave that Muller had to be his contact man. Now all Bill had to do was to respond properly with the coded reply that Edwards had provided.

156

This, he promptly did.

"On a night such as this, you could call me 'Eve' if you wanted too."

"So at long last! Good! My mission will be completed as soon as I turn these documents over to you. However, yours, unfortunately, won't terminate until you manage somehow to get these out of Denmark and back to the United States."

Then, replacing his gun in his holster, Muller lifted the right pant-leg of his army uniform, unstrapped a leather pouch wrapped around his calf, and reached over to hand it to Bill.

"Guard it carefully. And be sure you don't get caught by the Germans with this in your possession. You'll be executed on the spot, if you are."

"And so will YOU! You traitor!", shouted an enraged Bergmann, who without warning, jumped out from nowhere, grabbed Muller around the neck from behind, pressed his loaded revolver to his right temple, and blew his brains out.

Bill was paralyzed with disbelieve. And as Muller slumped lifeless to the ground, Bill could only cry out,

"Why did you kill him? He's not the real traitor. You Are! You're a traitor to all decent mankind."

"The Fuhrer will be proud of me when he finds out what I have done for the Fatherland," Bergmann retorted contemptuously.

"When I uncovered what Muller was carrying in that pouch, I knew at once he must be a traitor. He was betraying us. But, for what country? I thought it would be for the Russians, not you dirty, peace-loving Americans."

After that outburst, he grabbed his gun by the barrel and ruthlessly slashed at Bill, smashing him on the head with the butt-end of the pistol. Then, as Bill reeled under the blow, Bergmann began hitting him unmercifully. On his chin. On his face. In his stomach. Blood oozed, then, flowed freely from Bill's nostrils and mouth, as Bergmann, still in his wild animal-like rage, kept striking his defenseless captive.

"When I get through with you. You'll be just a mashed pulp of human flesh!", he gloated.

Helpless, and beaten to unconsciousness, Bill fell to the ground with his head hanging over the top step of the spiral staircase. Arrogantly, Bergmann came up to him and raised his right leg, bent at the knee, high into the air. So high in fact, Bergmann teetered backwards as if he would lose his balance. He was so intent on crushing his boot into Bill's head, his crazed eyes didn't see the hand that reached upward in the dark, grabbed his elevated foot, and pushed him with such force that Bergmann was successfully flipped over on his back.

Bergmann's skull cracked hard on the concrete platform, momentarily stunning him. Consequently, he wasn't aware who his rival was until he opened his bleary eyes and saw Hansen standing over him. And when he did, Hansen kicked him in the groin with all the power of a frenzied mule. Bergmann cried out loudly in excruciating pain. But, unsympathetic Hansen showed him no mercy and kicked him in the balls again . . . but this time even harder, almost as if he was trying to castrate him.

"The first one was for Truelsen," he said. "The second one was for my friend Bill . . . And this one is for me!"

Then, after gladly keeping his promise, Hansen lifted Bergmann to an upright position, before using his enormous strength to raise him over his head. Bergmann, wincing in his well deserved pain, suddenly realized what Hansen was up too.

"Please . . . Please!" . . . Bergmann pleaded as he groped wildly with his flaily arms . . . desperately trying to grasp onto something . . . anything . . . that would prevent Hansen from tossing him over the siderail.

"Don't kill me! I don't want to die!"

"You filthy coward!" Hansen bellowed. "Neither did my buddy, Truelsen!"

And with that he moved over to the edge of the platform, grunted hard and long as he strained every muscle in his weary body to raise Bergman even higher . . . so as to be sure that his flapping arms could not grab the railing. Then, Hansen hurled him away . . . like a discus player unleashes the winning shotput in vying for a record toss.

Bergmann screeched . . . whined . . . and cried out in agony . . . as he catapulted through empty space and started tumbling to his certain death some 300 feet below.

Hansen, although short of breath from his miraculous feat, impulsively lifted his head over the side rail in order to witness the demise of his hated Nazi enemy. His dancing blue eyes gleefully followed the arching trajectory of Bergmann's body . . . and his ears rejoiced in hearing the fading woeful cries of despair emanating from the bastard, Bergmann . . . until the moment of impact . . . as his body became impaled on the pickets of an iron fence surrounding the lower base of the church.

"All of Copenhagen must have heard him," Hansen said smiling.

"All of Denmark will soon learn that tonight we have avenged the lost of our heroic Truelsen."

Satisfied that Bergmann was undoubtedly dead, Hansen turned and moved swiftly over to attend to his wounded friend, Bill, who showed only slight signs of recovering consciousness.

Yet, Hansen intuitively felt that his brave idol, Bill, would soon get well. Badly bruised for sure . . . but alive!

Without further delay he gathered up the Master Plan packet and stored it inside Bill's shirt for safe keeping.

"Right next to your heart Bill, where it belongs until we have you safely out of Denmark and into neutral Sweden."

And with that he again exerted himself to superhuman endurance and lifted Bill so that his limp body rested on his left shoulder. Then, he proceeded ever so slowly down the winding spiral staircase to its base.

Now, looking over to the ten foot high iron fence, Hansen not only could see Bergman's bloody body hanging upside down

159

impaled on two supporting pickets, but . . . he could also hear the low moans of sure death still oozing from Bergman's gapping mouth.

Carefully, he laid a limp Bill down on the concrete, and while drawing his knife from his belt, slowly walked over to Bergmann and said disgustingly,

"No! You son of a bitch! I'm not going to cut you down. You deserve a slow tortuous death. But, I wouldn't be able to ever have a good night's sleep again if I thought by some miracle you would survive and betray me or my friend, Bill."

And with that, he plunged the knife deep into Bergmann's throat, slit it widely across, withdrew his gagging tongue and cut it off at the root.

"There! That does it," he said matter-of-factly. "Now . . . I'll be able to sleep like a kitten!"

11B

Hitler erupted in a violent temper tantrum when informed by Heinrich Himmler, Reichsfuhrer of Secret Services, about the deaths of Muller and Bergmann.

Muller was not a traitor in Hitler's eyes . . . Nor was Bergmann a hero for killing him. After all . . . Hitler never found out the whole truth. All the German Fuhrer comprehended was that two of his best officers had been brutally murdered in Copenhagen.

And when Himmler bluntly told him that the Gestapo's investigation concluded that an American tourist, William Price, was the most likely culprit, Hitler became infuriated.

"It's a lie!" he screeched. "It was the Jews. It was Copenhagen's Jews!"

Himmler tried several times to point out the circumstantial evidence concerning the mysterious disappearance of Price from the Hotel d'Angleterre where he occupied a suite adjacent to the officers, and the eye-witness accounts of numerous German soldiers who had seen the American in the immediate area about the time of the killings. But . . . mercurial Hitler's degenerate mind was already made up. And, now glaring straight at Himmler through a pair of enraged eyes, he shouted,

"That's absurd! I tell you it's the Jews that are responsible!

"I want you to round up every Jew in Denmark. Then, exterminate them as you would rats in your barn. Show no mercy

... poison them ... club them ... gas them ... but kill all of them!"

As much as Himmler agreed with Hitler's philosophy that the Jews must be wasted, he feared that the public outcry of Danish citizens to this anti-Semitic vendetta might ferment an uprising throughout Denmark. Such a populous revolt, Himmler reasoned, could seriously compromise Germany's invasion operation in Norway ... simultaneously launched on April 9th with the attack on Denmark, but which now was being bitterly fought and contested by the Norwegians. So he tried to delay Hitler's insane edict by offering a compromise.

"My Fuhrer. No one ... but you ... hates the Jews more than I do. However, unlike our easy blitzgreig success in Denmark, our attack on Norway has posed grave military problems. The combat effectiveness of the Norwegians is much greater than we had ever anticipated. If we are to win that battle, we must not dilute our resources at this time by antagonizing the Danes into a rebellious uprising because of our desired elimination of the Jews. Believe me. The Danes will resist that endeavor more vehemently than our conquest of their country ... simply because the Danish people are fanatic idealist, who believe in treating all humans like humans ... even if they are Jewish."

Himmler detected an awareness of reality suddenly sweeping back into Hitler's satanic mind. Himmler had twitched one of his most sensitive psychotic cords. If Hitler feared anything, it was the humiliation of suffering a defeat in Norway. Such a catastrophe would virtually end his dreams for Germany's conquest of the world. So it wasn't surprising that he became more rational and listened intensely as Himmler presented his alternative.

"Ninety-five percent of Denmark's eight thousand Jews now live in Copenhagen. We already have them contained, without them knowing it.

"I promise you! I promise you my Fuhrer that, as soon as you deem it appropriate after our conquest of Norway, the Gestapo will quickly round them all up and extradite them in closed boxcars to our new concentration camps now in Theresienstadt(Terezin, Czechoslovakia).

"Meanwhile to save face with the Danes, we'll blame the American for this massacre. A massive search is already underway looking for him. We'll find him shortly . . . dead or alive!"

"Good! As long as you keep your promise . . . Good!"

Now warmly embracing Himmler's stratagem, Hitler calmly demanded,

"See to it that our press releases about this incident properly admonish the United States for the dastardly act perpetrated by one of its citizens . . . and for violating their policy of strict neutrality in our war with Great Britain and the Europeans. And send for the American Ambassador, here in Berlin . . . I want to personally ream his ass out for allowing this atrocity to occur."

Now rubbing his hands vehemently with glee, Hitler continued,

"I'll demand an immediate apology from President Roosevelt. And an explanation as to what motivated this William Price to commit such a heinous crime. If it's an act of sabotage, Roosevelt must be deliberately trying to provoke me into a declaration of war against the United States. He's been itching to get into this on the side of the British, but I'm too clever for that capitalist, Roosevelt. I'll be furious with the Ambassador. But I'll be magnanimous in my willingness to forgive . . . after I scare the shit out of him first."

Unfortunately, Hansen had been too optimistic in his assessment of Bill's ability to recover rapidly from the horrendous beating he sustained from Bergmann. Bill just drifted in and out of consciousness, for several days . . . completely unaware of the round-the-clock care that both Stig and Johan were providing in their noble effort to nurse him back to health.

In fact, more than a week past before Bill regained full

control of his senses, and could eat his meals by himself . . . instead of being spoon-fed as he was religiously by his faithful saviors.

And although still badly bruised, as evidence by his numerous black and blue blotches, nature's healing process had now lowered his pain to a tolerable level.

That morning, with the clearing of his mind, Bill looked to Hansen for searching answers to his questions.

"What happened? How did I get here? The last thing I remember was Bergmann swinging at me after he killed Muller."

Suddenly, Bill panicked. And with Hansen and Johan curiously watching, he started groping with his hands under the pillows, and under the sheets . . . frantically he scanned the room, searching for the leather packet containing the Master Plan copy.

Unsuccessful, he cried aloud,

"Oh, God! Don't tell me I lost it. Maybe it's still at the church."

Hansen quickly spoke out to relieve his anxiety,

"No, Bill. You didn't lose it. It's right here in my dresser drawer. I was only saving it for you until you recovered."

"Then you know!" . . . Bill exclaimed.

"Nothing!" Hansen replied. "I only know that these must be tremendously important papers for you to have subjected yourself to such danger . . . to such pain and misery. I didn't read them Bill. You know we Danes believe in minding our own business."

Johan nodded in agreement. And Bill's moistened eyes revealed how moved he was over the unquestioning loyalty of his two friends. Now clutching the pouch tightly with his hands, he was able to relax, vowing that it would never leave his possession again.

"But, what happened? Do you know, Stig? Who rescued me?"

Bill was astounded when Hansen filled in the gory details . . . and how he avenged Truelsen's demise. Astonished . . . but happy that the depraved Bergmann got everything he deserved. How he wished he could have witnessed Hansen's removal of Bergmann's arrogant tongue.

What he wouldn't have given for the opportunity to have held the knife that was plunged into Bergmann's throat.

But now . . . he was more deeply concerned realizing that both Hansen and Johan had put themselves at considerable risk to save him.

Especially, in light of the on going . . . house-by-house, systematic search being conducted by the Germans trying to find him.

Johan's acute apprehension, however, was solely for Bill, which prompted his warning,

"We must get you away from here, today. The German's grid-search is only two blocks away. They'll be here by tomorrow at the latest.

"We should have moved you sooner but your poor health prevented that. We can't wait any longer."

"Let me give myself up," Bill pleaded. "I don't want either you or Stig to suffer any repercussions because of me."

"Never! Did you risk your life . . . everything . . . just to give up now?" Hansen bellowed, almost in disgust.

"If those papers were that important to you before . . . they must still be just as significant now. Maybe more so . . . since now you have them, whereas before you were just anxious to get ahold of them."

Bill nodded in agreement, knowing only too well how meaningful they were to the eventual salvation of the world.

"I told you once before Bill," Johan said softly. "Danes don't fight . . . but treasure freedom. You must not give up. You must escape. You owe it to yourself . . . and to us who remain under captivity by the wicked Third Reich. Someday. Somehow. Our Nation will be rescued from Hitler's tyranny by freedom loving countries, like yours, that have the wherewithal to defeat Hitler.

165

That's why we must start the process by first saving you from the German butchers. Because if you escape, All Denmark is escaping with you . . . even if we have to stay a little longer to appease the madman."

Bill acquiesced immediately,

"You're right. Of coarse you're right. But how?"

Johan knew . . . so he quickly retorted,

"By boat. That's the only way. A fishing boat to Sweden. Still neutral. Still free. And not invaded or coerced by Hitler. At least . . . not yet. But the German Army and Gestapo units have saturated Copenhagen looking for you. They're like swarming bees seeking vengeance against the predator who has destroyed their hive.

"We can't risk your taking a boat from here. We are taking you out of the city to a small fishing village along the Sound. At least then, the odds will be tipped more in your favor. Still heavily weighted against you, but infinitely better than trying to debark from Copenhagen,"

"Elsinore!" Hansen offered without hesitation.

"That's about 25 miles north, along the coastline of the Sound, where the blue waters of the Baltic separate Denmark from Sweden by only two and a half miles.

"And more importantly, my cousin, Peter, lives there. He owns his own fishing boat. We'll arrange for him to take you to Sweden. Tonight!"

"Are you sure, Stig?" Won't he be worried about the German's retaliation?"

"Bill. I can see you still have a lot to learn about us Danes. We stick together like glue when it comes to a human's rights. You're my friend. That's all that will matter to him. And to the others that have already agreed to help us."

Obviously moved by Hansen's remark, Bill felt a strong kinship . . . not only towards Stig . . . but towards all Danish people that he was growing to respect and admire . . . more and more with each passing moment.

"Bill. It's time to brace yourself for the trip. We'll be leaving in broad daylight as soon as our vehicle transportation arrives."

"In broad daylight! Wouldn't it be best to travel in the dark of night?" Bill asked anxiously.

"Not the way we're traveling."

"What do you mean.?"

"Well . . . it's a bit 'unorthodox'. But, the Germans are searching every car, taxi, or truck leaving Copenhagen.

"And since they also have copies of your photograph from the passport you left in your room, they are also scrutinizing everybody walking, or bicycling. The only way to fool them . . . if we can fool them at all . . . is to feed on their natural hatred of the Jews."

Bill's deep frown indicated his confusion and perplexedness . . . as did his simple comment,

"I still don't understand, Stig."

"As I said before 'brace yourself'. We're driving to Elsinore in a funeral hearse . . . with you as the corpse!"

Bill cringed. Knowing all too well that the Germans might soon succeed in making him one.

"A dead Jew . . . Bill. That's our best chance. The Germans want to rid the world of Jews. They'll be more than happy to start by letting a dead one out of Copenhagen."

At that moment there was a soft rap on the door. The sequence of the knocks seemed to be a prearranged code that both Johan and Hansen recognized. It was Johan that left the bedroom and quickly moved downstairs to let in their expected guests.

When Johan returned to the room, he was followed by two gentlemen. The stark contrast between them reminded Bill of the old-time comic strip 'Mutt and Jeff'.

One, apparently Jewish, was short, plump, dark-eyed, and wore black clothes, in harmony with the similar coloring of his full-face beard. The other was over 6 feet tall, thin-railed, blue-eyed, nattily outfitted in a grey suit that blended smartly with his greying hair, and carried what obviously was a black medical bag.

"Bill this is Dr. Alex Olsen and Mr. David Belin. Mr. Belin is a Jewish funeral director, who has willingly agreed to loan us his hearse, a coffin, and the traditional funeral garments worn by the Jew's at burial. We've got to make your dress look authentic . . . or else we'll probably fail if the Germans stop and interrogate us."

"And Dr Olsen . . . why is he here?" Bill asked somewhat apprehensively.

"To make you a believable corpse. Just before we put you in the coffin, Dr. Olsen will inject you with a tranquilizer. It will knock you out for a couple of hours, and make you appear as dead as a doornail until you wake up."

Bill's fright was apparent. So the doctor immediately spoke up to calm his fears.

"I can assure you Bill, you have nothing to be concerned about. It's an absolutely safe technique. I've used it many times before on hysterical patients . . . even on children that had to be sedated for their own good . . . for reasons that I won't dwell on now."

Still somewhat dubious and a bit reluctant . . . Bill hesitated . . . before acquiescing. Knowing that in his dire situation, he had no other choice but to leave his destiny in the hands of his trusted friends.

And so the mock funeral began. Hansen and Johan brought in the wooden coffin on its wheeled-carrier, and rolled it into the living room, while Belin carried in the paraphernalia required to appropriately dress Bill for a Jewish burial.

As Bill prepared to be redressed, Belin seemed to relish that he had this opportunity to explain some of the detail of the Jewish ritual to everyone in the room.

"All Jews . . . regardless of how rich or poor they maybe . . . are buried in the same type garment . . . because before God . . . everyone is equal," he began.

"As you see, these are homemade, white, and not ornate at

all. They are symbolic to us of dignity . . . purity . . . and simplicity. These seven shrouds, referred to as the 'tachrichim' must be put on in a very specific order.

"First, the head dress, called 'mitznephet' is placed on the head . . . like this Bill . . . and is drawn down to cover the neck. Next comes these trousers or 'michnasayim' . . . ."

However, before Bill donned them, he first took out the leather pouch . . . and made sure it was securely wrapped and bound around the calf of his right leg.

Then, the michnasayim was put on and tied at the belly as required.

Fascinated. Bill eagerly listened and cooperated as the 'k'tonet', a chemise long enough to cover his entire body, and the 'kittel', an upper garment with sleeves for the arms was also drawn down over his body, but left open at his neck . . . like a shirt. Then, Belin took the white 'avnet', used as a belt, and wrapped it three times around Bill's stomach and knotted it at the belly before saying,

"There. That does it. Now, as soon as I spread the 'sovev' or linen sheet in the casket, and place the 'tallit', a prayer shawl over the sovev, I'll be ready for you to lie down in the casket so that I can finish by wrapping the tallit and the sovev around your body."

Thoughts of being placed in the coffin made Bill very edgy. In fact, something had been bothering him about this ever since being told that he would be. No longer could he keep his concern suppressed.

"Can I ask one question? Is the casket going to be left open or will it be closed?"

"Closed! It must be closed," replied Belin.

"But won't I suffocate?"

Hansen answered by hastily jumping into the conversation to allay his friend's fear.

"No Bill . . . You're lucky. The Jewish custom is to bore a multiplicity of holes in the bottom of the wooden casket so as to

169

fulfill the guiding principle of Genesis, 'For dust thou art . . . and unto dust thou shall return'. But . . . just to be sure there won't be a problem . . . we drilled even more . . . so you'll have all the air you'll need to breathe normally.

"And don't worry about the holes getting plugged or clogged. We're going to keep the casket elevated at all times on that stand . . . whether you're in or out of the hearse. See! We've thought of everything."

"I sure hope so," Bill responded tensely.

"So do I,"Hansen replied matter-of factly, before adding, "Bill . . . if you're ready. We are. All the doctor has to do is give you the shot of sedative, Then we'll do the rest."

"To put it mildly Stig, I'm frightened to death. But I have faith in you . . . all of you. So let's get on with it."

Dr. Olsen quickly administered the drug. All Bill really felt was a slight prick of the sharp needle as it penetrated the flesh of his right arm, followed by a woozy sensation that swept over him, just before his eyelids fluttered and then shut.

Almost comatose . . . Bill now laid serenely in the casket. Hansen, on the other hand, was deeply perturbed as he grudgingly assisted Belin in closing it.

"Don't be alarmed," Dr. Olsen said. "Although Bill's been heavily sedated and appears dead in his unconscious state, he's still very much alive. He's breathing . . . almost imperceptibly . . . but quite adequately for him to survive."

Belin volunteered to accompany Stig and Johan to Elsinore, despite the fact this would put his own life in jeopardy. His insistence prevailed because his logic was indisputable.

"Everything hinges on my being with you. The Gestapo knows all too well that our custom requires a Jew to stay with the corpse until its burial. The body must never be left alone, but must be constantly watched by the so-called 'shomer'."

Now scanning both Cilborg and Hansen, while grinning profusely, he mused,

"The two of you certainly won't deceive the Germans if they stop and inspect the hearse. You're both Danes.And certainly look it.Whereas I . . . I fit the Jewish mold, and definitely will not have any trouble in looking like the real shomer."

So on that dry note of humor, the coffin was carefully loaded into the hearse and everyone nervously departed for Elsinore.

11C

All three comfortably rode in the front seat as they left Copenhagen. But Hansen drove. The choice, at the time, seemed appropriate, considering that his taxi-driver experience provided him with intimate knowledge of both the main and back roads leading out of Copenhagen and up the coast of the Sound. However, as it turned out, this proved to be a mistake . . .

For as soon as the outskirt of the city was reached, and the uncongested road loomed invitingly up ahead, Hansen instinctively pushed the vehicle's gas pedal to the floor. His speed of travel soon resembled that which was normal for him in his profession . . . Not fast enough for the customer running late for an appointment . . . but too fast . . . much too fast for a funeral hearse. This oversight precipitated their downfall.

Within minutes of its execution, sirens started blaring and horns began honking. Looking into the rear view mirror, Hansen's blue eyes bulged with fright as he suddenly comprehended the stupidity of his action. Two black sedans were now in hot pursuit and gaining on them. Hansen's first reaction was to accelerate, and try to escape from his pursuers.

"That would be asinine," he muttered in disgust, slamming on his brakes.

And he was so right. For the Gestapo cars had already pulled alongside, moved out in front, and then veered in to cut him off and block the road. In a mountainous cloud of swirling dust, all cars screeched to a halt. Miraculously, Hansen avoided ramming into the sedans. No small tribute to his learned skill ... mastered by his numerous near misses over many years with zealous Danish taxi drivers.

Even before the dust had settled, the front doors of both sedans swung open, and four Gestapo agents disembarked abruptly, two from each car. One of the four, apparently the officer in charge, with revolver in-hand, ran rapidly over to the hearse while the other three, menacingly holding sub-machine guns in a ready position, spread out slightly and stood about 20 feet away.

"Out! Everybody out and stand over there," the Gestapo officer ordered, waving his pistol ominously in the direction of his command.

Hansen, Cilborg, and Belin wasted no time in quickly complying to the officer's demand.

"Now then. Who are you? Where are you going? And why are you in such a hurry?"

Having asked these questions, the officer conveniently began to eliminate some alibi answers.

"Certainly not to the synagogue or, to the Jewish cemetery. We've been following you for several miles, and you passed both of them about a mile back without even pausing to stop."

Hansen calmly spoke up, trying to bluff their way out of this predicament.

"I'm Stig Hansen. That's my father-in-law Johan Cilborg ... and this is David Belin, the funeral director that owns the hearse."

While Hansen was talking, the Gestapo officer was not only listening ... but also was peering. Glaring first at the flyer held in his left hand containing both the descriptive material and a photograph of Bill. And then scrutinizing each of his hostages closely ... as if he was a medical student dissecting a cadaver. Observing that both Stig and Johan had blue eyes, not brown like Price's, he dismissed them

173

as being the wanted suspect. One more analyzing glance at Belin's short and robust figure, compared to the tall and well-built physique possessed by Price, the sought after murderer, was sufficient to convince him that none of these strangers remotely resembled the fugitive.

Satisfied with his observation, he now impatiently asked, while placing his gun back into his shoulder-strap holster,

"Why the speed?"

Hansen lied. He hoped convincingly.

"My dead Jewish friend is from Elsinore. He got into a brawl yesterday, and died before dark last evening from a concussion. We were rushing because he must be buried today in Elsinore before sundown. You must know . . . that's the sacred custom of the Jews . . . "

Annoyed by what Hansen just said, the officer belligerently interrupted and said,

"Yes . . . I know . . . I know full well all their damn traditions. And as far as I'm concerned, sundown is not soon enough. But first. Before I let you all go. Let's see if you're lying to me. Let's see if you're hiding anyone else in the back of the hearse besides the dead Jew."

With that he directed everyone, including the other three Gestapo agents to follow, which they all did. Then, he strategically positioned the agents in an arc before commanding Hansen to open the hearse's rear door. Everyone's tension was relieved when the only thing present inside was the unadorned wooden coffin. Still suspicious however, the officer demanded,

"Bring out the coffin! So I can take a good look at it."

Hansen and Cilborg both began sweating Not so much from the exertion of lifting the casket out and setting it down gingerly on its stand in the road, but from the imminent threat of exposure by this unrelenting Gestapo officer, who was slowly walking around the coffin and inspecting it carefully.

His next command wasn't at all what Hansen had expected. "Open it up!" he bellowed.

Hansen shuddered. But still had the courage to refute the order.

"We can't do that! Once a Jewish coffin has been closed, it is never opened. You know their custom."

"And I say 'to hell with Jews and their laws'.

"Now damn it. Open it up before I have my men riddle it open with their bullets."

And with that he motioned to his agents to aim their machine guns at the casket.

"But! . . . Hansen started to say.

"No ands . . . ifs . . . or buts. Now!", he screamed angrily. "I won't ask you again."

Hansen dreaded what he was doing. However, he knew the officer would delight in carrying out his threat to shoot-up the coffin. Bill would be killed, for sure. Obeying was his only choice.

With the top of the casket now opened, Bill was immediately exposed to detection, without any real opportunity . . . because of his immobility . . . to escape. How peaceful Bill looked. Unaware that at that very moment, the Gestapo officer was bending over and staring directly at him. How Christ-like he looked . . . all decked out in white linen, with a ten day stubble of whiskers covering his ashen cheeks and chin.

"Must have been quite a fight," remarked the officer. "Judging from these bruise marks, he took quite a beating. Got what every Jew justly deserves."

Suddenly, the officer pulled out his gun and pointed it at Bill's head. Hansen almost rushed to stop him from firing. But before he did, the Gestapo officer raised the pistol's barrel towards the sky . . . and fired five times into the air. The noise was frightening and deafening. However, Bill still did not stir a muscle,

"He's dead all right," he said gleefully. Before bending over

175

again, hacking a few times, and then spitting with tremendous volume and force directly into Bill's face.

Hansen had the urge to kill him for what he had just done to Bill. Somehow, he controlled his impulsive emotion by clenching his fists tightly. So tightly his blood circulation was cut off temporarily.

Now the officer stood erect, and turned deliberately so as to confront Belin. He cocked his eye-brow meanly, and gloated,

"A dead Jew is a good Jew!"

Then he shouted loudly to Hansen,

"Get all of this garbage out of here. That includes him too," as he pointed over to Belin.

Shortly after that order the Germans left. Scurrying away amid rising cyclonic dust clouds generated by their squealing tires.

Tears welled on Hansen's eyelids as he removed his handkerchief and slowly, but gently cleansed Bill's face. As he did, he whispered,

"I'll never forget him, Bill . . . for what he did to you. As soon as I get you to a safe haven, I'll be back for him. I'm going to strangle him with my bare hands. His going to die . . . choking on his own fuck'en saliva. I promise you. I'll get the swine . . . just like I got that bastard Bergmann."

They moved on. But a gloomy cloud of deathly silence hung over them. Hansen was embarrassed. For Bill. For Belin. For the whole human race that allows such bias and prejudice to exist between its fellow men. Danes appreciate the sanctity of life . . . as the Jews do. How then could the world be so polluted, Hansen wondered, by the blood-curdling rhetoric of one man?

A crazy, unbalanced man whose evil thoughts . . . evil actions . . . and evil deeds inspire such hatred for Jews throughout Germany and her occupied territories. His psychotic babbling about purifying the world by creating a super race of 'Ayrans', Hansen realized would only lead to chaos and untold suffering for all mankind. Not just the Jews.

Man against man. Brother against brother. And soul pitted against soul. Certainly not the beginning of a new world as Hitler wanted Hansen to believe. But surely the end of a world of compassion . . . understanding . . . and love of all humans.

Hansen was shuddering again. No longer out of fear for the safety of Bill's life . . . or his own. But out of the realization that millions of Jews would die before their wanton persecution ceased. And millions more before the world's society could be once again restored to peace-loving . . . freedom-loving people.

As they crawled forward towards Elsinore, unchallenged by the Germans, the wind started to kick up suddenly. Followed by a light drizzle . . . then heavier rain. Cilborg broke the silence with his comment,

"The Germans don't like to get their feet wet. So I think we'll all have safe passage to Elsinore now."

And they did.

Hansen was edgy and couldn't relax. And didn't . . . until Bill's body was lifted out of the casket, and set down gently on his cousin's bed. Only then did the stress that was twanging his taut nerves slowly dissipate, disappearing all together when Bill stirred a little and showed signs of soon waking up from his deep sleep.

Meanwhile, Belin, at Hansen's suggestion, departed immediately with the hearse and coffin for the local synagogue, where he had planned to seek shelter for the night, before making a solo return trip to Copenhagen in the morning.

"At least Belin will no longer be exposed to danger of being caught for assisting us with Bill's escape attempt," Hansen remarked to Johan.

Bill blinked his eyes open. Once . . . Then again. The third time with a long sigh of relief. He was happy to be safe. Happier yet to be alive! With no ill effects from the drug. No headache. No disorientation. No dulled senses or stupor feeling. Just a keen sensation of being unusually alert . . . well rested . . . and raring to go.

Naturally, his first question to Hansen concerned their journey from Copenhagen to Elsinore. Optimistically, Bill hoped to hear that all went well . . . without a hitch.

However, after being informed by Hansen about the harrowing exploit . . . everything except the part about the German officer having spat in his face . . . his cheerful attitude collapsed. A delayed reaction of intense shivers swept over him as he reflected on the dire consequences of what might have been.

Hansen's had his own reason for excluding the spitting episode. It was understandable . . . if not noble.

It was now a personal matter. Strictly between the Gestapo officer and himself. A grudge . . . a revenge that would only be satisfied after the officer had paid with his life for his filthy action and vile tongue.

"Soon. Very soon," Hansen muttered to himself, "He's going to wish that he hadn't humiliated Bill and my Jewish friend, Belin. My hands are itching for that moment . . . so I can even the score again."

Hansen's deep meditation was abruptly disrupted when Bill recovered from his chills and prophesied,

"I feel like a cat who has nine lives. So far I've only lost two. With seven to go I should make it . Shouldn't I Stig?"

"You damn well better. So that someday you can tell us what this was all about."

Everyone smiled. Even Peter, who was now noticed for the first time by Bill . . . Peter was tall and very muscular . . . with much broader shoulders than Hansen. But, looked much older . . . like all Danish fishermen who are aged with facial skin that appears tougher-than-rawhide Seasoned by the wind and salt. Calloused by endless hours of baking in the summer suns. And by years of exposure to the icy cold Arctic blasts of harsh winters that all Danish fishermen can somehow silently endure in their passionate quest to reap harvests of fish from the fertile seas.

Then Hansen, in a serious vain, added,

"Peter says, 'It's best that you and he leave for Sweden as soon as possible'. However, if we're going to pretend you're a fisherman on this trip to freedom, the least we can do is dress you like one."

So without further delay, Bill took off the Jewish burial shrouds, folded them neatly so that they could be returned to Belin, and redressed himself, putting on a pair of heavy long-john underwear, a heavy woolen shirt, socks, pants, a sweater, and a pair of sea boots. And finally, because of the prevailing inclement weather, he was oilskinned from head to toe, including a watertight wrapping for the leather packet, which was still tied securely to the calf of his right leg.

After being completely outfitted, Hansen stared at Bill for a split second. Then chuckled, while saying,

"Jesus, Bill. You sure could fool me. You look just like an old salt. All you need is a hand-carved pipe, a pole, and some bait and you'd be able to double for a Danish fisherman anytime."

On that confident note, Bill, Hansen, and Peter left the cottage and sloshed in the pouring rain about 200 yards to the wharf, where the boat was docked.

Peter's boat was Danish designed and Danish built. And, for him and his normal working crew of three, fit . . . like a glove . . . to the unique demands of fishing for a livelihood in the seas along Denmark's coasts.

She was 'clinker' constructed, with the side-planks overlapping and riveted together, analogous to the appearance of siding on a clapboarded house. Looking down, her horizontal cross section, at the deck line, projected as an oval, twice as long as it was wide. With large elliptical contours At first glance, Bill guessed that she was only about 32 feet long and about 13 feet wide. Too small he thought to challenge the whims of nature on the high seas, or even on the Sound on a stormy night.

This negative feeling about its size sprung up suddenly while Bill peered out towards the sea, in a darkness so black nothing could be seen beyond a hundred yards from shore. Certainly not Halsingborg . . . their destination . . . which on a clear day Hansen had said was so close it could be reached with outstretched arms. Something akin to thinking as a child the sparkling stars could be readily plucked from the sky at night.

Worried. To be honest real scared. Bill didn't particularly care to venture out into the rough Sound, in what he now perceived was just an overgrown rowboat. A fisherman's courage was something he definitely lacked and made no bones about it. But, then, he recalled that the Mayflower was only twice as long at the keel, and less than twice as wide at the beam as Peter's boat. And since that vessel successfully conquered the ravages of the Atlantic ocean back in the seventeenth century, he forced himself to take another hard look at Peter's boat. One, he hoped, that would be more optimistic than his first impression.

In spite of her modest size, Bill had to confess she appeared strong and robust. And the sound of her throbbing 8 HP motor, located below deck just aft of midship that Peter had just started by stepping inside the engine control deckhouse, was very reassuring . . . even if its power did make the boat quiver slightly. Although her long spruce mainmast was, for some reason, now down, and anchored to the top of the rear deckhouse, Bill felt secure just knowing an alternate source of propulsion was available in the advent of an emergency.

And, aft was the all important rudder, with its long tiller handle projecting at least 5 feet forward. Just far enough, Bill surmized, so that Peter, or whoever else was the helmsman, could be sheltered from the elements, while still controlling the rudder, by standing under the umbrella-like extension of the deckhouse roof.

Finally, looking forward, Bill sighted a small deckhouse with a sliding hatch that he later found out contained two bunk beds, a small table, a clothes locker, and a small coal-burning stove.

Apparently, she showed no outward signs of deterioration. On the contrary, she had been recently painted. Her topside white, the bulwark yellow, the deckhouse white with a green roof, and the bottom a deep fire-engine red. Even her deck and hatches were freshly varnished. All in all, she carried a new look about her, in spite of the fact she plowed the seas daily. A good omen Bill thought for his new beginning, once he got to Sweden.

But as Bill continued to watch the boat as it jumped up and down in resonance with the choppy sea, like a cork bobbing freely on the crests and troughs of agitated waves, he couldn't restrain from asking,

"Can Peter operate the boat all alone, Stig? I did some sailing in Long Island Sound when I was at college, but I always was more of a liability than an asset to the rest of the crew."

"When he goes out to the North sea . . . under sail . . . he has to have at least two fellow fishermen aboard to help. But tonight Peter plans to cross the Sound under diesel power. That's why the mast is down. You should be glad. When it is down, the pitching is at a minimum."

Just the thought of a rocking boat caused Bill to respond,

"Too bad Dr. Olsen isn't here. I'm sure he'd have a home-remedy concoction to keep me from getting seasick."

Bill's outward projection of a buoyant mood, impressed Hansen, even though he knew Bill was as apprehensive as he was over the adverse weather that now seemed to him to be developing into a full blown squall, prompting his concerned statement,

"The wind is really getting fierce, Peter. Don't you want to wait until it dies down before leaving?"

"Hell no, Stig. I've fished in the North Sea in much worse than this. Besides . . . the gale winds and rain might be a godsend. I've noticed that the German trawlers always stay nestled in the coves . . .

181

instead of patrolling the Sound . . . whenever the weather closes in, or the seas get too rough. It's much safer to leave now. After all it's only about three miles across. We'll be there in a less than an hour."

"So near. Yet . . . so very far," Bill said spontaneously as he turned to face Hansen. Then, meditating deeply, he began searching for appropriate words of farewell to Stig. Ones that would somehow convey his strong feelings and appreciation for what he had done for him.

But, it was Hansen that spoke first,

"Bill . . . Peter would give his life for me. And since you are my friend, he would do no less for you. Nothing would please him more than to assist you in your escape.

"This is one small way we have of getting back at the Germans for their invasion of our country.They may have conquered Denmark. But they haven't conquered us. Nor will they ever." Then, Hansen hopefully said, "God willing you will be on the free shores of Sweden before morning."

Bill now reached over gladly for Hansen's outstretched hand. And shook it warmly, saying,

"Stig. I can't begin to thank all those who have helped me. Especially you. You saved my life when Bergmann tried to kill me. And you risked your lives in bringing me to Elsinore. Thank God the Gestapo didn't discover I was alive in the coffin. Everyone would have been shot, just for trying to save me.

"I won't forget what all of you have done for me . . . a perfect stranger. If . . . if I do make it safely to the United States . . . I want you to know I'm coming back after this war is over to see you again. Friends like you are rare. Much rarer than precious metals . . . And infinitely more valuable."

With that they both dropped all their manly composure. And embraced . . . with arms wrapped around each other in a bear hug, trying but failing in a futile attempt to hold back their tears of regret over parting. As well as tears of longing since they might never see each other again. Impossible as it may seem, in less than a month's time, each had developed such a strong bond of companionship for the other, each felt welded as one. For now. For life. No matter how long . . . or how short that time span was actually going to be.

And then, as the boat slipped out of its mooring with Bill aboard, Peter grabbed hold of the tiller and began steering her slowly out towards Halsingborg. Observing Bill's anxiety as he watch the dock quickly disappear from view, he felt compelled to shout above the wind's roar,

"Nothing to worry about Bill. You'll soon see how seaworthy she is!"

CHAPTER 12

Bill tried to have a positive attitude . . . as he sat on the edge of a narrow bunk bed, below deck on Peter's boat. After all, he was on his way to Sweden and to freedom. Freedom from being captured by the Nazis. And, most certainly, freedom from being executed by them for his role in securing a copy of Germany's Master Plan. His thin optimism even had him taking the first flight tomorrow out of Sweden, to London, to Washington,D.C., to Boston and home. Home, at last, to Jonathon and Cathy.

These were all positive thoughts that really should have lifted his spirits and given him cause to rejoice. But, as Peter's trawler began rocking and swaying more violently, with each passing moment . . . in resonance with the mountainous swells building in a raging sea, his hopes waned dramatically.

As the cold, raging sea boiled ever more ferociously . . . driven mad by the shearing forces of winds now exceeding hurricane velocity . . . gigantic waves formed and began swamping the boat with ever increasing frequency, The sea heaved . . . and so did Bill, whose stomach never did get acclimated to the sea's random up, down, and sideways oscillations of the boat as it traversed obediently in the sea's huge valleys and troughs.

Peter had assured him that the boat was very seaworthy. Just as Blake Edwards assured him that he'd have no problem in securing a copy of the secret Plan. So it was no wonder that Bill began losing confidence in Peter's judgment when the boat's engine started to cough and wheeze as it labored to keep running. If it had just continued doing so, Bill might have adjusted to what he realized was a terrible situation.

But, when, suddenly, it died and wouldn't respond to several frantic efforts of Peter to restart it, Bill panicked! Hastily, he charged up the stairs leading to the deck.

As he anxiously pushed open the hatch door, Bill bellowed loudly so Peter could hear him above the roar of the breaking waves and thunderous booming of a lightning discharged atmosphere,

"Peter! What's wrong? Why can't you restart the engine?"

Immediately Bill guessed from Peter's ominous response that they were in serious trouble.

"I don't know! The damn fuel must be contaminated with seawater. From seepage into the tank. If it's polluted. We're done for! I'll never be able to get the engine to restart."

Now, with the loss of all mechanical propulsion power, the trawler stopped dead in the water and, its radical movements were completely dependent upon the whim and mercy of the sea's wild, agitated currents. She rolled. She lurched. She pitched. All of her motions . . . without the thrust provided by her now defunct engine, were unpredictable.

Peter struggled valiantly with the gyrating tiller in an effort to keep the bow heading directly into the breaking waves. As he tried to do so, without much success, the fright in his eyes betrayed his true feeling about their plight, when he shouted,

"Never! Never in all my years of sailing have I ever experienced anything like this, Bill. I know now we should have waited 'til the storm passed over before leaving port. But, I was thinking only of your safety . . . and getting you to Sweden before the Germans had a chance to pick you up.

"All I've succeeded in doing is putting you in greater jeopardy! Unless, this foul weather subsides . . . and quickly, at that . . .

we may capsize. I'd lash myself to the tiller if I thought it would help, because I'm losing control of her rudder."

"No wonder," replied Bill. "The waves are kicking us around as if we were the soccer ball on a playing field."

Hoping a question he was about to pose wasn't too stupid, he blushingly asked,

"Can't we hoist the sail?"

"God, I wish we could, Bill. But, in these fierce winds, the spar will snap, faster than you can take a breath. I'm afraid all we can depend on now is mother nature or, a miracle to save us and my vessel."

No sooner had Peter spoken those words, when an enormous tidal wave suddenly hit the boat broadside, The long tiller bar jerked out of Peter's hands spontaneously. Then, after first swinging out over the rough sea, it swung back again rapidly . . . smashing into Peter with such momentum that it knocked him overboard. The savage wave that washed across the entire deck of the teetering boat, not only drove Bill's body aft but, almost succeeded in washing him overboard also.

Now, as he laid prostrate on his belly, completely stunned by his impact collision into the rear railing, his startled eyes locked onto Peter's not six feet below and away from him, as he wallowed hopelessly in the great troughs of the turbulent sea. Bill immediately reacted instinctively,

"Grab my hands!" he yelled. "Reach up and latch onto my hands when the stern dips down beneath the water."

Incredibly, the combination of the boat's pitching motion, Peter's desperation reach, and Bill's outstretched arms, all culminated in grasping hands capturing clinging hands in a life or death grip.

"Hang on, Peter!" pleaded, Bill. "I've got you."

The rescue was agonizingly slow and tedious. But successful. Once Peter was pulled onto the deck, he immediately broke the high tension by joking,

"I was suppose to save you! Not the other way around. Stig will surely tease me about this ... the next time I see him in Copenhagen."

And, with Peter's rescue also came a reprieve from the storm, as the tornado-like winds now diminished rapidly. Calm seas returned and left in its wake a trawler that hadn't overturned. And two thankful and humble souls, Peter and Bill.

They were blessed and knew it. Both had been scared out of their wits ... and now readily admitted that emotional fear to each other.

But, there situation was still very critical as Peter's boat continued to drift at the mercy of an unfriendly tide. A tidal current that was now carrying them back towards Denmark, instead of towards Sweden.

"I feel as if we're on a yo-yo ride, Peter. Here we are less than a half of a mile from Halsingborg and, sliding much further away. Isn't there anything we can do about it?"

"Now's the time to put the sail up, Bill. Want to give me a hand?"

"Gladly," responded Bill, in an optimistic mood again.

"With my tacking expertise, we'll be there in less than an hour. I'll bet you can't wa ... "

Peter abruptly halted his conversation ... as soon as his supersensitive ears picked up the whining sounds of a very powerful engine approaching. Then, while pivoting his head in all directions to pinpoint its source, he urgently shouted to Bill,

"Quick! Get below deck and hide. If that noise is what I think it is, we're about to encounter a German Trawler."

Chalk-white with fear, Bill jumped up, dashed for the hatch, opened,then closed it behind him, and scurried down the rungs two at a time. And, just in the nick of time. For no sooner had he hurriedly disappeared from sight, when a powerful searchlight suddenly was turned on by the Germans. It turned night into day ... in a split second. And, almost blinded Peter while doing it.

Then, as the trawler pulled alongside, within ten feet of Peter's, its Captain screamed through a bullhorn,

"Jawohl! Quite a storm, Yes." Followed rapidly, before Peter could even reply, with his curious inquiry,

"How come you're adrift and not under power? Do you need help?"

"I was but my engine quit on me. The sea swamped my boat and contaminated the fuel. As soon as I get my sail raised, I'll be underway again . . . now that the storm has abated."

"Throw me a line and we'll tow you. Where are you heading for anyway?"

Peter was trapped. He didn't want to say Denmark because if they towed him there, Bill was as good as dead. So, he had to gamble everything on the improbable.

"Off the shore of Halsingborg. After a big storm, the fish always bite at a place I go to that's only about a 100 yards offshore."

While under his breath he whispered,

"If they tow me towards Sweden, Bill will have a chance. Maybe slim . . . but a chance to make it. But if they refuse, its going to be curtains for both of us . . . anyway."

The German Captain only hesitated for a brief moment before stating,

"If it's fishing off Halsingborg that you want . . . it's Halsingborg you'll get. Now throw me a line before I come aboard and get one."

From below deck, Bill was astonished at what he had just heard. And, once the tow line was secured, couldn't believe what he was seeing, as he cautiously peeked outside the porthole. Peter's boat was being towed. And towards Sweden as promised.

If, for any reason, the German Captain had decided to search Peter's vessel instead of assisting him, Bill would have been captured. And held for the firing squad. But, instead, they were now in tow, and rapidly approaching Halsingborg's shoreline.

Bill shook his head in utter amazement as he exclaimed,

189

"I could swim from here if I had to. Maybe, Blake was right after all. These Germans are making it easy. Almost too easy," sighed Bill.

As soon as both boats reached within a hundred yards of the spot designated by Peter off Halsingborg's coast, the German trawler stopped, quickly released the towline to Peter's boat, and then after waving a friendly good-by, just as quickly sped away, heading towards Copenhagen.

Bill, on the other hand, wasted no time in getting onto the free shore of Sweden. And, after his thankful good-byes to Peter, he went directly to the U. S. embassy in Stockholm . . . in order to obtain a new passport. As soon as this was accomplished, Bill set out for the airport and, upon his arrival there, promptly made all necessary reservations for his flights back to the States.

Two days later, he landed safely in Washington, D.C . . . and immediately handed the secret Master Plans to Blake. After which, in a relaxed mood for the first time in months, Bill rambled on for hours telling Blake about his many harrowing escapes from the Germans.

"Unbelievable," Blake commented . . . nodding his head from side to side . . . right after learning how the German Captain assisted them in getting to Sweden. Followed by his usual, astute observation,

"Sometimes, Bill, truth IS stranger than fiction!"

CHAPTER 13

Bill didn't call Cathy to tell her he was back in the States and would be home Friday evening. He wanted it to be a big surprise.

And now as he approached the front door of his home, he was full of anticipation and joy. Brushing back his wavy brown hair with the fingers of his right hand, he entered quickly without knocking, singing happily,

"Cathy . . . I'm home!"

A song he repeated . . . as he walked swiftly into the living room and found not only an amazed Cathy, but a bewildered young gentleman sitting on the couch . . . embracing her.

"Oh . . . I'm very sorry, Cathy," Bill, embarrassingly uttered. "For some reason, I just expected that you would be alone."

"Bill!" Cathy exclaimed in a startled, yet, exhilarating voice. Then . . . sensing Bill's disappointment in seeing her in this innocent but, compromising situation, she began blushing profusely while immediately starting to react defensively,

"Why didn't you write . . . or at least call? Do you know the number of sleepless nights I spent wondering if Jonathon still had a father? Wondering if you were dead or alive!. But not a word. Not a single word in all those agonizing months. Only the constant pain of worrying about you twenty four hours a day."

After pausing briefly to catch a breath, she turned her head toward her visitor and continued,

191

"If it wasn't for Tom, here, to comfort me, I would have gone out of my mind. I don't know what I would have done without him. But, I do know . . . he was always here when I needed him."

Bill felt like an absolute fool. Certainly a fool for not notifying Cathy immediately as he wanted to as soon as he was safe in Sweden. But, now a bigger fool for barging in on her privacy in what he perceived was going to be an intimate moment with Tom.

Obviously shocked by the biting impact of Cathy's emotional remarks,Bill was momentarily stunned into silence. Sheepishly, he apologized again. This time for being so insensitive to Cathy's needs and concerns with these words of atonement,

"Cathy, I will try to explain everything to you tomorrow. I hope, then, you'll understand the reasons for my unusual behavior."

From the compassionate way that Cathy now reached out to Bill with her misty green eyes, he knew that she really felt badly about hurting him with her outburst . . . even though she was the one that obviously had suffered the most during his absence.

Bill really didn't want to leave Cathy alone with Tom because he jealously detested the thought that she might end up in his arms again. However, his presence only seemed to be contributing more to the awkwardness of an already befuddled situation. Therefore, he had little or no choice but to excuse himself politely and to proceed slowly upstairs to look in at sleeping Jonathon, before retiring himself for the night.

Very early the next morning, as soon as Cathy came downstairs, Bill asked her to come into the living room so that they might discuss several things that were on his mind. She more than willingly accepted his invitation as she was anxious to ease any residual tensions from the night before.

Bill began tentatively because he was about to breech security regulations by revealing all that happen to him since last February. But, he just didn't care. He had to win back Cathy's trust in him . . . and more importantly, he had to win back Cathy.

Cathy was spellbound by what Bill had to tell her. And, the

more he described his hair-raising, life-threatening overseas experiences, the more she realized how lucky she was just to have Bill home safe and sound.

When he finished his narrative, she was now lost for words and only could say,

"It's a miracle, Bill! A miracle that you came back to us alive."

Then, she broke down in tears. Ashamed of all the doubts she ever had about this man that she loved so much.

Bill instantly moved over to comfort Cathy and, cupping her hands in his, decided not to wait a moment longer to ask her a question that he had to have answered.

"Cathy darling. Will you marry me? I know I should have proposed to you months ago . . . before I left for Europe. But I'm asking you now . . . before I lose you to Tom."

Overwhelmed by this wonderful but, sudden and unexpected request, Cathy remained speechless for what Bill thought was an eternity. And why not. Her delay appropriately reflected both her surprise . . . and shock.

The last thing in the world she had expected was a proposal from Bill. And, as a consequence, had buried her obsession for him months ago, when he failed to respond to her overture of affection.

To control her frustration . . . to retain her sanity . . . she begrudgingly had accepted the fact that Bill would never love her. That Bill would never release himself from Karen's shackles. Having succeeded in reconciling herself to that reality, as she perceived it to be, she was now totally bewildered by his sudden change of heart, and desire to marry her.

Unable to give him an unqualified 'yes', even though her heart urged her to do so, . . . but, unwilling to emphatically say 'no', thereby closing the door forever on her opportunity for the Cinderella-type happiness she fantasied would be hers with Bill . . . she had only one choice. That was to hedge her reply, so as not to seal her destiny prematurely.

193

"Bill. You're probably just over-reacting to Tom's presence in my life. If I wasn't seeing him, you wouldn't feel forced to ask me now . . . if ever. But . . . even if I'm wrong and you really do want me to marry you, I can't commit myself just yet. It's not that I don't care for you. God knows I do. I just can't decide so quickly until I sort it all out in my mind. I need more time."

Cathy noticed that Bill seemed be confused by her evasive reply. So she offered a further explanation in the hopes that he might appreciate her point of view.

"You always neglected me, Bill . . . by denying my amorous feelings for you for well over a year. Do you realize what that did to my self-respect? My self-esteem was shattered. I wanted to crawl into a hole and die.

"I was literally begging for some silent acknowledgement from you . . . some visible sign that you cared for me. Even just a tiny bit. When you didn't respond at all, I was crushed. And humiliated. If it wasn't for Tom, I'd probably still be grieved and depressed by your lack of sensitivity to my needs. Tom has asked nothing of me. But . . . has made me feel like a woman again by the way he treats me . . . by his outward admiration of me . . . by his expressed desire to . . ."

Bill interrupted before her last analogy was completed in order to plead his case.

"Oh, Cathy. It isn't that I didn't care. For over a year, I've loved you deeply. Even if Karen's memory prevented me from revealing my true feelings, I desperately wanted to make you mine. But it was too soon after Karen's death. Especially, since I felt totally responsible for causing it by not being with her in her hour of need.

"That guilt seems to be a life sentence of denial for me . . . one that has always stood between us in the past. But no longer. You are right for Jonathon . . . and for me."

"Are you sure it isn't just Jonathon that motivates your marriage proposal? Maybe you're just afraid of losing his nanny to Tom . . . rather than wanting to win a new bride for yourself. Are you just blinding the truth from yourself, Bill?"

Bill frowned for a split-second, as if he had to meditate on her astute statements before answering.

"No . . . I don't think so. No! I am sure. It's not Jonathon or Tom. My feeling now is solely for you. Selfishly for you. I love you!"

Cathy never thought she would ever hear those wonderful words from Bill. How she ever resisted the impulse to throw her arms around him and smother him with kisses and say 'yes' was something even she couldn't comprehend. But she did with her plea,

"Bill . . . Please give me more time. Tom also has asked me to marry him . . . just last night in fact. I can't believe it. Just imagine. Two proposals in less than twelve hours. And, for the first twenty-six years of my life . . . none. Is it any wonder my head is spinning like a top? Frankly . . . I'm perplexed. I really need more time to think it over."

Then, her Irish eyes danced as she mischievously said suddenly,

"Until then! Until I do decide. You can start courting me like a lover should. The change will do wonders for my ego. And who knows? It might just make the difference. And in a weak moment, I just might impetuously say 'yes'."

Bill was quick to seize this opening just provided by Cathy.

"Well! If it's courting that you want. At least let's begin right now."

And with that he reached out, took Cathy's hand, gently pulled her to him, and kissed her. Their first kiss. One that stirred anew her passionate feelings. One that almost succeeded in winning her total submission immediately. It took all her willpower . . . and then some . . . for her to break away from his embrace, and softly murmur,

"Now Bill. Be fair. A one hour whirlwind courtship is not exactly what I had in mind."

They smiled. Then, both chuckled loudly. Bill readily acquiesced to her wishes. He was more than willing now to wait just a little longer . . . because he knew when they kissed . . . from the lingering tell-tale protrusions in her blouse made by her emotionally aroused nipples . . . that it was only a matter of time before he would possess her.

"Poor Tom," he gloated. "He doesn't have a ghost of a chance. Cathy is going to be mine. I'd bet my life on that. She loves me. Even if she isn't ready to admit it, just yet. She's all mine."

And she was. For on Christmas day, when Bill proposed again, Cathy eagerly accepted. The date for the wedding was set for September 25, 1941.

"Enough time, Bill, for me to properly notify the clan. And also to dispel any rumors that we're rushing into marriage because . . . Well you know . . . because I must be in a family way."

Bill didn't elope this time. Instead, at Cathy's insistence, they had a traditional church wedding. And Tom was the best man. A magnanimous gesture on Bill's part, showing no resentment or residual jealousy towards Cathy's other suitor. Besides, Tom was a good loser. And Bill . . . a compassionate winner.

Bill's nervousness, as he waited in the alcove for the wedding ceremony to begin, was understandable. For he was a private person . . . not one who enjoyed being in the limelight in front of at least one hundred invited guests, almost all family relatives' of the bride.

But, when the organist started playing 'Hear Comes The Bride' and the wedding procession began, Bill's apprehensions quickly vanished. For as he slowly stepped out to take his position at the alter, his enamored brown eyes caught their first glimpse of Cathy, breath-takingly beautiful in her white satin and lace gown.

Cathy's jubilant green eyes, resonating in happiness, locked onto Bill's as she moved buoyantly down the aisle, silently passing 'I love you' messages that warmed his heart.

The 'I do' that Cathy and Bill exchanged were confidently expressed. And all reservations that either might have had in the past were forever smothered by the traditional kiss at the alter, after being pronounced 'husband and wife'. A very sensuous kiss that promised a future of intimate togetherness.

Cathy's radiant mood at the reception was contagious. Bill was extremely happy also. And so was Bill's mother and father, who now accepted Cathy as the ideal mate for their son, and the perfect step-mother for their grandson. No longer was there any rift between them and Cathy. In fact, they volunteered to baby-sit Jonathon while the newlyweds were honeymooning. Cathy graciously accepted, without having to bite down on her lip, in remembrance of past differences in days gone by.

Niagara Falls was where Cathy sentimentally wanted to go on their two week honeymoon trip. And since she wanted it. Bill wanted it also. So around 3 P.M., they drove rapidly off from the reception grounds, trailing the traditional 'Just Married' banner and strings of rattling noise-making cans, and headed west for a pre-arranged stop for the first evening in the quaint old town of Brattleboro, Vermont.

The sunset that they watched that twilight together, cuddled in each other's arms, highlighted nature's fall foliage in all its colorful glory. Both were enraptured by the awe-inspiring display and with each other. Both, mesmerized by the peaceful tranquility that is characteristically Vermont, were now in the mood to make love. And as Bill leaned down to kiss Cathy's sweet lips, he whispered softly,

"Oh, Karen. I love you so."

Suddenly . . . Cathy froze. Then, cringed . . . as her mouth dropped open with a gasp of pain.

"Karen? . . . Karen! Oh, Bill . . . how could you? How could you be so cruel . . . so insensitive? On this night of all nights!" she cried . . . running swiftly off in tears into the bedroom, slamming the door shut, and locking it.

As soon as the name, Karen, slipped off his tongue, Bill realized the mistake he regretfully made. But, the scenic view snapped his mind out of reality and back to '37, when Karen and he made their fall trip to Vermont to see the foliage. It was an innocent error. Even a forgivable oversight perhaps but, under different circumstances.

However ... as Bill soon discovered, the ominous consequences of this reversion in his thinking went far beyond just his wedding night. Naturally it started with Cathy refusing to sleep with him that evening. And no one could blame her for that ... And certainly Bill didn't.

Bill fitfully slept on the sofa, twisting, turning, and agonizing. If he could do one thing over, he never would have come back to Vermont. Cathy may have been in the next room, but Karen's presence was felt all around him again. Precious nostalgic moments of the past flashed temptingly before his weary eyes and threatened to mar, not only his happiness ... but most assuredly Cathy's.

Bill was torn between past and present. Yet, wanted desperately to rebuild his life, which explained his woeful cry,

"I need help. So I can separate the reality of today from my yesterdays. I can't let Karen choke-off my relationship with Cathy."

All the next day, as they drove towards Niagara Falls, the atmosphere surrounding Cathy and Bill was leadened with her bitterness and resentment. Cathy's normally bubbly mood was beaten into gloomy submission.

Bill tried to apologize several times, but Cathy turned deaf ear, as she mulled over yesterday's debacle. She wanted to find the compassion in her heart to forgive Bill again, but her Irish pride wouldn't let her. However, as the day wore on, her temper cooled down, and her mood switched to one of more understanding. She realized Bill's guilt-syndrome was a mental sickness that could only be cured with patience and love.

And Bill's love ... in spite of his relapses into past memories of Karen ... was something that she was sure of. Just as her love for him was uncompromising. In fact unequaled. And even stronger, she felt, than Karen's could ever have been for Bill.

If only Bill would give her a chance to prove it to him. But then, she would only have that chance if she stopped dwelling on last night's mistake and started her own offensive.

So, she decided to make light of what had happened with a smile that brightened her dimpled face, forcing her green eyes to sparkle again as she said,

"That was quite a performance I put on last night, wasn't it? Maybe I should think about becoming an actress."

Her humorous remark immediately eased all tensions, and both Bill and Cathy responded by bursting out in laughter.

"Wait until I tell our children what happened on our wedding night. They're not going to believe me. In fact, I don't believe it myself."

From that moment, the newlyweds drove on . . . cuddly close, with Cathy's head resting comfortably on Bill's shoulder. And from time to time, as Cathy raised her chin, Bill bent over an kissed her. Once again the newlyweds were happy. Exhausted from the long drive . . . but happy.

Cathy had promised herself . . . as she undressed and slipped into her sheer pink . . . see-through nightgown that she was going to be uninhibited in her love making with Bill. And she was. However, to no Avail. For while Bill could kiss her passionately, touch her softly, and hold her tenderly, he just couldn't get physically aroused.

Cathy was frustrated as never before, and felt like screaming. Instead, she bit down on her lip and jokingly said,

"You picked a fine time, Bill to tell me you're libido."

Bill couldn't laugh. He couldn't even manage a smile. He was too embarrassed. Mortified. Disgusted by the fact that he couldn't perform . . . that he was sexually inadequate . . . in spite of his strong desire to please Cathy.

As he stammered to make an excuse, Cathy sensed his personal humiliation and tried to shrug it off by saying,

"And our children will howl even louder when we tell them what happened on our second night."

199

For two weeks of their honeymoon, Bill and Cathy embraced, smooched and petted. But . . . because of Bill's mental block, they couldn't have physical intercourse. No matter how hard Bill tried.

Realizing Bill's dilemma, Cathy finally urged,

"I love you, Bill. But . . . you must know how frustrated I am. I need you. You've got to bury Karen once and for all. Please get help. Please help me. I feel more inadequate now than you. I'm devastated that I can't excite you. Please see a doctor."

The very day that they returned from their trip, Bill made an appointment and saw Dr. Goldman immediately. Sympathetically, the psychiatrist listened to Bill as he related his problem and its association with the past. Competently, the doctor advised Bill that his ability and willingness to recognize that the problem existed and knew its cause would ultimately lead to its solution.

"Suddenly . . . one day. You'll totally emerse yourself in the living of the present . . . instead of clinging to the past as you do. And when that day comes, as it will soon, seize the moment! Let yourself go. Emotionally! Physically! And from that moment on you'll be a new man . . . a virile man. Like you were before . . . if not more so, as you try to make up for lost time."

When Bill told Cathy what the doctor advised, she joyfully said,

"I'll wait for that moment. Even if it takes a lifetime, Bill."

October rolled by, then November . . . without any real change in the marital relationship that Cathy had to endure. She tried to adjust to the situation . . . and most of the time, she did. But, as time dragged on, she became more irritable . . . more tense, especially during and after their abortive attempts at intercourse.

She tried to control her frayed emotions . . . She tried, unsuccessfully, to convince herself that the sexual act was not all that important in a marriage. That the important thing was that two people be united with the love they had for each other. But she wasn't sure that she could wait a lifetime. Her craving . . . her denied satisfaction was gnawing away at the fiber of their marital bond. Her prayers . . . her deep religious belief that God would listen and act . . . were her only salvation.

And, while occasionally, she thought of calling Tom, Cathy never did. Her pride wouldn't let her. But more than that . . . she feared that her need might cause her, in a moment of indiscretion, to commit an adulterous act.

"I've got to be patient," she lamented, sobbing herself to sleep every night.

December started off like all her other married days . . . except on December 6th, Bill received an urgent call from Blake Edwards, asking if he could come over immediately to see him.

When he arrived, Blake was in a somber mood. And once again, as they moved into the library room, Blake closed and locked the door behind them.

This time Bill jested,

"Seems like you have a bad habit. Every time you come here, you go around locking doors. What's up this time? Although, I'm probably going to be sorry for asking."

"The Country is in trouble, Bill. Our worse fears are about to materialize. Intelligence reports indicate that the Japanese are going to attack Pearl Harbor tomorrow."

"Tomorrow!" Bill shouted in disbelieve. "My God! Can't you stop them before they do?"

"I'm sorry to say the President can't. We've broken their code. They'd know how we found out."

"So What! Think of the innocent lives that will be lost if the President doesn't act."

"Think of how foolish we'd look . . . if the report we've intercepted was just a hoax. The world would laugh at us. All that would accomplish would be a change in their code . . . to our disadvantage."

"I swear I don't understand politics," Bill said shaking his head from side to side.

"There is a great deal of that in our decision to ride out the attack . . . if it comes. The President feels the isolation mode of our Country can only be changed by a 'shock' treatment. Then, every full blooded American will quickly rally around the flag . . . and willingly accept his declaration of War."

"You mean we're not going to warn our troops or the populous stationed there . . . or the Captains of our naval vessels."

"No one is going to be alerted . . . even to the remote possibility that an attack may occur. Our ships are not going to be dispersed? Just be blasted out of the sea without any warning."

"That's the plan, Bill. A calculated risk that their forces won't inflict any serious damage. Yet, will provide us with a bonafide reason to get into this war . . . aiding the British of course."

"I just don't believe it. It sounds insane to me." Then Bill paused for a moment . . . finally, his face lit up as if he understood,

"Oh, I get it. You developed that atomic bomb . . . and plan to stop the War as soon as it starts."

"I wish it was as simple as that Bill. All I can say is that we're still actively working on it. You wouldn't believe the money and resources we've already poured into its research. The Master Plan you got for us has been invaluable in getting us started in the right direction. But, we're not there yet. And probably won't be for two years or, maybe more.

"Meanwhile, we have a couple of crises to tend to right in our own backyard. One is along our eastern seaboard. The German U-boats are having a field day sinking a high percentage of the merchant ships carrying cargo overseas from ports all along the eastern seaboard, from Maine to far below Cuba."

"What!" Bill said again, in surprise. "I haven't read anything about that, or even heard rumors that it was going on. We're not at war with Germany."

"Technically . . . you're right. But they sure are at war with our merchant marine operation. We've covered it up. We've kept the lid on it. But it's a kettle that's boiling and ready to blow its top.

However, there is no sense in arousing the ire of Americans by informing them of our inadequacy. Particularly, when we don't even have the wherewithal to correct it."

Bill's incredulous look, prompted Blake to quickly explain,

"The depression Bill . . . that's the main reason we haven't spent the money to upgrade and expand our fleet.

That and the Congress . . . unwilling to appropriate money for wartime material when we are at peace. It's those damn isolationist. That's the nub of the problem in a nutshell. But getting back to that mess in the Atlantic. We've got to get a handle on it . . . before Britain loses the war because of us."

"And how do you do that?"

"By seeing, first hand, what we are doing wrong out there. That would help us solve the problem.

"We're beginning to suspect the Commodores . . . the civilian commanders, who are in overall charge of the convoys. Some of them may have strong Nazi feelings . . . and are deliberately leading our merchant ships to their doom at the mercy of the wolf packs of German submarines. And . . . "

"And?"

"And that's where you come into the picture, Bill. We get you aboard with the Commodores on several of these trips to find out where their loyalty really lies."

"I get seasick!"

"Who doesn't. But I'm told after a few outings that's no longer a problem. You'll be an old salt with the best of them. Just like Denmark. Remember?"

"How the hell could I forget that. God! Why did you have to stir up those coals?"

"Sorry, Bill. I didn't mean to upset you. I know what a rough time you had over there. But you did the job for us. That's why we're back. The Country needs your help again."

"Do I have a choice?"

"No you don't. In fact you'll be pressed into service as a

Naval Lieutenant, on Special Assignment, as soon as war is declared on Monday. Your orders are already being cut."

"Where are you sending me to this time? New York City? The Port of Boston?"

"No such luck, Bill. Not this time! You'll report to the Gulfstream Frontier Station. That's headquartered in Key West, Florida."

"Why is it Blake that whenever you contact me, my family life is immediately thrown into turmoil?"

"Look at it this way Bill. Absence makes the heart grow fonder. Maybe this assignment will help."

Bill was flabbergasted by Blake's remark, and mulled it over further in his mind,

"What did he mean by that? Don't tell me they know about my problem with Cathy."

Then, he remembered . . . THEY find out everything. "Obviously, Dr. Goldman has been contacted. Confidentiality . . . between doctor and patient . . . doesn't mean a thing if the Government is making the inquiry"

"Any more questions, Bill?"

"Yea! What happens if Japan doesn't attack? Do I still have to go?"

"All I can say is . . . 'They will' and . . . "You will."

When Blake left, Bill immediately confided to Cathy that he would be leaving shortly to carry out an important assignment again for the Government. Naturally, Cathy was upset.

"I don't understand Bill. Why?"

"You will tomorrow. I can't tell you anymore because Blake swore me to secrecy."

The news of the Japanese sneak attack on Pearl Harbor shook both Cathy and Bill to the core. Both clung to each other in fear of what was to come. Cathy couldn't contain her tears because she knew that Bill was once more going to risk his life for his Country.

"Oh Bill!" she sobbed. "Please take care of yourself and come back to me alive. My life won't mean a thing without you. Just like our problem now seems so trivial compared to what lies before you. Promise me you'll be careful."

"Don't worry Cathy. I'll be safe. I'm going to be stationed in Florida. I'm sure I'll be able to get back to Boston quite frequently to see you and Jonathon. This is going to be tough on you Cathy. Are you sorry now that you married me, instead of Tom?"

"Bill . . . don't talk that way. I love you. Oh God! I love you!"

With that they held onto each other for an eternity. Both dreaded tomorrow's coming. Both already hated a war that was forcing them to be separated from each other. But sacrifice and suffering seem to be the fundamental building blocks of all good marriages.

CHAPTER 14

"Bill, I have my own suspicion as to why you've been assigned to sail with me. However, I don't really expect you to admit it if I'm correct. You've probably been sworn to secrecy, anyway."

After concluding his uncanny, provocative statement, the Commodore peered over to see if Bill's reflex reactions would give him away. A smile. A frown. Maybe, even a cocked eyebrow was all he needed as a sign to know he was on the right track.

But, Bill was like ice. Cool. Cold. Solid. Not showing any visible changes in any of his facial expressions. So the Commodore just continued,

"Topside thinks it's all my fault that my convoys have had such bad luck . . . And that I've lost so much tonnage to the U-boats. Probably are convinced I must be collaborating with the Germans. With Hitler's Nazis! Just because my parents emigrated from there, at the turn of the century, doesn't mean I'm one of them. If they really believe that, they have their heads buried in the sand . . . I'm no Nazi sympathizer! Telling the German agents when, and where my convoys are heading."

Then after pausing, in deep meditation, and, almost feeling sorry for himself, he proudly stated,

"I'm an American! As loyal as you are.I served in World War I and, just retired as a Navy Captain, about four years ago. Tell them . . . for me . . . to remember this! They called me back to be a Commodore. They needed me ... I no longer needed them."

Bill didn't say anything but, he sure was listening attentively.

"Bill. Believe me. It's not the loyalty of our Commodores that we have to worry about. I'll wager my life that well over 99.99% of them would never betray the United States.

"No! It's not us. Never was. However, It is the damn incompetency of our own Government's intelligence and defensive organizations."

Now, staring directly into Bill's informed eyes, the Commodore ordered,

"When you report back to them, tell them we need more protection out here! We're like sitting ducks in a caged pond. Our convoys have 40 or 50 vessels plodding forward at only 8 to 10 knots. And, what do we have for protection.? One ... maybe two destroyers and, if we're real lucky . . . maybe a couple of wornout PT boats.

"Hell, by the time they all make one loop around our convoys, searching for U-boats, we've lost 10 to 20% of our convoy numbers to the wolf packs."

Then, clearing his throat, and waiting for a brief moment, he added,

"I'd rather sail alone . . . and take my own chances than be bottled up inside a damn convoy that doesn't even have adequate antisubmarine capabilities to protect my flanks and rear."

Bill almost gave himself away, when he started to nod his head in the affirmative. Fortunately, he controlled this reaction immediately . . . without its observation.

Then, the Commodore continued with an ominous prediction,

"But, you'll see what I mean, first hand, on this trip. Its not going to be any different than the last one . . . or, the one before that . . . or, even the one before that. I've lost over 50 vessels in my convoys in nine months. I hope, we can come through this one without adding too many more to the total. But, I doubt it!"

Again peering at Bill, and almost through him, the Commodore offered his final words of wisdom ,

"Just tell them I said they should put as much tonnage into new antisubmarine destroyers as we've lost in one year to the wolf packs. Then, this convoy concept might have a chance of succeeding. A small one. But, a lot better than they have now."

Throwing up his hands . . . as if both disgusted and frustrated, he concluded in a more conciliatory tone,

"But, in the meantime, don't blame me! Don't blame the rest of the Commodores. Just blame the guys upstairs. Now, Bill, Let's move out with this convoy and meet our predators head on!"

Bill felt sick. Nauseous, not due to the undulating motions of the ship as she sailed to sea. But, due to the ominous prediction of the Commodore.

"Jesus!", Bill blasphemed, "What did Blake get me into this time!"

The first several hours of their outward passage were uneventful, as all ships tracked slowly forward at a speed of ten knots, under a rising full moon.

Bill learned by peering through his binoculars from the deck of the Commodore's vessel that a convoy is truly a majestic sight to behold . . . as the array of freighters and tankers steamed ahead in column after column, from horizon to horizon, as if marching in a Veteran's Day parade. Bill, also, learned that a Commodore's job is anything but easy, as he listened to him bellowing out commands angrily to his delinquent convoy captains.

"Number seventeen. You're still off station. Get back . . . damn it. And fall in line! Number fourteen. Are you sailing on your own? Or, are you on my team? Keep on your station. Remember on this trip, I'm the Commodore. Not you!"

From his cursory observations, Bill neither coveted or envied the Commodore and his awesome responsibilities.

"Its like trying to exert parental control over a bunch of spoiled brats. All wanting to be king of the mountain."

209

As dusk faded into darkness, those on watch kept searching the vast ocean of the Atlantic that surrounded them, just 20 miles from Cuba, for the tell-tale periscopes of the U-boats. Hoping to find none. Dreading to see one. But, because of the relatively calm sea and because the moon was full, an attack could be expected at any moment. For the weather conditions were just too perfect for any wolf pack commander too ignore, if they were out there laying in wait to ambush the convoy. They couldn't want for a moment more ideal than this.

And, they didn't. For suddenly, all hell broke loose. And, the resulting barrage of fireworks soon resembled that of a Fourth of July celebration. But, instead of rockets soaring through the air, torpedoes were streaking though the cold ocean waters. And, instead of rockets bursting in air. Torpedo after torpedo exploded into the keels of their prey. Lighting up the sky with a spectacular display of shimmering red hues emanating from the flames of the burning ships.

The wolf pack was exacting its terrible toll as the multitude of fired torpedoes blasted successfully into several of the merchant ships and oiltankers on the outer flanks of the convoy. In fact,, so many ships were taking hits, the status quo of the situation became extremely critical. Reluctantly, but correctly, the Commodore ordered all ships to scatter and clear the area at top speed.

Too late, however, to save the easy targets of the U-boat attack that already had suffered gaping holes in their hulls, or were split apart by the destructive power of the torpedoes.

Too late, also, for the hundreds of seamen blown asunder and now were fighting for survival in a hostile ocean, whose surface, coated with oil slicks oozing from the holes of damaged tankers, quickly ignited into galloping infernos, and spread radially, like wildfire, in all directions.

Too late for Bill, who was also blasted into the cold sea by the force of a direct hit on the Commodores vessel. A violent explosion that ripped his ship apart . . . as easily as one tears paper . . . and sprayed pieces of metal shrapnel everywhere.

Unfortunately, some of those fragments penetrated into Bill's torso, before his flying body broke the surface of the flaming water.

Bill certainly wasn't alone in this dire predicament. Scores of his fellow seamen were also fighting for survival, as he was. Trying to escape, as he was, the viscous layers of burning fuel, which threatened to engulf everyone.

Too many . . . especially those who never learned how to swim or, became too exhausted from trying to swim to safety, simply gave up. They all could be seen raising their arms vertically . . . as if praying to the stars for their salvation, and now crying out in anguish, one last time, before disappearing forever . . . when swallowed up by the hungry sea . . .

By some miracle, Bill was still afloat, but just barely. For his shrapnel wounds made it impossible for him to swim effectively. Or, for that matter to swim at all. And, as if that situation wasn't serious enough, the red tinge of the surface water that immediately surrounded him, as revealed by the bright lights from the oil fires and full moon, convinced Bill that he must be bleeding profusely.

"Only the cold water," he reasoned "Can save me now . . . if it helps to coagulate my blood."

The searing pain now being experienced by Bill on his upper torso could mean only one thing. His skin had been badly scorched by the burning oil. A firewall that still threatened to cremate him, unless he was able to maneuver out of its path.

So tolerating the excruciating pain being experienced as a consequence of his present, necessary physical movements, Bill began thrashing his arms and legs in an awkward gyrating motion that somehow did succeed in propelling him out of harm's way. And, free him from the burning holocaust that had already entrapped so many of his fellow comrades in distress.

Gritting his teeth as a means of coping with his unbearable suffering, Bill turned his thoughts to Jonathon. This provided him with the will, determination, and inspiration to stay alive. To survive . . . even though the cause appeared hopeless.

All of a sudden, Bill was faced with a more immediate danger.

One of the freighters fleeing the scene of carnage was steaming directly towards him. Realizing that he could easily be sucked under the sea by the churning action of its wash or, worse yet, shredded to pieces by its propellers, Bill quivered with fear and trepidation. Only a last second, planned, evasive change of course by the ship's captain, saved his life.

Now, as Bill gratefully looked up at the freighter as it was passing, about 75 yards to his starboard, he determine that it was named 'Hulsey'.

Then, as his eyes scanned along its deck from bow to stern, he detected a lone seaman leaning over the side rail, peering directly at him, before he stepped away and disappeared. But, within seconds reappeared. And, with one tremendous hurling effort, heaved a large, white, circular object overboard towards Bill. Even in his semi-conscious state, Bill immediately recognized it to be a lifepreserver, as it arched upward into the smoked-filled air and,then downward, landing in the ocean about fifty yards from him.

Joy! Then, panic gripped Bill. Joy . . . because with it . . . he had a chance to survive. Panic . . . because he was too incompaci-tated to swim over to it.

"It might as well be a mile away." Bill said disgustedly. "There is no way that I can ever retrieve it, even at this short distance."

Fate, however, was on his side. For as he struggled to reach it, the tidal stream created by the wash of the passing Hulsey pushed it to within ten feet of him.

Grasping for it with outstretched arms, Bill failed to grab it. Failed by only inches! Lunging for it, in spite of the torturing pain that grated every nerve fiber of his body, rewarded him with its successful capture. Bill hugged the lifepreserver tenaciously, as if it was Jonathon he was clinging onto.

Then, breaking down and weeping with delight, Bill lifted it over his head, and put it under his arms. Finally, his exhausted body was buoyed . . . No longer did he have to worry about sinking. Nor drowning. For the moment . . . at least . . . Bill felt safe.

Soon after accomplishing this remarkable feat, Bill became awful dizzy, drooped his head forward, and lost consciousness.

1 4 B

Bill didn't know how long he drifted aimlessly in the calm sea. Whether it was minutes or hours was irrelevant, Bill had passed out. Maybe, from exhaustion. Probably, from shock. Surely, from loss of blood. And, most likely, from all three. So he didn't witness, the Coast Guard Cutter, Dione, drawing alongside after spotting him bobbing up and down in the water. Apparently, those aboard her detected some sign of life emanating from the floating body. Because within minutes, after discovering him, they succeeded in rescuing him . . . as they had so many other seamen on this tragic night.

Then, at full speed ahead, they rushed their victims towards Cuba. Within hours, the Dione docked safely at Guantanamo. All survivors were put immediately into waiting ambulances and, transported to the Guantanamo Naval Hospital.

Bill's stretcher was wheeled into the Emergency room, hastily rolled onto an elevator, and, then, taken directly to the operating room on the fourth floor. Within minutes, of his arrival, anesthesia was applied and the surgeons commenced the long operation to remove the shrapnel pieces lodged in Bill's chest and thighs.

One might have thought he had been peppered with machine gun bullets, except the individual fragments were larger and more jaggered. Fortunately, no vital organs had been pierced, even though the fragments had come very close to severing several major arteries.

After finishing the suturing of all wounds, the doctors completed the operation by tending to the severe burns on Bill's body, caused as a result of his brief immersion into a sea of burning oil.

As soon as Bill regained consciousness in the recovery room, he was transferred to a private room on the second floor of the hospital. As he laid in bed, he shook his head in disbelief, wondering,

"How did I ever survive?"

Bill's doctor filled him in on the missing details of his rescue at sea and, also, told him how lucky he was not to have bleed to death. Then, Bill was informed that the operation was a complete success, and that he would probably be released from the hospital in a week. Two at the most.

"Great! shouted Bill excitedly. "That means I'll be back with my family real soon."

Home to Cathy. Home to Jonathon. Bill couldn't be happier. Tomorrow, he promised himself, he would call them, just to hear their voices, just to let them know he loved them, and just to let them know he was coming home.

But, often the expected turns out to be the unexpected. And, as Bill's temperature skyrocketed during the night, the intern on duty became extremely apprehensive. This type of post operative symptom is ominous. For it usually signals the onset of a serious infection. When Bill's temperature reached 105 degrees, he became incoherent and delirious. The intern, under direct orders from the Chief of Staff, immediately moved Bill to the intensive care unit, under 24 hour nurses' care and surveillance.

One of these nurses, a volunteer on the first shift assigned to Bill, was Sue Walker. A new Sue Walker that no longer was emaciated. No longer depressed. But now radiating her natural beauty and, an aura of complete confidence in herself as she deftly performed her duties for the sick and needy.

And, Bill was very needy for his condition rapidly deteriorated. His delirium worsened and, he began to experience prolonged

215

periods of unconsciousness. In fact, Bill was almost comatose! Burning up once again but, this time, with the ravages of an uncontrolled fever.

Sue did everything she could to comfort Bill in his distress. And, hour after hour, as sweat poured profusely out of the pores of his body, she would bathe him with alcohol in an effort to lower his temperature.

And, hour after hour, she would also gently rub his brow . . . as she had done many times for her son, Steve, whenever he was sick with a high fever. From Bill's stirring, Sue got the impression that this pleased him.

The preliminary diagnosis, suspected, and ultimately confirmed was a staphylococcal infection. A deadly infection. An infection caused by a bacteria that, all too often, invades the sanctuary of the hospital operating rooms, and causes havoc until brought under control.

This was a new outbreak for the Naval Hospital. No patient had experienced this type of infection in over a year. But now, many others, besides Bill, would surely come down with it.

Most will die. The combat is between the bacteria and the immune system. And, right now Bill's immune system was losing the battle.

For days, the only treatment given Bill for his sickness was the traditional one. One that relied only on appropriate drainage of pus, and on proper sterilization of the affected area.But, with this conventional treatment, Bill's condition showed no signs of improvement. Still incoherent. Still burning up. Still trying to fight off the debilitating effects of a bacterial infection that seemed to be gaining the upper hand.

All appeared lost because there were no other alternatives.

But on the tenth day, Bill was finally given something else for his infection . . . A new medicine. One that arrived only moments before . . . after being flown directly to the hospital from Washing-

216

ton, D.C. One researched and developed recently at Oxford University, in England, and first demonstrated on an experimental basis, only six months ago, to have curative properties on human patients suffering from staphlococcal infections.

This miracle drug was called Penicillin. Never before used on the American Continent because Penicillin was a new discovery . . . still highly experimental in very limited usage . . . And because pharmaceutical manufacture of it in England had not yet been undertaken on any meaningful scale.

It was much much rarer than diamonds. And, it was more precious . . . because it provided hope. At a moment when all hope had dissipated.

No one asked why Bill was selected to be the first American to receive it. Nor who supplied it to the hospital for him. The doctors were just thankful to have it. Grateful to have any medicine that might possible be effective as a cure for a 'staph' infection.

The Chief of Staff, however, was curious and astutely commented,

"He must be important, with friends of influence and power. Only someone high up in an important organization would be able to beg, borrow, or steal this rare Penicillin for him."

Bill certainly did have one such friend, Blake Edwards. Blake pulled every string at his disposal to have the Penicillin vial flown from London, England to his office in Washington, D.C . . . And from there, rerouted, with all urgency to Guantanomo.

Blakes' ulterior motives were twofold. Humanitarian. And, selfishness. The first is obvious. The second involves an extremely important mission that both Bill and he would soon be undertaking. Provided, of course, Bill recovered. And, Blake left no stone unturned to assure that that objective was achieved.

So on the morning of Bill's tenth day in the hospital, Sue careful measured out the prescribed dosage of Penicillin, gently lifted Bill's head up, and then fed the first spoonful of it to him.

She knew from the doctor's comments that this was his last hope. And, she didn't want Bill to die. She never wanted any patient to die. But, she, especially, didn't want Bill to die.

Twice more that day, Sue gave Bill his Penicillin. But, since she detected no change in his physical condition, her hope waned. So, as she was getting ready to leave for the day, she uttered, yet, another prayer,

"PLEASE GOD! Make this medicine work. He's too young to die."

The next day, a personal emergency came up involving Sue's adopted son, Steve. And, as a consequence, of her taking the day off, she was unable to be with Bill. When she did return to work on the following day, she ever so quietly opened his door to enter. Only to be greeted by a strong, coherent voice. One she hadn't heard before. And, one she was amazed to hear now.

"I missed you yesterday."

"Bill!" Sue exclaimed in a tone of sheer surprise and delight. "You're finally out of your coma. That's so wonderful!"

Bill's reply was just a simple repetition of his previous statement.

"I missed you yesterday."

"Oh, I'm sorry. Bill, my son, Steve, was sick with an upset stomach, and I had to take care of him. I wanted so to come in. But couldn't leave him. He's only three and a half years old. I hope you understand. You were still delirious the day before when I left you, I didn't think you'd even know I wasn't here, yesterday. What ever gave me away?"

"Your hands."

"What!"

"Your special touch. Even though I was out of it most of the time, I knew when you were by my side . . . tending to me. The other nurses, including your replacement yesterday, just don't have that same gentleness that your hands have. When my fever broke last night and I blinked opened my eyes with a clear head, all I could think about was you. Wondering who you were and what you looked like. By the way . . . what is your name?"

"Sue. Sue Walker. My husband and I have been living in Cuba for almost three years. I've been a volunteer nurse at the hospital since before the war began."

"Oh, then your husband is also a navy man . . . assigned to Guantanano."

"You're half right. He's a merchant seaman and just shipped out on the tanker, Hulsey, two weeks ago,"

"That's a strange coincidence!"

"What do you mean?"

"Well, his ship was in our convoy. In fact, I owe my life to some seaman aboard her."

"Why?"

"Well . . . after we were torpedoed, I was thrown overboard by the force of the blast into a sea ablaze with burning oil.

"Then, just as I lost all hope of surviving, the Hulsey passed by. Someone on board her saw me floundering in the sea and threw a lifepreserver in my direction. Fortunately, the tide brought it close enough for me to grab hold of it. Someday, I'd like to meet the man that threw it, and thank him for saving my life."

Bill didn't know that it was Joe, his wife's murderer, he'd have to thank for rescuing him. What irony! A man who took the love of his life . . . now saved his life. The despot that killed Karen, suddenly, is a saint in Bill's eyes for his heroic deed. Only, Bill didn't know . . . and never would know the whole truth.

"You must worry all the time about your husband crossing the Atlantic with all those damn U-boats out there, creating havoc with the convoys."

"I do, Bill. But, Joe was a broken man before he got this job. It is something he has to do, in spite of the risks, to restore his self-worth . . . even if he dies doing it."

"War is hell. Isn't it? . . . I can't think of anything worse."

Sue meditated for a brief moment before answering, but, then, sadly said,

"I can . . . Mental torture."

Bill seemed perplexed by her remark, but didn't dwell on it since Sue had immediately changed the subject.

"Obviously, from the ring on the finger of your left hand, you must be married."

"I am. And I can't wait until I get back to Boston to my Cathy."

"Cathy? I would have sworn her name was going to be Karen . . . not Cathy. When you were delirious you kept calling out for Karen."

Bill blushed . . . frowned . . . then looked away while replying softly,

"Karen . . . Karen was my first wife. She died in childbirth three and a half years ago, delivering my son, Jonathon. Cathy and I are newly weds. I married her just last September."

Sue notice the sadness coming over Bill, so she quickly said,

"Enough talking for now. Let me just change your bandage and give you your medicine. This Penicillin was a life-saver for you. Before you started taking it, the doctors thought that, barring a miracle, you would die. "

"That means I only have four lives left," Bill responded nonchalantly.

"Whatever are you taking about, Bill? Are you teasing me or, are you still delirious?"

"Neither," Bill replied with a sheepish grin. "I've just been lucky and have had my life saved a number of times lately. It's uncanny. Almost as if a guardian angel was watching over me."

What Bill didn't say was what he honestly believed. That somehow Karen was his protector . . . constantly saving his life for the sake of Jonathon. Saving him . . . even though he had failed her. The guilt returned, and with it a somber mood.

Sue said nothing, but seemed to know everything. After giving Bill his medication, she tenderly placed her hand onto Bill's forehead and ever so slowly kept moving it across his brow, as she had done so many times before when he was comatose . The movement was so soothing to Bill, he closed his weary eyes in contentment and fell right off into a much needed sleep. Even after he had, Sue was reluctant to stop physically massaging his soft brow. Reluctant because, for some strange reason, she knew she was attracted to him from the first moment she started to nurse him in the intensive care unit.

"He so reminds me of my son, Steve," she whispered to herself, as if to excuse her actions.

Then, she dismissed her fantasy by now extracting her hand and gently covering Bill's masculine shoulders with the bed sheet. Quietly, she turned to leave. Then, impulsively, Sue looked back again to admire this stranger that had suddenly stirred within her a long lost emotion.

"Stop daydreaming," she berated herself. "He'll be discharge soon and will be going back to his love ones. Just be grateful you have Steve to love. And, Joe to love you."

Over the next two weeks, as Bill recovered completely, they spent endless hours conversing with each other. Each had come to know the other intimately, as if they had been friends since birth. Each looked forward with great anticipation to each days visit. And at the end of every nursing shift that brought them together, each regretted deeply the need to part.

But, Bill's return to perfect health was rewarded with a medical discharge from the hospital. And, with it came his new orders.

Two competing emotions hit him, almost simultaneously, when Bill received them late in the afternoon after Sue had left . . . Elation! Then, sorrow. Initially, he was thrilled because being shipped back to Boston meant that he would be with Jonathon and Cathy again. But, the after thought was one of sadness because this meant he was leaving Sue. That part of him yearned to stay in Cuba. That part pleaded with him to remain with Sue.

And, as often as he tried to suppress that kindled emotion of affection, the more it kept surfacing anew in his thoughts.

But, this was crazy! This wasn't right. And he knew it. He was married to Cathy. He loved her. And never, never could hurt her. Any thoughts of infidelity on his part would not only destroy the mutual trust they had in each other, but would also compound his debilitating guilt-complex. Fortunately, this sobering reflection succeeded in quickly diluting his yearning for Sue.

Even if his marriage to Cathy was still not consummated, Bill felt that the bond between them was unbreakable. And, while his impotency may temporarily deny them the physical pleasure of intimacy they both desired, Bill still worshipped Cathy. For no other reason than that, Bill felt confident that any temptation to betray . . . to cheat on her . . . would be successfully resisted by him.

Yet, Sue was still something special to him. And, he'd really be a hypocrite to deny that truth. She was a compassionate woman, whom he had come to admire and respect immensely during his convalescence as she benevolently gave so much of herself to nurse him back to good health. Her beauty and charm had nothing to do with his present feelings. Or, did they? No, he concluded. Sue had become a good friend. A good friend and . . . and so much more. It was the 'much more' part that now concerned him most. Worried him most. Excited him most . . . in spite of all his efforts to quash these disturbing emotions.

On the spur of the moment, Bill decided he had to see Sue right away, rationalizing that since his plane took off at dawn, he wouldn't have the opportunity to say goodbye to her personally if he didn't. It had to be tonight. And it had to be now. Before he lost his courage. Before he changed his mind.

"Just to thank her for everything she has so unselfishly and so willingly done for me," he, convincingly, lied to himself.

However, as he was being taxied from the Officer's quarters

towards Sue's home, Bill began having second thoughts about what he was doing. And why he was doing it.

However, since he steadfastly refused to admit to himself what his real motivation was for wanting to see her, Bill's reservations could not be honestly resolved.

Nor, could he back out now before it was too late. For at 9 P.M., when Bill knocked softly on her door, he was irrevocably committed.

Sue opened the door almost immediately. Her surprised expression, then instantaneous welcoming smile, and joyful exclamation sealed Bill's fate.

"Bill! . . . Oh, Bill. You can't imagine how happy I am to see you! Come in. Please come in. I've been thinking about you all evening."

Upon entering, Bill quickly offered a rational explanation for his presence,

"My orders came through today. I have to leave at dawn tomorrow."

"I know," Sue sighed so longingly. "I heard through the grapevine that you were going, but didn't know where. My intuition tells me, however, that you must be going back to the States."

"You're right Sue. But, I couldn't leave without saying 'good-bye' to you first." Then. he hesitated a long moment before adding, "For some reason . . . I just hate to go. Funny isn't it. When I first came to the hospital, all I could think about was getting back to Boston. Back to Jonathon. And, back to Cathy. Now . . . now . . . I'm all mixed up. I no longer feel that same desire to leave A part of me wants to stay right here. And, I know why. It has everything to do with you . . . and the kindness you have shown me during my recovery."

"How sweet of you to think that way, Bill. And, I don't have to tell you how much I've treasured being near you this past month. Just watching you mend completely, and sharing so many wonderful moments with you. Talking so openly about everything in our lives has been a very rewarding experience for me.

223

"I'm certainly going to miss you, Bill. I hope you always remember those shared moments. And, more than that, I hope you never forget me."

Bill could have left at that point . . . But didn't. And then couldn't when Sue timidly asked,

"Do you have time to sit and chat for the last time? My son is sound asleep, and if we keep our voices down I'm sure we won't disturb him."

"Now, I wish I had come earlier so I could have seen him romping about. Since he and Jonathon are the same age, maybe someday . . . after this war is over . . . Cathy and I can vacation in Cuba so that our two rascals can get to know each other."

And so for the next two hours, Bill and Sue sipped wine while they talked together seriously . . . while they laughed together happily . . . while they unexpectantly lost themselves in the pleasure of each other's company. All the time relishing every moment of it, including the red wine. Much too much wine!

Then, around 11 P.M., as Bill stood up to leave, Sue uncharacteristically complained,

"It's not fair. You're leaving me, and my husband's ship won't be returning for a couple of weeks or more. I'll be all alone again."

"I'm sure you've missed Joe."

"On other trips . . . yes. But this time . . . this time your presence has more than eased the loneliness that I carry in my heart when he's away. And oftentimes . . . even when he's around."

"Bill was moved by her confession. And because he was he started to say,

"I better leave before . . . "

He didn't have a chance to finish his remark. For Sue got up, walked over, and now stood directly in front of him . . . so close their bodies almost touched. Her misty, hazel eyes looked up wistfully, locked deeply into his, and spoke without her speaking.

Impulsively, Bill gently put his arms around her, drew her

slowly to him, and met her open lips as they rose to meet his. What was meant to be only a 'goodbye peck' was now a burning . . . passionate kiss. Then another. And another.

Bill couldn't understand what compelled him to behave as he did. Not since Karen had such a lust possessed him. Not since Cathy had such a strong desire boiled inside him, crying for sensual relief. But, just as he couldn't get sexually intimate with Cathy because of his guilt concerning Karen, he knew that this craving, now felt for Sue, would rapidly dissipate.

However, this time he was wrong!

For the urge grew ever stronger . . . And, for the first time since Karen's death, he no longer was limp . . . but was bulging.

They didn't move into the bedroom. Both knew, if they had . . . the spell would have been broken. They would have come to their senses. And stopped. But instead, they slowly undressed each other where they stood. Now nude. Each absorbed the beauty of the other's naked physique through lustful eyes.

Then, craving fingers began to softly touch, roaming freely over each other's bodies, as their sex-hungry lips clung together again. Aroused as never before, Bill now placed his hands firmly atop Sue's shoulders and pressed gently downward. Sue responded. Knowingly. Willingly.

Slowly she slid down Bill's body and with closed lips began kissing. First, his nipples. Then, along the centerline of his chest towards his thighs. Bill started to quiver as he moaned with pleasure. And as her open lips now mouthed the warmth of his excited manhood . . . Bill tensed . . . Shuddered. Then, thrashed his lower torso forward . . . as he violently exploded away all his constrained inhibitions . . . all his suppressed desires . . . all his years of sexual denial, self-imposed since Karen's demise. Freed. Finally, freed from his torturous guilt, his animal instincts demanded even more satisfaction.

With Sue now laying alongside of him, they each searched deeply into each other's longing eyes. Then, Sue twisted her body so

225

as to lay flat on her back. Unable to resist her obvious invitation, Bill gently got on top of her. And as they kissed ferociously, Sue's heart pounded in great expectation. She wanted Bill to take her, and showed her submissiveness by consciously spreading her thighs wide apart so that Bill could enter easily. Bill eagerly did.

Then . . . after vigorously rocking up and down in rhythmic harmony for several minutes . . . Sue sensed that her moment of ecstasy was near. Quickly, she wrapped her legs around Bill's pulsating buttocks and squeezed tightly, drawing him closer and forcing him deeper. Then . . . panting and moaning cries of sheer delight as the feeling of elation swept through them . . . they both climaxed simultaneously.

Never before had Sue experienced such an exotic orgasm. But, before the evening was over . . . before her lover's insatiable sexual appetite was fully satisfied, She was rewarded time and time again . . . with many, many more.

Bill was intoxicated . . . by the wine and by the realization that he was once again able to copulate. Sue had accomplished the impossible. She had unleashed him from Karen's strangulation hold on his physical ability to perform sexually.

Yet, as he participated in his orgies with Sue, Bill sometimes fantasied that he was really having intercourse with Cathy. No wonder his mind now shared the delight his body was feeling. No wonder he felt ten feet tall . . . a man again . . . a whole man. Able to love without restriction. Able to be intimate again, without any sexual hang-ups.

But, Bill knew that what he and Sue were doing was morally wrong. Both were married. Both were committing adultery. However, Bill justified his action. Convincing himself that by being intimate with Sue his marriage to Cathy now would be saved.

"Two wrongs never make a right," he philosophized, "But, damn it. This time is the exception!"

Neither Sue nor Bill had any regrets as they parted around 4 A.M. . . . Neither was embarrassed. Neither apologized for their passionate behavior. Both felt that their uncontrolled fervor had at last given them the freedom to physically love their respective mates with renewed vitality. Sue once again with Joe. Bill . . . for the first time with Cathy.

They vowed to always remember this night that they shared together. And, although they probably would never meet again . . . or ever allow themselves to be passionate with each other again, even if they did meet . . . they would never forget the beauty of their shared embrace. The thrill of their romantic encounter would live forever in their liberated hearts.

But, each knew that with the sunrise would come a new day . . . A new beginning. Without their togetherness . . . except in nostalgic memories of their past.

Bill left. And, Joe returned three weeks later, just a few days after Sue started having morning sickness and realized immediately that she was pregnant. She prayed,

"Please God! Don't let me abort this time. Let me have Bill's child." Sue begged often for this treasured gift that would forever bond her to Bill. And give real meaning to their brief . . . but intimate relationship, even though it meant deceiving Joe and making him believe that he was really the father.

CHAPTER 15

As soon as Bill's plane landed in Boston at 7 P.M., he rushed home to Cathy and Jonathon. He felt reborn. And now anxiously looked forward to the new life he would be sharing with his wife. An uncompromising love . . . A fulfilling love. At long last, Cathy would no longer have to frustratingly accept him only in spirit . . . not in body. For Bill now knew, without any doubt, that their marriage would be finally consummated. Not humiliatingly aborted, as in the past, because of his inability to successfully perform the intimate act.

"Tonight!", he promised as he let himself in the front door. "Right after we put Jonathon to bed. We'll have the honeymoon night we never had."

Bill felt elated. Emotionally high . . . like an alcoholic who had just been handed a bottle of booze. And as he wrapped his arms around Cathy and smothered her with deep kisses, he quickly became sexually aroused. Bill was ecstatic. Knowing that Cathy . . . his patient, loving wife . . . would soon be able to judge for herself his adequacy to satisfy her physically.

Thoughts of Karen's demise vanished, along with all residual guilt feelings of her that had plagued him for so many years. Even the new one, associated with his lustful affair with Sue, less than 20 hours ago, was already buried deep in his subconscious mind.

After all, he had already dismissed that guilt, under the

pretense it was really a virtue, since his copulating with Sue was responsible for setting him free emotionally. And surely Cathy would not only understand, but would also appreciate what Sue had accomplished in unshackling him from all of his sensual inhibitions. For that reason, he was momentarily tempted to make a full confession to her. But wisely, Bill vowed instead never to even mention Sue's name, or anything about Sue, to her.

"No. Not tonight. Or ever! Tonight is going to be just ours . . . Nothing is going to come between my virgin bride and me, tonight."

And, as promised, as soon as Jonathon fell asleep, Cathy and he made passionate love until the wee hours of the morning.

Cathy was deliriously happy when she woke up about 8 A.M . . . Content at last with herself . . . and with her marriage. No longer tortured by Karen's uncanny possession of Bill's emotions. At long last, everything that she had every hoped for and wanted from her husband was uncompromisingly given to her. Given zealously. Passionately. Satisfyingly . . . by the one and only man she ever loved.

But, still, it was only natural for her to marvel at the sudden change in Bill's sexual behavior. One that finally consumed her virginity, and consummated their marriage.

"I feel like a whole woman again," she sighed. "Not rejected by my lover, but cherished by him."

And no longer did she have to cry herself to sleep, aching for fulfillment. Not now that the ecstasy of intercourse was being realized with Bill . . . time and time again.

"Whatever could have happened while Bill was hospitalized in Cuba to bring about this radical change?" she continually questioned.

"Whatever it was . . . it certainly has made him a new man. A virile man. A very . . . very sexy man. He must be keeping something secret from me."

Cathy's curiosity grew and kept growing until it dominated her every thought. She was determined to know what caused her husband's sudden reversal of behavior from one of total abstinence of intimacy with her to an almost insatiable obsession . . . several times a day . . . for sexual gratification.

Finally, one evening about two weeks later, she could wait no longer in her quest for an answer. So she cuddled up close to Bill, just after they had been intimate again, and coyly asked,

"Was it that new medicine . . . Penicillin? Is an increased sexual drive one of its dangerous side-effects?"

Both Cathy and Bill roared with laughter. And Bill later wished that he had said 'yes' and simply dropped the subject. But, he didn't . . . and so Cathy persisted,

"Seriously, Bill. What was it? Please tell me. I'm not complaining mind you. I'm just dying of curiosity to know why!"

Bill's reply to his wife was as naive as putting one's hand into a bee's hive to keep the bees inside. There was no way he could escape the consequences . . . once he started,

"Cathy. Don't ask! You know I can't lie to you. I don't think you really want to find out. Let's drop it. Let's just be thankful I'm normal again . . . in every way!"

Bill got stung immediately . . . over and over again with her piercing barbs,

"Oh, Don't I! Now I must know what it was." Then frowning, when a new, more worrisome perception came to mind, she spontaneously added, "Or, who it was!"

Trapped . . . Bill felt hopelessly ensnared in a quagmire. He had no option left. So he broke down and reluctantly said,

"It was Sue."

Cathy's green eyes dilated immediately with fierce jealousy, and she lost all semblance of docile composure when she instantly responded in a scornful rage,

"Sue? Who the hell is Sue? You never mentioned Sue before!"

Cathy's mind and heart might have accepted any other explanation, but not the one that Bill now was confessing to her. And after he had, she screamed out in agonizing disgust,

"Oh, Bill! How could you? Didn't our vows mean anything to you? Wasn't my love for you strong enough for both of us? Wasn't it pure enough to resist any temptation?

"It was for me. Why wasn't it enough for you?" she sobbed uncontrollably.

"Do you think I've longed . . . and suffered . . . and waited for you all this time, just to have you betray me like that? God, Bill! How could you? How could you do that to me?"

Cathy never gave Bill a chance to explain his irrational behavior. Besides, her mind was sealed shut to any excuse he might have offered. None would ever suffice. None could justify, in her mind, his sinful act . . . even if it did finally release Bill from his guilt about Karen. Nothing he said could appease her tortured mind . . . now that she knew the truth.

Cathy was able to live with Bill and his memories of a dead Karen but . . . she could never live with Bill and his reminiscences of a live Sue. So, she ranted on vehemently,

"You violated my trust in you. You violated everything sacred to me . . . including my love for you. Even worse . . . you violated my body by fucking me after your adulterous affair.

"God! I'd have more compassion and forgiveness in my heart for a perfect stranger who just raped me, then I have for you at this moment. I HATE YOU! I hate you for destroying our marriage. Destroying whatever future we could have shared together. But most of all . . . I hate you for deceiving me by being unfaithful. How could you come rushing home to me and steal my virginity, not even hours after you had made out with Sue, in your moment of filthy lust?"

Now jumping out of bed, Cathy raised her right arm, and pointed her extended index finger repeatedly . . . first, at Bill and, then, at the bedroom door . . . as she started to spit out her poisonous venom like a wounded rattlesnake,

"You Bastard! Go back to your whore. Go back to the sexpot that freed you of all guilt. She's the only one that's ever going to satisfy your sexual urges from now on. Not me! You're never going to have the chance to hold me . . . to touch me . . . to have me. I'll never let you fuck me again . . . ever . . . ever . . . EVER! The only way I can cleanse my mind and my vagina is to rid myself of you forever. So get out! And stay out!"

Bill was stunned. He tried to plead with Cathy. But nothing he said made any difference now that Cathy's righteous Irish temper had reached full boil. She was adamant in her stand and scornfully rebuked him again by announcing,

"I don't want to stay married to you anymore. And If I had only known about your affair before you seduced me, I would never have let you be intimate with me . . . no matter how hard your cock ached for satisfaction and relief.

"You've made me feel so dirty by cheating on me. I only wish we had never consummated this marriage. At least then, I could have gotten an annulment and lived with myself within my religion. Now . . . I want a divorce . . . in spite of my religious beliefs."

Unfortunately, the die was cast. There was no turning back for Cathy or Bill . . . even though Bill wished he could use all the money he had to buy back the time spent that evening with Sue. But life is unforgiven with its spent time, be it an hour or a second. Once dispensed, there is no second chance to roll back the hands of time to redeem one's acts or misdeeds.

No second chance to fully nullify a mistake, or eradicate a wrong. In that way, Nature always holds all the aces. Humans are allowed to play the game of life . . . but by the Master's rules which seem to demand perfection during every nanosecond of one's existence.

Bill failed!. At least in Cathy's eyes he did. And, as a result, she wanted . . . she demanded her freedom. Nothing less would suffice.Not a temporary separation . . . but a permanent one. And certainly not a reconciliation EVER! Not even a financial settlement. Her despair . . . her hurt could only be healed with an amputation of her bond of marriage to Bill. An immediate divorce. That's what she asked for.And she would accept nothing less.

Through his lawyer, Bill offered so much more. He wanted her to have the house and a large monetary settlement. But Cathy could never live in Bill's home again . . . even without Bill in it. For it contained too many hopes and dreams that almost became a reality . . . until they were smashed into bits by Bill's confession. And like a precious china vase that is suddenly cracked, nothing can ever be done to restore it to its original state of beauty and perfection. So too with the human scar that never heals.

"Nothing. Nothing at all but, my total independence!" Cathy steadfastly reiterated . . . up until the time her uncontested divorce degree was about to become final, exactly three months after her violent argument with Bill.

That's what her Irish pride wanted, even after the doctor first informed her that she was pregnant. But, then, she reluctantly considered changing her mind when the doctor later said 'he wasn't sure, but that he thought he detected two separate heart beats'.

She knew then, she might have to swallow her pride because her children . . . Bill's children . . . deserved more than she could ever provide as a single mother struggling to support her family.

Cathy could have opt for an abortion. But as much as she detested Bill, she couldn't bring herself to willfully taking a life. Her religion . . . her morals . . . her principles . . . and, especially, her conscience, all negated this course of action as a viable choice . . . immediately after the thought surfaced in her mind.

Bill never found out why Cathy finally allowed him to set up a large financial trust for her. But, he was relieved that she had.

And, he never found out that Cathy was pregnant with his children. And Cathy 'thanked God' for that . . . along with her fervent prayer that she someday would be provided with a good father for her children.

"And it isn't going to be Bill!" she swore.

The divorce was a traumatic experience for both Bill and Cathy. But, Cathy knew it was an even worse one for three and a half year old Jonathon, who suddenly lost the only motherly love he ever had. This was causing Cathy so much anguish, she almost changed her mind. For while she was insensitive to Bill's remorse, she was unable to hold back her tears over Jonathon's.

But in the end, she knew if she stayed married to Bill for that reason, she might someday come to resent or hate Jonathon for keeping her tied to a man who she now loathed and despised. And she loved Jonathon too much to ever let that happen.

So Jonathon suffered! As only an innocent child can, who is living one day in a serene and stable world and, in the next, is having its heart torn out by the turmoil of parents separated. He was too young to understand why Cathy was no longer there to mother him. Why his cries for her always went unheeded. He only comprehended a depth of sadness and loneliness that was previously unknown to him. So all he could do was wail to ease the pain. As did Bill. Who cursed the day he was ever unfaithful to Cathy.

Cathy didn't have to convince Tom to marry her. It was the other way around. Tom begged her. However, Cathy kept resisting.

"Tom . . . You know I don't love you. You're my best friend. But it isn't love. If It was, I would have married you, instead of Bill, long ago. You must realize that Tom."

"I do Cathy. And I know that in spite of what you have done in divorcing Bill, I believe that you still do love him. I can never hope to take his place in your heart. But for the sake of your unborn children, let me be your husband. They'll soon need a father."

"But, I don't love you. I don't know if I ever could."

"It doesn't matter to me. I have enough love for both of us. Maybe someday my love will spill over, and you'll begin to cherish me . . . like you did Bill. But even if you never do, I need you."

Not getting a positive response from Cathy, as he had hoped, Tom decided to use a different approach to convince her.

"And let's be honest, Cathy. You say you don't want Bill ever to know you're carrying his children. But, if they're born before you get married again, you'll either have to acknowledge that they are his, or that they were conceived with someone else, while you were still married to him."

Then, Tom paused . . . a deliberate drawn out pause . . . so that the impact of his next statement might finally sway Cathy to say 'yes'.

"Or, worse yet, that the children were conceived out of wedlock, after your divorce. You and I know the truth Cathy. But, people love to gossip . . . and always believe the worse . . . not the best . . . of those that they are gossiping about. Marry me now . . . and avoid all that. We'll leave Boston. That way we'll protect your reputation. And the children will carry my name, instead of the stigma of being illegitimate."

So for the sake of her unborn children, Cathy did marry Tom immediately. And in the fourth month of her pregnancy, they moved to Washington, D.C . . .

At first Cathy thought it sinful to sleep with a man . . . to have relations with a man . . . she didn't love. However, time tempered her feelings. Not only because of Tom's devotion to her, but also because Tom was right! For in spite of herself . . . In spite of the fact she wished otherwise . . . she still did love Bill. He remained in her every thought . . . every day. And, as a result, she became more receptive to Tom's lovemaking because of her fantasies that she was being intimate with Bill.

1 5 B

Although Joe was at sea most of the time during Sue's pregnancy, when he was back home, he was a completely new man. No longer despondent, or bitter at the world for the cruel hardships that plagued him since they abandoned their farm in Kansas. And best of all, no longer an alcoholic, having given that vice up cold-turkey the very same day he learned of Sue's expectancy.

Naturally, Sue was truly elated over the reformation of her Joe. But, at the same time, torn because his euphoria resulted from his mistaken belief that he had impregnated her. But, how could she tell Joe about her act of infidelity without destroying him? How? . . . When she knew that Joe, in spite of all his faults, never doubted for a moment that Sue remained faithful to him, as he did to her.

How? When, she knew that her Joe took the conception as an omen that . . . after all those years . . . God had forgiven him for killing Steve's mother. And, now showed his forgiveness by allowing Sue's pregnancy to reach it's eighth month, instead of having her abort after three months as she usually did.

However, Joe was wrong! But, for the wrong reason. For the baby girl that Sue had just delivered 'prematurely' was his in name only. And Bill, not he, was the true father. Even so, a deceived Joe couldn't be happier at the moment as he cradled the new born baby girl in his arms. Well . . . maybe he was a little disappointed that Sue hadn't named the child, Joan . . . after his mother . . . as he had hoped

237

she would. However, over Joe's mild objection, Sue decided to call her daughter, Wilma . . . obviously in memory of her unforgettable night of passion with Bill.

Ironically, Cathy also went into labor and delivered her fraternal twins, a boy, Michael, and a girl, Sharon, just two days after Sue did. So in that one momentous week, Bill had become the father, in absentia, of three healthy children. None of whom, he was aware that he had ever conceived. But, all of whom carried his genes and, undeniably displayed many of his physical characteristics. And, all of whom were blood connected to each other. Either, as siblings . . . like Jonathon and Steve, like Sharon and Michael . . . or, unknowingly, as halfbrothers and halfsisters.

Both Sue and Cathy couldn't have been happier as they breast-fed their babies at this precious moment of motherhood. Their only secret regret was that Bill was not there with them to share their happiness. However, both resisted the urge to write or call Bill and tell him the good news.

Cathy, especially, was torn. Torn with compassion for Tom . . . with love for Bill, which caused her to lament,

"Oh, God! I shouldn't have been so impetuous. I should have controlled my temper and my hurt. However, it's too late now for Bill and I. I've got to think only of Tom and my children. I've got to erase Bill from my mind forever and never let him know about the daughter and son we've created. Instead, I've got to make myself believe he's dead. Dead like Karen. And buried with her!

CHAPTER 16

The World was at war! Consequently, the family bonds of almost every soul living on the Five Continents were either strained or broken.

"What hypocrisy!" Bill thought. "A World at War . . . killing supposedly to save humanity. Somehow, it just doesn't make any sense."

There is no doubt that war is hell! And that forced separations must be endured . . . like Bill's from Jonathon as he served by continuing his espionage activities overseas. Like Joe's from Sue and his children, Steve and Wilma, as he continued risking his life as a merchant seaman. And, like Tom's separation from Cathy and his family, after he enlisted and was assigned to General Patton's U.S. 3rd Army Tank Corps in Europe, in 1943.

Sadness always accompanies separations. Whether they be long or short. But along with it . . . springs the eternally hope of being reunited again . . . someday soon . . . as one.

Unfortunately, however, such was not the case for Joe's family. Their sadness quickly degenerated into prolonged suffering and hardship . . . starting in June of 1944, just before the Allies D-Day invasion of Europe, when Joe's cargo ship was sunk off the coast of England.

Joe's luck ran out and he joined thousands of other heroic merchant marines who lost their lives during the war attempting, unsuccessfully, to transport vital war material across the U-boat infested North Atlantic.

All courageous seaman who could only cope with the mental torture of their daily routine by clinging to the false belief that the German's deadly torpedoes would never strike their ship . . . but were destined instead to hit others in their convoy. But the odds of survival were stacked too heavily against most of them. And, thus it was no great surprise that they were suddenly and brutally blown asunder when the killer hunter's powerful explosive penetrated their ship's hull.

Joe actually survived the blast after being blown overboard. But, unlike Bill, no one threw a life preserver to him to keep him afloat in the cold, hostile sea. So, all Joe could do was to drift helplessly . . . and hopelessly . . . at the mercy of the angry tide waters. Drift and pray! As he did now, with arms fluttering wildly, in a frantic effort to save his life . . . for Sue . . . for Steve . . . for his precious little daughter, Wilma, who was only a year and a half old.

Miraculously, he endured exposure to the cold Atlantic for almost an hour . . . before his teeth-chattering, shivering body succumbed to exhaustion. No longer able to hold his head above water, Joe realized his fate was sealed, and that God's will had to be done. So, gasping his last breath, he murmured pathetically,

"A life . . . for a life!"

Then, in a final act of supreme courage, Joe sacrificed himself to the inevitable by deliberately drowning himself.

Tom Foley was a worry wart once he got into combat overseas. Not about the fighting . . . because he quickly got that apprehension under control. What he was having a hard time handling, however, was constantly fretting about Cathy, who was alone in Washington, D.C., taking care of Michael and Sharon. Just thinking about her always made his eyes blink with tears.

Tom loved Cathy with all his heart. But, he was no fool. For he knew that Cathy still didn't love him . . . or need him. Not the way she did Bill! Certainly not financially, since she had received over a million dollars from Bill when they got divorced.

And she didn't need him physically either to satisfy her yearnings in their intimate moments. Tom soon realized that Cathy faked her orgasms. And, no matter how loving or considerate he was, Cathy still was possessed by her deep feelings for Bill . . .

So, no wonder Tom was worried as his tank rolled along the hilly and wooded countryside of the Ardennes toward Bastongne on a mission of great urgency brought about by a German counteroffensive which threatened to break through to Antwerp, and annihilate tens of thousands of British and American soldiers. Only the heroic stand by the outflanked U.S. detachments, holding Bastongne and several other important bottlenecks, in the snow covered fields of Ardennes, were annoyingly hindering the German's rapid advance.

"A hell of a way to spend the Christmas holidays," Tom bellowed in disgust. Almost loud enough to be heard above the constant din of cannon fire, and the squeaking clatter of his noisy tank treads.

Tom now was having second thoughts about his decision to enlist for overseas duty. The Army wanted to keep him in the States, and assign him to a staff job in Washington, D.C . . . But Tom didn't want that . . . even though that option would have allowed him to be home with Cathy every night. No! He had to go overseas . . . to give Cathy a chance to come to terms with herself and their relationship with each other . . . Tom still was clinging to the hope that by being away, until the War was over, Cathy would come to miss him. Come to love him . . . as he did her . . . as she did Bill.

"Then again!", he muttered alarmingly, "Cathy may grow to hate me for leaving her alone. If that happens, I'm a loser either way."

That last thought caused him to frown deeply, increasing his concern about Cathy even more, as his tank continued to rumble on relentlessly towards Bastonge.

241

However, on a bitter cold winter day, January 8, 1945 . . . after Tom succeeded in personally destroying six of the enemy's tanks in a surprise attack on the Germans and helped break the strangulation hold on the beleaguered American forces at Bastongne, all of his worries were finally put to rest. For Tom was killed by shrapnel from an exploding German artillery shell, just as he was dismounting from his tank, with the loud resounding cheers of the relieved U.S. soldiers still ringing in his ear.

At midnight . . . on May 8, 1945, the War in Europe officially came to an end. And, to Bill's utter amazement, the tyrant Hitler and the German's invincible war machine were defeated. Crushingly defeated. And, in less than a year from the time the Allied Forces stormed ashore on the coast of Normandy, on June 6, 1944.

It was inconceivable to Bill that the Allies could ever accomplish this feat so quickly . . . especially, in light of Germany's total dominance of the European continent since the days of Denmark's demise on April 9,1940. A day Bill always so vividly remembered because of his harrowing adventure in obtaining a copy of Germany's Master Plan for development of the atom bomb. An adventure which almost cost him his life.

And, if it wasn't for Stig . . . Johan . . . and Joe, he wouldn't be rejoicing now with the tumultuous crowds of happy, waving, cheering people that filled every street of every city in every country of Europe celebrating this tremendous victory.

But, unfortunately, V-E day (Victory in Europe) did not mark the end of World War II for Bill. For his new orders, sending him to the Pacific and into the War with Japan, had already been received. Orders that allowed him only six weeks leave in the States before he had to begin his new clandestine assignment. Almost too short a period of time to get reacquainted with Jonathon, who Bill hadn't seen for over two years.

However, Jonathon . . . now 6 years old, instantly recognized his father when Bill stepped out of a cab at the front door of their home in Boston. Excitedly, he ran to him with both arms opened wide . . . his dark, wavy hair glistening in the bright sunlight, and his misty blue eyes starting to weep with joy as he screamed happily,

"Daddy! Daddy. You're home. You're home!"

Bill wrapped his arms around Jonathon, lifted him up gently, and hugged him tightly. Affectionately. Bill cried for joy on this extremely emotional occasion. Unashamedly. His tears flowed . . . like a steady spring rain . . . as did Jonathon's.

For Jonathon, having his father home again was the best treat of all . . . better than all the presents he ever got at Christmas time. For Bill, it was the perfect panacea for all the loneliness he had endured . . . while away.

And so, for nearly six weeks, Jonathon and Bill were inseparable. Like two pieces of similar metal welded together, they bonded, once more, as one. Then, the dreaded day of departure arrived again,

"Too soon," Bill moaned. "Always too soon."

Leaving Jonathon again was the hardest thing in the world for Bill to do, causing him to lament,

"The War is half won. Why do I have to continue risking my life for the other half?"

In spite of his complaining, Bill already knew the answer. As always, it was for his son, Jonathon! Jonathon's right to have a future in a serene, peaceful world . . . free of all tyrants. This, and only this naive belief gave Bill the necessary strength to face the hardship of saying 'good-bye', which he now reluctantly did by holding his son close, kissing him several times, and praying that this time would be the last time they would ever have to be parted.

1 6 B

Bill's plane landed at the Guantanamo Naval Base, on the Island of Cuba, about 8 P.M. on the 6th of July. His itinerary called for him to leave at noon the next day for Panama City, where he would rendezvous briefly with Blake Edwards, before both boarded a cruiser heading directly to Pearl Harbor, after passing through the Canal.

Suddenly Bill's curiosity got the best of him. And to satisfy his burning craving for the missing knowledge, he quickly logged in at the Officer's quarters, hired a cab, and immediately headed for Sue's house. Bill wasn't even sure that Sue still lived in Cuba, but his unrestrained desire motivated him to find out. Once again Bill was denying the truth of his feelings for Sue ... by not admitting to himself that he was drawn to her like iron is to a magnet.

By not admitting that the driving force was strictly one with sexually overtones. Even after all these years, Bill couldn't forget the lustful night they had spent together. Even though he wanted to ... even though he should have. He never was quite able to erase that episode from his mind.

Memories of that affair rushed forth and surface anew, as soon as the cab stopped at its destination to let Bill out in front of Sue's house. Immediately, Bill started fantasying a little. Maybe too much! Definitely the latter, since even his nostalgic memories of Cathy now quickly dimmed out.

But, as he briskly strolled up the flag-stone sidewalk, his

jubilant, excited, passionate mood turned to one of somber dismay. The sign post still said, 'The Walker's—Sue and Joe', but the house was pitch black. Looking at his wrist watch, Bill was somewhat perplexed because it was only 9 P.M., which prompted his remark of dejection,

"Just my luck. She's probably out. Damn it!"

Then, Bill had a further thought . . . one which rapidly cooled his fantasies down to the icy range of reality.

"God! Maybe Joe's home," he blurted with just a slight twinge of jealousy in his voice. "If that's so, I'd look pretty darn foolish barging in on them. Joe doesn't know me from a hole in the wall. And as much as I want to see Sue, it would be just too frustrating for me to visit if Joe is home, and I couldn't be with her alone."

So with that, Bill disappointingly ambled down to the street corner, hailed another cab, and decided on the spur of the moment to drown his sorrows at the local bar in town. It's true that Bill had heard that 'Charly's' was also a hangout for prostitutes. Since 'Charly's' was the only place to get liquor so close to the Naval Base that bit of gossip certainly didn't surprise him . . . nor did it bother him.

After all, he wasn't interested in having another women at the moment. It was the whiskey he really needed tonight . . . if he couldn't be with Sue.

When he arrived at the bar, he found it to be as rowdy and as full of Naval personnel as he had expected. Everywhere he peered, he saw carefree sailors and Naval officers . . . either fondling their dates, or busy propositioning the available women-of-the-evening, who were only too eager to accommodate any male companion, as long as he could afford the price for an hour's fornication. What Bill never expected to see in a million years, however, was Sue, wearing a sleazy sexy outfit, obviously trying to entice an inebriated Navy Lieutenant to pay for her sexual favors.

Sue didn't have the opportunity to see Bill because he

quickly covered his face with his hat ... until he moved some distance away. Staying in the background ... Bill kept his startled brown eyes glued on Sue, who flitted and flirted with man after man ... until apparently one horny soul did make her the right offer. Then, arm-in-arm, the two went off together, walking up the steps leading to the hotel rooms on the second floor.

Meanwhile, Bill waited anxiously for Sue to return. Waited agonizingly ... needing to prove to himself that his eyes had deceived him. That he must somehow be wrong.

"It was just someone that looked like Sue," he lied. "Sue would never be caught dead in a place like this."

Then, Bill suddenly remembered Cathy's biting words of admonishment,

"Go back to your whore!"

And when Bill saw Sue return in a half hour to begin her solicitation of men again, his faith in her and in himself was completely shattered. .

"God! Cathy was right ... instinctively right! Sue is just a slut ... a common ordinary slut. She must have been one ... even before she came to me that night. What a jerk I was. Too naive to know that she must be an old master at seducing men. Especially ... jack asses like me."

Dejectedly, Bill left 'Charly's' without having his drink, even though he needed one now ... more than ever.

"There's just got to be an explanation," Bill said as he walked away sadly. "That's not the Sue I once knew. I'd bet my life on that."

Bill was so distraught over this discovery, he couldn't think straight. He was not only totally confused. But also totally disillusioned. And, totally disgusted at what he had just witnessed. His peace of mind would forever elude him, he concluded ... until he found out just how long Sue had been a loose woman.

"Was she one before our affair?" he wondered.

It wasn't just his ego that was crushed. Although that certainly was deflated to absolute zero. But, what really bothered him was an odd feeling of having been betrayed.

The uncontrolled smirk that now ran across his face was precipitated instantly by the irony of his thought,

"What the hell am I thinking about? I'm the betrayer.

"Not Sue. I'm the one that cheated on Cathy."

Still the thought persisted. Probably because of his deep conviction that what Sue and he had shared that night was a once in a lifetime moment of no regrets. At least, he thought so. Apparently, however, to Sue it was nothing more than a quick fuck with no real emotional significance.

"She definitely fooled me! Only I didn't have to pay for it. I got it for free."

Then, his mind dwelled on all the negatives of having had an intimate relation with an immoral woman and not wearing the appropriate protection.

"God! If she was as sexually active before she met me as she is today, she could have been a carrier of gonorrhea, or, God-forbid, even syphilis."

Bill shuddered at that distressing new thought . . . realizing that if he had acquired either disease that night from Sue, he would have totally destroyed pure, innocent Cathy. Not only morally, as he did, but also physically.

"I've got to know!", he demanded of himself. "Not just sometime but . . . now. Before I leave Cuba tomorrow."

So with his mind made up, Bill didn't return to the Officer's quarters to get some sleep. But, instead, went directly back to Sue's house, sat himself down on her porch step, and waited . . . and waited.

Several times he almost dozed off. However, his unrepenting anger kept him awake. Then, about 3 A.M., Sue's car came weaving onto her driveway. After parking, she got out and slowly staggered towards her front door.

247

"Who's there?" she called out in a startled voice, somewhat frightened by seeing a stranger sitting on her front steps.

She was dumbfounded, when under the glare of the street light, Sue thought she recognized her visitor.

"Bill! Bill is that you?"

For a moment there was deathly silence. Then, Bill responded . . . not by answering her question . . . but by asking his own.

"Why . . . Sue? Why? I have to know why!"

Sue was completely mystified by Bill's inquiry. But being so happy to see him . . . she went over, tried to bend down, tried to put her arms on his shoulders and, then, tried to kiss him.

However, she failed on all three accounts. For all she accomplished, in her intoxicated condition, was to fall over, landing on her backside, in a sitting position, facing Bill.

Uncharacteristically, Bill didn't even move a muscle to assist her to get up. So, Sue just draped her arms awkwardly around her raised knees, and stayed sat, while looking at Bill distressfully. However, all she got from Bill in return was the same question.

"Why Sue? I saw you tonight at 'Charly's' . . . "

Before he could utter another word, Sue gasped and cried out,

"Oh! God! No! . . . You didn't!"

"You were prostituting yourself. I wish I was blind so that I couldn't have seen you doing it. But I did. And now Sue, I have to know why?"

Sobbing profusely over Bill's discovery, Sue . . . painfully . . . began to explain her actions,

"Oh! Bill. I never did anything like this before Joe was lost at sea. Believe me Bill. I never was with anyone but Joe . . . except with you that wonderful evening. But I was destitute . . . I had no means of supporting my two children . . . "

"Two children?", interrupted Bill.

248

"Yes! Steve . . . and a daughter born in '42. You'd love her Bill. After all she's . . . "

Sue was going to say 'ours' but she didn't then . . . and couldn't ever, now that Bill knew she was a prostitute. It was obvious from Bill's tone of voice that he had nothing but disdain for her. So Sue just completed her remark by saying,

" . . . so beautiful. Joe idolized her. She was his pride and joy. And every moment that he was with us, between his cross-Atlantic trips, he would spend cuddling her, as if she was the answer to all his prayers."

Bill was deeply moved. And while he had remained silent about Joe's demise before, he repented now by saying,

"I'm so sorry about Joe, Sue. But, I've seen so many deaths since this War started, I've become immune to its reality."

"I understand Bill. But please understand the predicament I was in because of it. Don't you see? I had nothing. I had no one I could turn to for help. I was broke . . . with hungry mouths to feed. I couldn't work days because I had to take care of my children.

"The only way I did survive and support them is the way you saw me tonight. Don't you think I hate it? It repulses me more than it ever could you. Its my body that they use and abuse. They've destroyed my self image . . . they've made me look at sex as some ugly thing. Not the beautiful intimacy that we shared once."

Sue paused . . . long enough to struggle up and to sit alongside Bill. Then, she continued,

"Three months after finding out about Joe being lost at sea, I found out about the real world. There just was no other way. Not unless I wanted my children to starve to death . . . or be taken away from me. 'Charly's' was the only answer for me. So each night, I'd put them to bed, wait until they were asleep, and then go out for a few hours to sell myself for a few lousy dollars. Just enough to buy the food and clothes we needed, and enough to pay for the rent."

Sue was too humiliated to look at Bill. She felt as dirty as her conscience told her she was.

"Why didn't you write me for help? I gave you my address before I left. You brought me back to good health when I needed you. Didn't you think I would do the same for you? Oh, Sue! Why didn't you? Before going out and selling your body to the highest bidder."

"I wanted to . . . I almost did. But, then, I thought that your wife, Cathy, might not understand. Might wonder why I would be asking you for assistance. I just didn't want to come between you two. I'd rather die first than have something like that on my conscience."

Bill certainly understood. And Sue was right! Even if Sue didn't know it, Cathy's jealousy over her had split them apart. However, Bill just didn't have the heart to tell her. For Sue certainly would blame herself for the divorce, when in truth, Bill knew it was all his fault by committing adultery. So he lied to Sue,

"You're really wrong Sue. Cathy wouldn't have minded in the least. You should have asked for help."

"It's too late now anyway, Bill. Can you ever forgive me for destroying your idyllic image of me? I swear to you Bill . . . It never would have happened if Joe was still alive. And may God strike me dead if I'm lying . . . I was a virgin when I married Joe. And I never . . . never . . . never slept with another man until after he died . . . except that one time that I know both of us will never forget."

Now Sue had the courage to look directly at Bill, searching for compassion . . . her eyes pleading for forgiveness.

"I believe you Sue. And now I want to help fund you so that you'll never have to sell your beautiful body again."

"I can't take your money, Bill."

"You must and you will. For the sake of the children . . . if not yourself. Joe would have wanted it that way. He wouldn't want his children growing up knowing their mother is a prostitute. And neither do I. I have plenty of money . . . that's the one thing I do have. Before I leave tomorrow, I'll set up a savings account in your name at the local bank for two hundred thousand dollars. Use the money wisely . . . but use it to get off the streets."

250

"Two hundred thousand dollars! Bill, I'd live like a queen with that much money."

"Well . . . that's great," said Bill. "Because that's exactly what you are."

No further words were spoken. They didn't have to be. For the chemistry in their eyes said it all . . . just before they embraced!

CHAPTER 17

When Bill's plane landed at the Panama City Airport on July 7th, he immediately surmised that something was very wrong. A premonition that arose while observing Blake Edwards . . . normally calm, cool, and collected, rushing out to meet him as he debarked from the DC-3. Blake was not only sweating profusely . . . but, also, was not puffing his pipe, which always dangled from his pursed lips, come hell or high water. Running in the steamy mist, a natural by-product of the unbearable tropical heat, could obviously explain the former. However, the latter could only be attributed to Blake Edwards' internally charged state of emotion.

"Are things as hot as you portray them to be?" Bill asked in greeting Blake.

Edwards, deeply impressed by Bill's astute intuitive remark, couldn't help thinking to himself, "He's come a long way since our first meeting in Boston." What he replied, however, only confirmed Bill's speculation.

"Hotter than blazes! And, it's not this stifling humidity. There's been a sudden revision of our agenda. Let's go over there . . . where we can talk without being overheard."

And with that they both moved to an isolated area outside of the Airport terminal building. Then, Blake amplified his terse remark,

"It's all because of what's happening back in the States. I

253

received a coded message just an hour ago. Our orders have been changed. We have to report to Los Alamos, New Mexico as soon as possible.

"Why? What's up? What's so damn urgent, Blake?" Bill inquired in rapid sequence.

"They're going to test fire the atom bomb! We're finally going to find out if we have a real 'firecracker', or just a colossal 'dud', at an enormous expense of two billion dollars."

"Two billion dollars! You've got to be kidding me Blake . . . You are joshing . . . Aren't you?"

"No . . . I'm not! Two billion is what it has cost so far. Who knows how much more it'll run if this shot fizzles. Even President Roosevelt was so concerned about the escalating cost of its development, just before dying in April, he was seriously weighing the option of pulling the plug and flushing the entire Manhattan Project. In fact, the day the good Lord took him, he had decided to do just that. No one would have blamed him if he had. The War is now over in Europe and, it appears, with our recent successes in the Pacific, that the War with Japan could end soon. Probably long before the 'monster' is ever made operational."

Blake paused, took a white handkerchief out of his back pocket, swiped away several times at the beads of sweat on his brow, cautiously looked around again to be sure of their privacy, then continued,

"Roosevelt concluded that even if there was a good chance of the bomb becoming a reality in a year or so, we'd have no further use for it by then. And certainly, no viable excuse for wasting anymore of our nation's resources, other than the two billion already down the drain. Just try to picture it, Bill . . . 2 plus nine zeros.

"I can't. But, I do understand, Blake, why Roosevelt would feel awful squeamish about trying to justify that kind of expenditure to American citizens."

"He knew even he couldn't. War or, no war. That's why the Project was going to be stamped 'Canceled'. Lucky for us, however, he passed away before making it official. And even luckier that he hadn't breathed a word about the top secret Manhattan Project to his Vice President, Harry Truman. Now, Harry's the President.

"Of course, we had to brief him about it as soon as he was sworn in. However, we skipped most of the details . . . except emphasizing that we had something that could shorten the War with Japan, if funds were made available for another six months of development. Nobody lied to him about the two billion dollars already spent. But, since he didn't asked about it, no one offered to volunteer that information either. Or, the fact that Roosevelt had decided to terminate the project."

Bill just shook his head in utter disbelief.

"He fell for the time extension request hook, line, and sinker. So General Groves, who has been heading up the Project since '42, really put the heat on the 'eggheads'. He told them in no uncertain terms' to get their asses moving and produce something that works before President Truman got back from his talks with Churchill and Stalin . . . being held at Potsdam in the middle of July. That must have shook them up real good . . . because they've scheduled an experimental test of the 'Fat Man', which is an implosion-type plutonium bomb, at Alamogordo on July 16th."

"But that's only nine days from now!" Bill countered.

"I know . . . and that's not all. Without even waiting for the results of that test, they're packaging our 'Little Boy', which is a gun-type uranium bomb, for shipment to Tinian in the Mariana Islands of the Pacific. It's going to be dropped on Japan, even if the test bomb is a failure!"

"What!", Bill exhaled in amazement.

"Yep. I guess top brass figures 'why the hell not'. If it doesn't work, the Project's dead anyway. However, If it does . . . they're heroes. And, undoubtedly, all will be in line for promotions. So that's why we're heading back to the States. First to Los Alamos to oversee security on the transfer of the 'target'(code named for Little Boy) to Tinian. Next to watch the 'big show' being put on in the desert on July 16th. And, after that, we both take off promptly for Tinian. Any questions?"

Having listened in awe to Blake's long discourse, Bill, who obviously was curious about many things, started seeking answers by asking,

"What do you think the chances are that the test shot will be successful?"

Bill interpreted Blake's quick response to be nothing more than an attempt at a bit of dry humor,

"I'd say about one in two billion!"

They both smiled. And Blake seemed particularly pleased that Bill had caught the pun. Then, in a more serious vain, he confessed,

"I don't really know Bill . . . However, if it doesn't go 'Pop', heads will start rolling. Not only those of the thousands of eminent scientist and engineers directly involved, but, even those belonging to the poor Generals that first assured Roosevelt . . . and now Truman . . . that it would."

Then . . . giving a quick wink, he continued,

"And you know what a crotchety son-of-a- bitch President Truman can be if you cross him up. He's from Missouri and has to be shown. But, they'll only have this one chance to do it. It either goes 'BANG' . . . in a big way as promised . . . or the guillotine drops, the decapitations begin . . . and we have a little blood bath. Any other question?"

"Yea! Where's Tinian?"

"Tinian is a tiny speck of an island at the southern end of the Mariana chain, which itself is just a series of clumps of uplifted coral reefs and volcanic mountain peaks, located in an easterly curved, arc-like array spreading over a 425 mile stretch of the Pacific. Just 4 miles south of the Island of Saipan, and 1450 miles from Tokyo. The latter is what makes it so important for our regular Air Force bombing missions over Japan. And, the perfect site for training the 509th Composite Group, which is a specially selected Air Force unit of pilots and B-29s, having the responsibility for dropping the atom bombs on Japan. Tinian may be small, Bill. But, strategically it packs a hell of a wallop."

Bill seemed satisfied for the moment with the terse, background information just given to him by Blake. And now reacting to the unbearable humidity of Panama, said wistfully,

"I hope it's cooler there . . . than it is here."

"That's one thing I wouldn't count on, Bill.

Right now it's one of the hottest areas of military action in the Pacific. So is its weather."

On that very disheartening note, Bill and Blake wasted no time in getting to Los Alamos. And upon their arrival on July 9th, both immediately began intensive review and monitoring of the security procedures involved in the transport of the 'target' to the Pacific.

Then, they closely scrutinized the packaging of the fifteen foot wooden crate, which contained the atom bomb's inner cannon, and a lead-lined cylinder within which was the uranium projectile. While doing this, Bill suddenly remarked,

"I'm amazed how simple this thing really looks, Blake. It's hard to believe it could ever cost two billion dollars to develop."

"It's not just the parts, Bill . . . it's the enormous technology put together by thousands of engineers and scientists that ran up the tab. But, you're right! Operationally the Little Boy atom bomb couldn't be simpler in concept. It's just a big gun . . . I should say a big cannon, weighing all together about five tons . . . in which one subcritical mass of fissionable material, Uranium 235, called the 'bullet' is fired as a projectile into a second subcritical mass, called the 'target'.

"At the moment they come together, we have a combination, called a supercritical mass which produces the 'chain reaction' that results, instantaneously, in a nuclear explosion. That's it in a nut shell. Whether or not it's going to work . . . when theory is put into practice is anyone's guess, Bill."

"Yea . . . I know . . . One in two billion at least."

Blake couldn't hold back his grin. Nor could Bill keep from laughing.

On the morning of July l4th, both Bill and Blake sighed with relief when Little Boy was finally loaded onto a closed, black truck, which quickly departed from Los Alamos, accompanied by seven cars in convoy array. Each of the cars housed four well trained security men, heavily armed with rifles, pistols, shotguns, and thousands of rounds of ammunition.

Needless to say, the assigned security forces heeded the stern instructions to never let the crate out of their sight until it completed its long journey, which included truck transportation to Albuquerque, air transportation to San Francisco, and finally, sea transportation aboard a heavy cruiser, the Indianapolis, to Tinian.

As an additional safety precaution, Bill and Blake decided that the small lump of Uranium 235 that is placed at the muzzle end of the gun inside the bomb, serving as the bullet, should be packaged and shipped separately. This, they did by having it flown directly to Tinian, under the tightest security measure imaginable.

No one relaxed at Los Alamos . . . even though Little Boy was now racing towards its destination. In fact, the opposite occurred. Tensions mounted to fever pitch as extensive preparations were carried out for test firing of the plutonium-type atom bomb, which was scheduled to occur at 2 A.M. on the 16th.

Anxieties reached a crescendo in the wee morning hours of that day, as Bill, Blake, several scientists, and other key personnel, including Project Director, Dr. Robert Oppenheimer, and General Groves gathered at the Alamogordo base camp, situated just nine miles from 'Ground Zero' where the atom bomb sat, perched one hundred feet above ground on a platform of a high, structural-steel tower.

Everyone waited nervously . . . not knowing what to expect. Everyone waited fearfully . . . for the destructive power potential of the atom bomb was still an unknown factor. But everyone had to keep waiting impatiently . . . for what seemed like eternity . . . because the weather, which was blustery and misty with periods of light rain and lightning, had already forced a time-delay of several hours. The only thing right about the weather seemed to be the wind, which continued to blow in a direction that assured no radiation fallout over populated areas. At least, that was the naive hope of both Oppenheimer and Groves.

"It's almost dawn," Bill commented wearily to Blake.

"And the weather is still marginal. They'll have to postpone the test."

"No way, Bill! Not if I know General Groves. He's itching to explode it, and I'd bet my bottom dollar that he'll tell them to go ahead with it anyway . . . before a bolt of fork-lightning strikes the tower and detonates it for us."

Blake absolutely correct in his assessment of Groves! For within minutes, Groves reminded everyone to cover their eyes with the smoked glasses that each had been supplied for protection from the expected blinding light of the blast. And, then, announced that ignition would definitely occur at exactly 5:30 A.M., Mountain War Time.

Looking at his wrist watch, Bill exclaimed,

"Jesus, Blake! That's less than five minutes from now."

Bill was right. But, Groves was wrong by 15 seconds. The atom bomb detonated at 5:29:45 A.M., not 5:30 A.M. . . . Maybe God took over the controls at this point, having decided that if man was so anxious to develop the means of destroying himself . . . then, he would assist man by accelerating time for this tragic, but momentous event.

Bill's eyes were absolutely transfixed . . . Awed . . . Hypnotized . . . And repulsed by the simutaneous revelation of both beauty and ugliness caused by the fantastic atomic blast spectacle that unfolded before him.

No one spoke. In fact, everyone remained speechless for several moments. Staring. Praying. Wondering if the World might now come to an end.

"I . . . I . . . Bill stammered incoherently . . . unable to spit out any sensible dialogue conveying the impact of what his sight had registered in his mind by witnessing this truly majestic, frightening, cataclysmal explosion. Fortunately, words didn't fail everyone for an observer from 'The New York Times' later eloquently expressed what he saw.

"a light not of this world, the light of many suns in one. It was a sunrise such as the world had never seen, a great green super-sun climbing in a fraction of a second to a height of more than 8000 feet, rising ever higher until it touched the clouds, lighting up earth and sky all around with a dazzling luminosity. Up it went, a great ball of fire about a mile in diameter, changing colors as it kept shooting upward, from deep purple to orange, expanding, growing bigger, rising as it was expanding, an elemental force freed from its bonds after being chained for billions of years. For a fleeting instant the color was unearthly green,such as one only sees in the corona of the sun during a total eclipse. It was as though the earth had opened and the skies had split. One felt as though he had been privileged to witness the birth of the World-to be present at the moment of Creation when the Lord said: Let There Be Light."

Finally, Bill's voice-box was able to utter his dismal thoughts,

"It's the end of civilization, Blake! Certainly, as we know it. Oh! God! At least in conventional wars, one has the feeling of contained violence. Of limited destruction. Of limited human suffering and calamity. But . . . now . . . with the reality of this atom bomb, who knows what fate is in store for all mankind. Especially when you realize that this is just the beginning of nuclear technology exploitation."

Watching the massive, mushroom shape cloud continue to surge and billow upward with tremendous acceleration, and recalling two supplementary explosions that occurred in the cloud, shortly after the main explosion, Bill predicted in panic,

"If sane scientists have been able to create this terrible

weapon in less than four years, God only knows what the future holds if its advanced technology ever falls into the hands of the mad ones. Or . . . in the control of other crazy dictators, like Hitler. What type of bomb is next, Blake? Certainly, bigger ones . . . more powerful ones . . . ones that one day will have the capacity to wipe out all humanity with the flip of a single switch."

Tears welled in Bill's brown eyes. Welled . . . then flowed in a steady stream down his flushed cheeks.

"Surely . . . What we have here is a run away technology train. No one is going to be able to slow down or stop the madness of mankind now that this accomplishment was demonstrated. Every Nation on Earth is going to beg, borrow, or steal the technology to build one of these. Or two . . . or thousands! How do you control that type of human chain reaction, Blake? You Can't! The World is doomed!" Repeatedly shaking his head from side-to-side . . . Bill, anguishly, said,

"I only wish now the bomb had been a dud. Then maybe our scientists would all go home, and never interfere again with God's domain. Not tamper . . . where they don't belong. Why didn't President Roosevelt live long enough to kill the Project? Not just to save the money . . . but to save all our future generations. I even wish, I had never gotten hold of Germany's Master Plan for Atomic Bomb Development. Then, I wouldn't have contributed, even in a small way, to the success we've witnessed here today. My conscience would be pure and free of guilt. Now, all of us will be polluted by . . . and slaves to . . . its awesome power. Mark my words Blake. We may win the War with Japan with this ugly beast. But ultimately, we are going to lose the human race because of it. This thing isn't going to save Jonathon! Someday this technology will destroy him. Oh, God! I feel sick . . . I feel as if I could throw up."

But despite his morose feeling, Bill knew there was no way of turning back the hands of time. If there was . . . Karen would be alive today. If there was . . . he never would have had an adulterous affair with Sue, and still would be married to Cathy.

261

However, Bill had learned from his own tragic experiences that life must go on . . . even in spite of his premonition that darker days were yet to come. God may have said: 'Let There Be Light', but Bill now knew . . . without any doubt . . . that man's response by creating the 'Atom' bomb was to opt instead for the certain doom of pitch-blackness.

"We're heading back to the Dark Ages Blake. We're accelerating into chaos. How I wish we were still primitive cavemen. Then, at least, we could look forward to brighter tomorrows. But now we've come full circle by mastering this atomic technology.

"And because we have, 'The Shadow Of Death' will plague us from this moment on. Not to eternity either. Because someday . . . very soon . . . there will be a Nuclear War . . .

"And those of us that are left will all be primitive cavemen again. Because everything else will be destroyed. Most likely, those of us that initially do survive the Nuclear holocaust will experience a miserable death caused by the deadly radiation fallout that will accompany the 'big bang'. I don't mind telling you Blake . . . I'm scared. I'm scared for all humanity . . . not just for my Jonathon!"

17 B

Even after their plane departed for Tinian, a cloud of deep depression . . . of unbridled hopelessness . . . hung menacingly over Bill, who hadn't yet shaken the adverse psychological effects of witnessing the earth-shattering blast resulting from detonation of the plutonium bomb at Alamogordo.

Blake tried several times to free Bill from his solemn mood. But, his efforts were to no avail, until he philosophized,

"Even if it was just a remote possibility, Bill, It was inevitable that it would happen someday. The frontiers of science and technology are forever being thrust further forward into the unknown. That's why we now have the airplane . . . the submarine . . . the Penicillin that saved your life a few years ago.

"Sometimes technology grows slowly and carefully. Sometimes with reckless abandonment. But once Germany's scientists discovered that the nucleus of certain atoms could be split, and Dr. Fermi's research in the States demonstrated that the fission process could be made self-sustaining, it was only a matter of time before 'science-fiction' was turned into reality.

"Sure! It might have been postponed for a few years or a decade . . . However, Bill, it certainly would have happened anyway."

"Maybe so, Blake." Bill retorted. "But if it wasn't for the urgency of the War, no one in their right minds would have committed the massive scientific and engineering brain power needed to make it happen in the short run. It would have been delayed . . . maybe not forever . . . but likely until the 21st century."

"Possibly so, Bill. However, I've learned never to underestimate the ability of the scientific community. The scientists certainly would have accomplished it sooner or later. And in my judgment . . . sooner."

"And now that they have! Is there any doubt in your mind that it's going to be used?"

"No . . . none at all, Bill."

"Then, God help us all," Bill prayed again, as the special B-29 that they were flying in began its landing approach at Tinian on July 26th, after a grueling fifty-five hundred mile flight across the Pacific.

"Don't be such a pessimist Bill. While I'm convinced it will be used, there's no doubt in my mind that it will only be dropped on military targets. But, then, . . . you'll see for yourself!"

With a sudden stare of surprise, Bill glared at Blake saying "What do you mean . . . see for myself?"

"Well . . . I didn't want to tell you until we got to Tinian. And since we have arrived, now I can. You, my boy, are going to be an eyewitness to the atomic bombing of Japan."

"Damn it Blake. No! What for?"

"Because Intelligence wants a first hand report on its capabilities. It wasn't our doing, Bill. The President wants an unbias assessment from us. Not a pumped up military version that may be more imaginary than real. After all, I told you before, he's from Missouri!"

"Why me and not you?"

"Well for one thing I'm much older than you. Don't have the stamina, or reflexes required for this mission."

Then in a jovial mood, Blake laughingly said,

"Besides! I can't swim."

"Meaning What?"

"Well if the plane runs out of fuel on the way back and has to land in the Pacific, you'd have a better shot at making it. Remember . . . both times you've been involved with the sea, you've been saved."

"Oh sure! But you've forgotten one thing."

"What's that?"

"You're out after the third strike."

"Bill, I'm not worried. Not with your luck. I'm beginning to think you can walk on water."

Too exhausted from the long trip to respond further, Bill just accepted his upcoming fate, headed for the nearest Officer's quarters, logged in, and slept for almost eighteen hours.

When Bill finally awoke, his mind was clear. Fresh. And inquisitive. Like it or not, he was committed to fly aboard one of the B-29's chosen to drop the Little Boy atomic bomb on Japan and, therefore, reconciled himself to fulfilling that mission.

"But why from Tinian, Blake? Why not Guam?", he inquired over breakfast.

"Well . . . for one thing, Tinian is one hundred miles closer to Japan than Guam is to our south. That one hundred miles converts into at least a ½ hour shorter flight each way for our bombers. Besides saving on the wear and tear of the crews, whose endurances are already being stretched to their limits because a round trip to Tokyo takes about fourteen hours, it also provides a small safety cushion for them in terms of residual gasoline supplies.

"As it is, a lot of our planes run out of fuel on their return flight . . . some 50 or 100 miles out at sea . . . and some have needle gauges stuck on empty, when they hit the runways here at Tinian. Our losses, Bill, would be much heavier, if we didn't take advantage of the shorter distance from Tinian to the Japanese mainland."

Now stopping to gulp a last swallow of coffee from his cup, and, then, pausing to savor a deep drawn puff from his ever ready pipe, Blake continued the conversation from where he left off,

"Another reason is the topography of Tinian. Most of this

265

Island is just a softly undulating plateau jutting up from the Pacific. Rather ideally suited for the long, 8500 foot, runways required for the B-29 Superfortresses. Ideal, that is, when compared to the mountainous terrain of some of the other islands out here in this God-forsaken Pacific Theater of War."

Bill interrupted Blake by asking,

"How long have we been flying out of Tinian, Blake."

"Ever since our Marines stormed ashore and took Tinian, about a year ago. The Seabees went right to work and converted this tiny speck of coral into the 'World's largest operational aircraft carrier', with four airstrips at North Field, and three more at West Field.

"Now, we have the capability to have hundreds ... and hundreds ... and hundreds of B-29's take-off continuously. All loaded with high-explosive, or incendiary bombs to drop on selected Japanese targets.

"In fact yesterday afternoon, while you were sleeping, I watched two hundred and fifty of them lifting- off from North Field, four abreast ... every fifteen seconds. Like tightly packed pearl beads on endless strings, they flew-off in parallel lines towards the Northern horizon, and Japan.

" I must say, it was quite impressive. But, I'm sure it's just routine activity for our boys over here, who do it day after day ... in good weather or bad."

Then , leaning forward so as to get closer to Bill's ear, Blake whispered softly,

"And on the 31st of this month, they've scheduled a bombing mission involving the fly-off of nearly a thousand B-29's. Boy! That's going to be sight to behold, Bill."

Bill, wincing inwardly, replied,

"Nothing like the one we've already seen at Alamogordo, Blake."

Blake, puffing steadily on his pipe, first nodded several times in agreement, then, rose from his chair, saying,

"Come on. Let's take a 'cook's tour' of Tinian before getting down to work."

Bill was all for that, so they quickly commandeered a jeep, and a Seabee, named Tony Vito, to be their chauffeur and guide.

Tony's enthusiasm, gift for gab, and keen knowledge of Tinian reminded Bill of his first impression of Stig when he arrived in Copenhagen, way back in 1939. However, Bill quickly realized there was one major difference. Tony's accent and aggressive driving behavior were dead give-a-ways as to his place of birth and adolescent residency. But, he had to confirm his suspicion anyway by speculating,

"From the 'Yankee's' baseball cap that you're wearing, I'd guess that you were from New York City."

"Right on! So are most of my buddies here with me."

"Then that explains it." Blake interjected with a coy smile.

"Explains what?" Bill asked curiously.

"The names of all the streets here. Haven't you noticed? We're driving south on Broadway, and have just passed 42nd Street, and Canal Street. While up ahead is Wall Street. Doesn't that ring any bells in your mind, Bill?"

Before Bill could respond, Tony eagerly did,

"I bet you can't miss! All are historic landmarks in my home town, New York City. When our Seabee Brigade got here last July, we immediately realized that Tinian is shaped just like Manhattan. And it runs North to south . . . just like Manhattan . . . with approximately the same length, width, and land area. Close enough anyway for our home-sick imaginations to adopt her as our home-away-from-home. So . . . as we built the streets and roads . . . we had a field day in duplicating the names of those from the big City. It's been great for our moral . . . if nothing else. And, for as long as we're here, it's not going to be Tinian . . . but Manhattan Island ll."

Now turning left onto Wall Street, Tony drove straight ahead to its intersection with West Street . . . and then halted.

267

"Why are we stopping here?" Bill asked. "Let's drive up that mountain peak. I'll bet the view is inspiring from up there."

"No . . . No way! That mountain is the only part of the Island that's not New York."

"What do you mean?" Blake asked.

"That's Mount Lasso . . . 584 feet above sea level . . . but definitely out of bounds. Right now, it is probably the most dangerous part of the Island. Not because of its terrain. But, because there are over 500 Japanese soldiers still alive and holed up there."

Bill gasped. While Blake . . . startled by Tony's remark, had to stoop over to pick up his pipe that fell out of his gaping mouth.

"You mean the Island is still not secure?" Bill inquired, as soon as he recovered his composure.

"Oh . . . it's safe enough. As long as you and I don't tempt fate. The Japs are pretty harmless . . . They're scared. And starving to death. And because they are, every so often, some of them slip down to scrounge for food from our garbage piles. When they do . . . we pick them up . . . or pick them off. We've gotten over two hundred of them that way in less than a year."

Bill, somewhat perplexed, pointed his extended right index finger up towards Mount Lasso, and asked,

"Why don't the Marines just go up there and wipe them out . . . once and for all?"

"Well . . . One of these days, they probably will. But for now, we have an undeclared truce. We know they're up there. And they know . . . we know. But as long as they don't do something stupid, like bothering us, we're willing to bide our time, and give them a chance to surrender peacefully."

Both Bill and Blake were visibly disturbed by this revelation. Upset and frightened because any one of these Japanese soldiers could sneak into the 509th Restricted Compound Area, where Little Boy would soon be secretly assembled, and sabotage the atom bomb.

Such a 'kamikaze' raid at a critical time, after the bomb was

armed, would be disastrous, resulting in everyone . . . and everything, including most of Tinian, being blown to Kingdom come.

"How many Americans are on Tinian?" Blake asked anxiously.

"Oh . . . about 20,000," replied Tony.

Blake frowned . . . deep wrinkles crossed his worried brow as
he said impatiently,

"I guess Bill, we have more work cut out for us here than
either of anticipated."

Now, it was Bill's turn to nod in complete agreement, as Tony
rapidly accelerated their jeep northward along Riverside Drive,
rushing back to the 509th Composite Group's compound under
Blake's urgent command,

"And fast! As if you were late for the start of a New York
Yankee-Boston Red Sox baseball game."

Tony didn't have to be told twice. Pushing the gas pedal to
the floor, and holding it there for the entire trip, he drove the nine
miles from the base of Mount Lasso to the main gate of the compound, at the intersection of 8th Avenue and 125th Street in less than
eight minutes. A little slow by his standard, but much too rapidly for
Bill and Blake who, at times, found themselves hanging on for dear
life, as the bouncing . . . rocking . . . and swerving jeep nearly side-
swiped a dozen vehicles on their mad dash back along the congested
thoroughfares.

Blake wasted no time in calling an emergency meeting of the
509th Security Patrol Group, and quickly issued orders for a 24 hour
double-ring of guards to be placed around the perimeter of the
Technical Service Quonset hut, where the Little Boy was
stored.Then, he and Bill held a private, top secret meeting with
Naval Captain William 'Deke' Parsons, an explosive expert, who
was responsible for 'arming' the atom bomb.

"I'm horrified, Deke, at the risk we're taking by fusing the
bomb while it's still on the ground. Those Japanese soldiers, holed

up on Mount Lasso, are all devoted fanatics. If they even got a hint of what we have down here, they wouldn't hesitate for a moment to try and sneak pass our guards and attempt to destroy it. Remember! They may be out of food, but I'll bet they're not out of hand-grenades . . . or courage. If they ever launch a surprise suicidal attack, all hell's going to break loose around here.

If they blow up the Tech hut . . . the ATOM BOMB COULD EXPLODE!"

Now, searching for a sought after answer, Blake asked,

"Is it absolutely necessary to arm Little Boy on the ground? Isn't it possible to do that after you're airborne?"

A stunned Captain Parsons immediately replied,

"It's uncanny Blake! Just as if you've been reading my mind. For sometime now, I too have been very apprehensive. In fact, worried sick about loading Little Boy on the ground, and having us lift-off with it fully armed. My concern, however, was for the real possibility of us crashing on take-off, which undoubtedly would trigger the bomb to detonate."

Then, slapping his forehead with the palm of his right hand, he added,

"It hadn't dawned on me that a desperation attack by the Japanese soldiers up on Mount Lasso is also a real cause for alarm. Not only possible . . . but probable. Because all Japanese soldiers are just what you say they are . . . 'fanatics', who wouldn't even think twice about sacrificing themselves for the glory of the 'Emperor'. Either way. Yours. Or, mine. The end result would be the same. Complete annihilation of Tinian and over 20,000 of our American service men . . . But . . ."

Parsons paused. Such a long, drawn out pause that Bill's curiosity had to be satisfied.

"But what?"

"General Groves would never approve the change . . . letting us 'arm' the atom bomb after we're airborne. I know that because about two months ago, at a Los Alamos conference, one of my staff personnel proposed doing just that. Neither Groves or Oppemheimer liked the idea. They both felt it was too risky. Their recommendation was to stick to the original plan."

"Good!", said Blake without hesitation.

"Why Good? If we both agree we shouldn't arm it until we have lifted-off safely."

"I mean good . . . because they didn't adamantly say 'no you can't do that Parsons'. And since they didn't, we'll just play the 'waiting game' before we play 'pass the buck'."

"I must confess Blake, I'm more than a little bit confused."

"Well then, let me explain. Don't tell anyone what you're going to do until the last possible moment . . . just after the bomb is placed on board the B-29. That obviously is the waiting game. Then, you don't notify Groves directly as to what you plan to do. Instead . . . You tell his Deputy, Gen. Farrell. Don't you see, you've passed the buck to him. Farrell won't say 'no you can't do that' . . . without first passing the buck again, and checking it out with Groves. By that time, it will be too late to change anything that you want to do. And, you will have accomplished two important things,

"Huh?"

"First . . . You don't have to worry about facing a court-martial for disobeying orders because you've properly notified your superior as to the what action you plan to take. And secondly, Groves won't be able to interfere because you'll be off the ground, heading for the target, before Groves can countermand you. Once the flight has been committed, no one . . . not even Groves . . . is going to abort the mission and order your B-29 to return to Tinian in order to arm the bomb on the ground. Gen. Groves may cuss like hell . . . may steam . . . may even kick a wall or two . . . but, believe me, that's all he'll be able to do."

"Blake. I like you! You're my kind of devious man, one who knows how to get something done without a lot of red tape."

"Well in our line of work, we sometimes have to rely strictly on our own gut feeling to survive. And I'd say this situation certainly

271

fits into that category. I take it then . . . we have a deal. But, don't forget. Only notify General Farrell at the last moment. After . . . not before Little Boy is put into the B-29."

At precisely 3:30 P.M., on August 5th, an assembled Little Boy, dangling motionlessly four feet above the floor of the air-conditioned Tech Service hut was carefully lowered by its chain hoist onto a trolley. Then, after being completely enshrouded with a canvas tarpaulin for concealment, the approximately 10,000 pound bomb was pulled by a tractor, ever so slowly, out of the large exit door of the Quonset onto a narrow coral apron leading to the North Field runways. Almost immediately, eight white-helmeted MP's, cradling fully loaded carbines in their folded arms, distributed them-selves along each side of the trailer, and crawled forward with it at a snail's pace. A small convoy of jeeps and army vehicles, carrying Parsons, Bill, Blake, and a handful of scientists fell in behind the trailer and, then in unison, the entire entourage moved forward. At a barely perceptible velocity, everyone followed the trailer in muffled silence.

The prevailing mood was so solemn, Bill couldn't help but remark to Blake in a whisper,

"Reminds me of a funeral cortege, Blake. Only the corpse is missing. However, I have a feeling that if this drop is at all successful . . . we'll have tens of thousands of them."

"I think you're wrong, Bill. As I said before, They're not going to waste this atomic bomb on people . . . they'll be directing it at the military installations."

"I wish I could believe you, Blake. But for some reason, I just don't."

It took almost forty-five minutes to transport the bomb a distance of only a half-a-mile from the Tech hut to the specially built loading pit on North Field, into which Little Boy was lowered with extreme care. As soon as that operation was completed, the Enola Gay . . . the B-29 chosen for this historic flight . . . was then towed over and jockeyed into position so that its forward bomb bay lay directly above the pit, housing the bomb. Once this was accomplished, the time consuming procedure of loading the bomb aboard the Enola Gay began.

Slowly . . . inch by inch . . . a noisy hoist winched the massive nuclear weapon into the huge cavity of the Superfortress' bombbay. Then, after securely clamping it into place with special shackles, the fifteen foot bombbay doors closed and clanged shut. Only then did Bill, Blake, and Deke Parsons expel a sigh of relief. And as the few on-lookers finally dispersed, Blake pulled Parsons aside and said,

"I guess the waiting game's over. It's time to tell General Farrell of your plan."

Parsons' eyelid twitched. An apparent nervous reaction from the anticipation of having to confront Farrell with the fact that the bomb had been installed unarmed.

Reaching out for some moral support, Deke searchingly asked,

"Do either of you have any good ideas on how I should do it?"

Bill did. And didn't hesitate to offer it.

"Why don't you just tell him the truth? Don't beat about the bush. Just tell him you were scared to death that the Enola Gay might crash on take-off. After all that is a real probability . . . considering the fact that she'll be overloaded, carrying that five-ton bomb and 7000 gallons of fuel needed to reach Japan."

"You're right, Bill! And to sweeten it up with a little psychological flavoring, I'll just remind him about the accidents we had last night, when four of our bombers couldn't lift-off and crashed on the runways in a burst of flame."

Parsons was surprised that Farrell didn't resist his idea at all. Maybe, he thought, the clincher was his closing remark,

"If we do crash before getting airborne, and Little Boy explodes, the nuclear blast will blow up half the Island. And kill us all!"

But the truth was that Farrell had been concerned about a take-off failure also. And its dire consequences. He didn't need any convincing, and readily agreed to go to bat for Parsons and notify Groves as to his modified plans.

"He's going to be pissed," Farrell said, "at being told after-the-fact.

"Especially since there isn't enough time for him to countermand your action without delaying the mission. And Groves certainly won't do that."

Parsons smiled sheepishly, knowing that Blake and Bill would be glad to hear that the 'buck' now had been successfully passed up the ladder.

"Oh, by the way," General Farrell asked Parsons as they parted. "Have you ever armed the bomb in such tight quarters as you're going to have up there in the bombbay?"

Parsons grimaced. Twitched once . . . then again. Finally, after swallowing a deep breath of hot tropical air, he replied confidently,

"No! . . . But, I've got a few hours to learn how . . . before we take-off."

And he did.

17 C

Officially, there were only twelve members of the Enola Gay crew taking part in Special Mission No.13. Bill was the uninvited guest, who had to travel incognito with Colonel Paul Tibbetts, pilot, Captain Robert Lewis, co-pilot, Major Thomas Ferebee, bombardier, Captain Theodore Van Kirk, Navigator, Lieutenant Jacob Beser, radar operator, Lieutenant Morris Jeppson, electronics specialty officer, Captain William Deke Parsons, supervisor of final delivery and assembly, and Sergeants; Joseph Stiborik, tail gunner, George Caron, tail gunner, Richard Nelson, radioman, Whatt Duzenbury, flight engineer, and Robert Shumard, waist blister gunner.

However, Bill didn't mind. Thirteen was his lucky number. The only thing that did disturb him about his presence not being acknowledged aboard was the possibility of the plane not returning safely. Then, even Jonathon wouldn't know where he died or, for that matter, why.

"Maybe they will list me as 'Lost at Sea'. Like Joe Walker was," Bill said dejectedly, as the Enola Gay lifted-off from the North Field runway at 2;45 A.M. Tinian Time on the 6th of August.

There destination was Hiroshima, the primary target, if weather conditions over that City permitted a visual bombing run. Otherwise, the first alternate was Kokura and the second alternate was Nagasaki. Unfortunately, for all the unsuspecting inhabitants of Hiroshima, a sudden break in the overcast clouds not only let in the warm glow of the morning sunlight but, also, triggered the 'all clear' signal to the Enola Gay that Hiroshima was the unlucky city . . . now destined to receive the World's first atomic bomb. And so at 8:15:17 A.M., Japanese time, the bomb of doom was dropped out of the open forward bay doors of the B-29 Superfortress. Forty-five seconds later, nearly 350,000 civilians watched in horror as sixty percent of their beautiful City was laid to ruin by the explosion of a single atomic bomb. As a testimony to its awesome power of destruction, almost all buildings and people, within a 1500 foot radius, were vaporized.

The twelve crew members on the Enola Gay were elated! Each one was exuberant . . . and now showed their joy . . . with cheering . . . with congratulatory back slapping over their success. One closed his eyes . . . in deep shame . . . over what had just been done. That one was Bill.

Now, boiling over with exhilaration, Deke Parsons quickly sent a short coded message to General Farrell,

"Results clear cut. Successful in all respects. Visible effects greater than Alamogordo . . . "

On the other hand, Bill, filled with dismay, and appalled at watching most of Hiroshima evaporate before his astonished eyes in an ever-expanding fireball of searing flames, mulled over the contents of the coded message that he was wiring to Tinian.

This one was to Blake. This one was more poignant. This one was more perceptive of the ultimate calamity that someday would be inflicted on the human race. Deciphered it read,

"Hell has no greater fury! The Devil is now in control of the World."

The atmosphere of doom that Bill's message conveyed was based on his observations and conjectures . . . as the Enola Gay circled three times around the rising, ominous mushroom cloud of the atomic explosion . . . as he reluctantly peered into the vast chasm of a Hiroshima that once was! He was convinced of one thing.

Hiroshima was dead! And so too must be the thousands upon thousands of innocent women and children who, unfortunately, were the first victims of the World's first nuclear explosion.

Bill's heart cried out for them . . . in spite of his anger felt towards the Japanese for causing the War. But, his sympathy was in vain. For no amount of pity could appease the terrible agony and horrible suffering being endured by the panicking residents of Hiroshima, who were now being mutilated by the invisible death-rays of radiation inundating their scorched and screeching bodies.

Bill knew the death toll had to be enormous. And he was intuitively right. For later he would learn that over 80,000 died instantly, or within a few hours after the blast. And another 80,000 perished due to effects of nuclear fallout. However, the former were the lucky ones. For the degree that they had to suffer was minuscule . . . some for only a millionth of a second. While the deaths of those irradiated, measured in suffering-time, were slow. Torturous. And unbearably painful.

Shocked and totally bewildered by the catastrophic event unfolding before him, Bill was stunned into silence and did not utter another word until the Enola Gay had landed safely back at Tinian over seven hours later. Now, recalling the havoc wreaked on Hiroshima by the atom bomb, he groaned,

"Blake . . . We thought Hitler was the madman. But look at what we just did. Hiroshima was totally destroyed.Thousands of innocent Japanese civilians must have been suddenly vaporized by the bomb. Mothers! Children! Helpless babies! All without any warning of impending doom. Without any chance for survival.How can we say we are the sane ones? We're all mad too! Just as crazy as Hitler. If not more so!"

Bill left Tinian for the States on August 9th the very same day that another B-29 was dropping its lethal weapon, a plutonium bomb of the Fat Man type on Japan. This time it was helpless Nagasaki.

277

And, before his plane landed in Boston, on Aug. 14,1945 after his one day debriefing session with the President at the White House, the Japanese government had already agreed to end the War.

Bill speculated that many historians will surely boast that only two atomic bombs were needed to bring the once mighty Japanese Nation to her knees ... duly begging and accepting an unconditional surrender.

A surrender that undoubtedly saved the lives of hundreds of thousands of additional American military men ... who would have been killed or maimed if the invasion of Japan had proceeded as planned, on November 1, 1945.

Then again, some historians may argue that dropping the bombs was unnecessary since the War was drawing to a successful conclusion and destined to be won by the United States, anyway.

But, Bill also wondered if the stain ... the stench ... the brutality of this display of man's inhumanity towards his fellow man could ever be justified ... forgiven or, forgotten.

What was bothering him most of all, however, was the burden of shame and guilt that he personally carried because of his small contribution to atomic technology development that ultimately resulted in sealing the fate of all those who died, or were critically wounded by the horrendous nuclear explosions.

An event that will certainly live in infamy. One that forever would dramatically alter the course of history of man's so-called civilized society.

In this respect, nothing had really changed for Bill since Karen's death. He still faced an uncertain future with a heavy heart and an even heavier guilty conscience.

Not even having Jonathon rushing out to greet him and holding him in his arms as he arrived home ... at last ... could relieve Bill's despair, or satisfy the longing that he once again felt for his lost loves ... Karen and Cathy.

Nor the affection and lust, he still had for Sue. And even for Marie ... who he met briefly while in France on a clandestine operation conducted with a French underground unit, during the summer of 1943.

Now, in reflection, Bill wondered just what role each of them would be playing in his and Jonathon's life in the years to come.

And, as he searched his mind also for answers to life's mysteries and purpose, in this very troublesome new atomic age something Dr. Jordan Brown told him that tragic night in the hospital came back to haunt him. It kept resonating in his perplexed mind,

'Nature's strange dichotomy . . . seeds of life and death'.